C000171569

The Island in
Bramble Bay

Victoria Walker

ISBN: 978-1-7399441-1-7

For Claudia
The Rory to my Lorelei
x

1

Maggie stood on the quay watching the ferry grow bigger as it made its way towards her. She took a deep breath. Wavering now was not an option. Heading off to live on an island, albeit only a stone's throw from the mainland, was the only way to leave everything behind and that was exactly what she wanted. The odds of making bad decisions had to be smaller on an island. But despite her fantastic powers of reasoning, doubt niggled.

She turned and walked to the end of the quay, hoping to release some of her anxiety. Why was she so worried? It was a sound, practical decision not driven by emotion or consideration of anyone except herself, and that was how everything would be from now on.

Once the ferry had docked, Maggie stood aside until everyone was off before grabbing her assortment of bags and cases and heaving them onto the boat.

'Blimey, love. Are you moving in?' asked the young man who was collecting the tickets.

'I am, actually. I'm the new park manager on Bramble Island, Maggie Cassidy.' She grinned and held out her hand which he took enthusiastically.

'Nice to meet you, Maggie. I'm William, first mate and

general dogsbody on the Bramble Bay Ferry.'

Maggie handed over her ticket and began to pick up her bags again.

'Hold on a minute, I can help you with those.' William grabbed the bags as easily as if they were filled with air and carried them into the cabin below, where he left them in a neat pile in the corner. 'They'll be safe here,' he said, before heading up the steep narrow stairs to the top deck. 'Best place to travel on a day like today.'

Maggie wholeheartedly agreed and thanked William before taking a seat on the port side which gave her a wonderful view of Bramble Bay. Once the boat was moving, the refreshing breeze that Maggie had enjoyed on the quay felt more like a force nine gale but it was a bright spring day and she didn't mind the elements at all. Years of working outdoors had taught her to be well prepared, whatever the weather, and today she was wearing numerous layers underneath her waterproof coat and her feet were toasty warm in her favourite hiking boots thanks to a pair of hand-knitted socks her sister had made.

She clasped her dark chestnut hair in one hand at the nape of her neck while with the other hand, did her best to keep the tendrils that were whipping across her face out of her eyes. She moved to the starboard side which was sheltered from the wind by the roof of the cabin, losing the view of the beautiful bay and gaining instead a peek at the exclusive properties that bordered the water in prestigious Sandbanks.

After a few minutes of sailing, the butterflies that had been with her since early that morning were threatening to turn into full-blown seasickness. Not wanting to make that kind of first impression on anyone, she forced herself to stop looking at the incredible houses they were passing and instead she tried to focus on the horizon.

From this far away, Bramble Island looked as if it were covered with trees but Maggie remembered the first time she had been to Bramble Island and knew there was more to it than that. She had been a teenager on holiday with her parents and older sister, Beth. They had visited the island for the day and she remembered feeling as if it were a place that time had forgotten. Back then, the park and woodland weren't managed like they were now and the island was still recovering from having been left to its own devices for too many years by a previous owner who thought that nature could look after itself. But there were so many species that weren't native to the island, having been introduced by the Victorians, that doing nothing meant that some of them ran wild, overwhelming the island. Through careful management by the Trust, it was now a beautiful place where everything thrived. Maggie was thrilled to be working with them and was excited to see how far it had come since her last visit.

When she'd been offered the job as park manager, not only had it been perfect timing as she was looking to move on — she needed to move on — but the fact that it was an island held a sense of adventure and intrigue that was tempting in itself. Living on an island was just what she needed. Especially because, from what she gathered, it would just be her and the odd holiday cottage tenant until she recruited some volunteers.

As the ferry approached the harbour, Maggie saw the large crenellated manor house, Bramble Castle, which was now a country retreat leased to a large company and not open to the public, although she hoped that island residents might be exempt from that rule, and on the other side of the quay was a row of small cottages.

William had told her to stay where she was until the other passengers had disembarked so that he could help her with her bags again. She made her way down the steps to the main deck and waited for William. As soon as the last passenger had disembarked, he skipped back onto the ferry, grabbed her bags from the cabin and deposited them on the quayside before jumping back onto the boat. 'See you soon! Good luck!' he called.

After shouting her thanks, Maggie turned and surveyed the quayside, wondering what to do next. She'd expected the general manager would be there to meet her although she would have been quite happy to go off and find someone, save for the thought of having to lug all her bags with her again. But as the ferry was about to leave on its return journey, she reasoned that if anyone tried to steal them at least they wouldn't be able to escape the island for another hour or two, so she shoved them next to the harbour wall and headed beyond the cafe and souvenir shop towards the Trust's visitor reception.

A harassed looking woman behind the desk planted a smile on her face with some effort and said, 'Good morning, welcome to Bramble Island. Have you visited us before?' As she spoke, she held out an information leaflet and map which Maggie took.

'Not for many years. I'm not actually a visitor, I'm Maggie Cassidy. Could you tell me where I can find…'

'Clare Francis. I'm so sorry I didn't meet you as planned. We're a member of staff short today so I had to help with the influx of visitors from the ferry.' She shook Maggie's hand and breathed a sigh of relief. 'Good grief, it's been one of those days already. Anyway, first things first, let's get your things to the cottage and then I'll show you around.'

Maggie's new home was the end cottage of the little terrace she had seen from the ferry. It was the one furthest from the quay, next to three others which were holiday lets. It was whitewashed, with tiny windows and a little patio area to the side, which faced the sea. The shingle beach reached almost to the doorstep and Maggie was sure that the waves must batter the cottage in the winter.

Clare opened the front door and the familiar musty smell of a house which has been shut up for a while greeted them.

'I meant to come and air it out before you arrived but you know how it is,' Clare said apologetically.

'Oh no, it's lovely,' said Maggie, taking in the flagstone floor and open fireplace in the small living room. She moved through to the kitchen which was surprisingly spacious and had a large scrubbed pine table in the middle. After all the places she had lived before, Maggie recognised this cottage for what it was; a slightly unloved but cosy little sanctuary that she could make her own. Upstairs was one bedroom overlooking the harbour and a small bathroom with pink sanitary ware which made her smile. It was perfect. She just wanted to stay, unpack and savour the fact that she had her own space for the first time but Clare was waiting to show her around the rest of the island.

From the quayside, they walked through the reception building towards the centre of the island. The mature hedging and trees shaded them from the spring sunshine and made for an enticing entrance to Bramble Island. Maggie imagined that as the greenery thickened in the warmer weather, it would become almost like a tunnel. Once they had moved away from the shore it became less obvious that it was an island at all. The woodland was quite dense and hid the sea from view very quickly. The water in the harbour was relatively calm which probably explained why the smell of the sea wasn't there to remind you where you were and there was no sound of waves crashing, at least not today.

They arrived at a large shed on the edge of the woodland where the sea came into view again but it was off the beaten track and away from the many footpaths that led visitors around the island.

'This is the headquarters of the park team and where you'll be based,' explained Clare. Inside, it really was no more than a glorified shed furnished with a couple of untidy desks, various overloaded notice boards and a handful of mismatched armchairs and wooden chairs arranged in one corner facing a wood-burning stove. In the opposite corner was a partitioned area which would be Maggie's office. 'Maggie, I hate to leave you in the lurch but the next ferry is due any minute and I could do with getting back.'

'Don't worry Clare. I'm happy to find my way around.'

'Thanks so much. I don't know if you remember, but you can walk around the main path which loops the island in an hour or so. That might be a good start,' Clare said, visibly relieved at being off the hook and backing out of the office as she spoke. 'Feel free to do whatever you think needs doing, it's your domain and it's only you and Charlie at the moment anyway. Perhaps pop into reception if you need anything or have any questions.'

Maggie stood in the middle of the room taking it all in. It was typical of most of the places she'd worked before; organised chaos. But now that she was in charge she wanted it to be properly organised, tidy and welcoming. There was nothing worse as a volunteer than turning up to work somewhere and not having a clue where to start or what was what and she was determined that her volunteers would feel like a valued part of a well-organised team.

And who was Charlie?

2

From his vantage point in the canopy of an ancient oak tree, Charlie watched the ferry cross the harbour wondering whether any of the teeny people he could see was the new park manager. As the boat docked, he leaned out from the tree, trusting his weight to his harness and the safety ropes so that he could get a better look.

The most likely candidate, he decided, was a woman with a mane of brown hair which glinted with hints of red when it caught the sun. No one visited for the day or even for a week in a holiday cottage with as much luggage as she had. From a distance, it was hard to tell how old she was, but she looked fit and dressed appropriately which Charlie thought was a good start. He had already concluded that there was little point in expecting anything from her because no one ever stayed. The island rarely lived up to the dream that new residents arrived with unless they were holidaymakers. The two managers that Charlie had known in the almost two years he'd been there had been worn down by the isolation and the bad winter weather and eventually left, each having had only one summer season on the island. He didn't imagine it would be any different with this person.

Charlie didn't mind the weather or the isolation, he loved

the island all year round. It helped that he lived close by rather than actually on the island. A bit of distance and the ability to get away from the place whenever he wanted were definitely good, but he still struggled to understand how people could come here without having considered what the reality might be of living on an essentially uninhabited little island. The first manager Charlie had worked with had left because he realised he was never going to meet a woman who would be willing to relocate to Bramble Island. The chances of him ever meeting a woman and getting to the point of being able to ask a woman to do that anyway were slim because he was the only inhabitant of the island for much of the year. That kind of predicament didn't matter to Charlie.

Once he'd finished checking the ancient oak for storm damage which was what he'd gone up there for, the view of the ferry being a handy coincidence, Charlie began to lower himself down. Still some ten metres from the ground, he paused. He could hear the crack of twigs as someone approached. It was the woman from the ferry, the new manager. Quickly debating whether to stay up in the tree to avoid having to meet her or whether to just get it over with, he plumped for the latter and carried on descending.

'Oh, hi!' she called, looking upwards and shading her eyes from the sun. She was smiling, she looked and sounded friendly, but Charlie was wary. He often found that first impressions were not always a good indication of what a person was like once you got to know them. Admittedly, it could go either way; better or worse, but best to be cautious, he thought.

As he reached the ground she made her way towards the tree, picking over the winter debris of twigs and branches, finally holding out her hand as she reached him.

'I'm Maggie Cassidy, the new park manager. I'm guessing you're part of the team?'

'Charlie,' he stated simply, ignoring her hand in favour of

unclipping his harness.

'You're the forester?' She'd lowered her hand and shoved it back into her coat pocket.

'Yes, that's right. Good to meet you,' he said curtly, aware that he sounded like it was anything but.

'Well, I look forward to working with you.' She smiled in a disarming way that made Charlie fleetingly wonder whether perhaps she was different to the others after all.

'Welcome to Bramble Island,' he said, finally holding out his hand to her and seeing a look of relief sweep briefly across her face as she took it.

'Thanks, Charlie. See you soon.' She walked off, still smiling.

He watched her as she went, noticing how she was scrutinising the woodland, taking everything in, briefly stopping to examine a plant and then gazing up into the trees as she walked. He was pleasantly surprised at how much she seemed to be enjoying the environment and wondered whether that would last once she properly started work.

He sat down on a nearby log and dug out his sandwiches from the depths of his rucksack. On days like this, it was the only place he wanted to be. The wood was quiet with the only activity coming from the trees busily unfurling their acid green leaves and the wildflowers forcing their way through the dense woodland floor. Soon enough the island would be invaded by hundreds of visitors every day and then Charlie knew he would start to long for the winter when the woods would be his again.

His mind wandered back to Maggie. It would be good to have a like-minded person around, someone he could share his love for the island with. On a professional level, of course. It didn't seem like too much to hope for. Then he shook his head and smiled ruefully to himself. He had based this hope on less than a minute of interaction with her, so not a lot to go on. She was trying to make a good first impression with her smiles and handshakes and could easily turn out to be a complete bitch. But something about her made him doubt that. She had seemed genuinely friendly and as out of practice as he was, he resolved to make an effort to be the same.

3

Maggie tried not to overthink Charlie's reaction to her. She wanted to concentrate on the island, get back to losing herself in the tiny details which made it special. In the sunshine, it was perfect. The bright green colours of fresh spring leaves were everywhere and she had even seen a carpet of wood anemones that were already in flower.

Spotting cyclamen tucked in between the roots of a huge sycamore tree, she left the main path and went to have a closer look. The ground became springy as she trod where nothing had yet compacted the leaf rot from the previous year. The damp smell of the wood closed around her and she was enveloped by the cooler air where the trees were closer together. She loved looking for these tiny plants which grew, unplanned, in the most perfect of places.

Once she left the woodland, the island opened up into a clearer, more cultivated landscape. She strolled down the path to the Scout and Guide campsite and carried on, following the shoreline, to where there were ruins of an old village. There was so much to know about this place. She was at the opposite side of the island to where she had started and it had only taken her about half an hour, even accounting for the awkward few minutes she spent talking to Charlie. It felt amazing to be living somewhere that had so much history to it and somewhere she could easily explore and end up knowing like the back of her hand.

After her stroll around the island, Maggie headed back to the office. It was difficult to know where to start because there were messy piles of paper everywhere. She sat down at her desk and trying to be methodical, began reading everything and stacking it into piles for either rubbish, filing or to-do.

As it was only her and Charlie at the moment, she would have to request some volunteers from head office. They would be students, probably studying for an ecology degree or something similar, who wanted to get some relevant experience over the summer. Bramble Island must be a popular destination with volunteers, so she didn't think it would be long before they would have some help.

She flicked the computer on to check the emails, already dreading the size of the inbox knowing that it had been a few months since her predecessor had left. As she waited for it to come to life, she picked up another pile of paper to tackle. It was several invoices from a tree surgery company in Poole for work they had done on the island. On closer inspection, it didn't appear that they had carried out any work but rather that they had been checking work carried out by someone else. Was it to check Charlie's work? At the moment, she knew so little of how everything operated on the island that although it seemed surprising that the Trust would employ a full-time forester and yet pay for his work to be checked, it was a possibility. From what she had seen, the woodland appeared to be well-managed and in good health and that must be, at least in some part, down to Charlie.

Charlie. Maggie hadn't known what to make of him. When she'd watched him lowering himself down from the trees, the harness tight around his thighs, her stomach had flipped. The dark hair that flopped down over his eyes was lovely and she had found herself suppressing a sudden desire to sweep it out of the way until he'd done it himself with a hand that told of the rugged nature of his work, tanned already by the spring sunshine, the muscles rippling along his forearms as he had unclipped himself from the harness. She thought she'd detected an American accent but he'd said so little that she couldn't be sure.

The fleeting moment of lust she'd felt had made her blush right down to her toes as it was replaced with embarrassment when she'd thought he wasn't going to shake her hand. In the end he had, but she was left feeling confused. Did he like her or not? What reason would he have for being unfriendly? Unless it was to do with the paper she held in her hand now. It would come to light eventually, she supposed. These things always did.

Maggie checked through some of the emails and flagged the ones which she'd need to address sooner rather than later, finishing off by emailing her request for volunteers to head office before she called it a day.

Back at the cottage, she flung open all the windows and doors and set about giving it a cursory clean; it wasn't dirty, it just needed freshening up. She unpacked the few home comforts she'd brought with her and placed them thoughtfully throughout the cottage. A woven woollen blanket was draped over the back of the squashy two-seater sofa, a blanket that her grandmother had crocheted for her when she went to university was folded across the foot of the bed and she dotted framed photographs and scented candles around the bedroom and lounge.

The spring sunshine had given the last of its heat as the afternoon headed towards dusk and Maggie closed the windows and lit a fire in the grate to make the cottage cosy. Luckily, she'd had the foresight to buy some milk from the café before it had closed so she made a welcome cup of tea and collapsed on the sofa.

On reflection, the first day had gone well. There were no disasters of her making and none had been waiting for her to discover as far as she could tell. She had a wonderful feeling of anticipation about what lay ahead. This was her chance to make a success of things on her own terms and to prove to herself that she could step up to the challenge that she'd taken on. It was a new start, away from everything and everyone.

She flipped open her laptop and sent emails to her parents and sister to let them know that she'd arrived and settled in. The few weeks she'd had between jobs meant that she'd briefly had to move back in with her mum and dad and they had fallen back into the habit of wanting to know her every move again. She loved them but had been glad to leave and get her independence back.

And should she email Ben? They'd had very little contact with each other since she'd moved out. It had been a relief to be able to leave once she'd finished working at Croftwood Court. The months of living together without being together had been tough on both of them. Now maybe she should let him know where she was. But the reality was that he wouldn't care where she was and although that hurt, it was more bearable than she'd expected.

She sat next to the fire, hugging her knees and smiled to herself as she poked the log she'd just added and it fell into the embers spraying sparks up the chimney. Her chimney, her cottage, her island, her life. From now on, everything was going to be amazing.

4

Charlie moored his little motorboat at the quay, glancing towards Maggie's cottage as he tied it off. It was still early but the curtains were open so perhaps she was an early riser like him. He had barely seen her since the first time they'd met in the woods a week ago, but today he needed to speak to her about the coppicing he planned to start.

The office door was unlocked which wasn't unusual, after all, there was no one other than himself and Maggie on the island. The residents of the Castle never ventured far from its comforts and everyone else, including Clare, came over on the ferry every day. He planned to leave Maggie a note explaining where she could find him working. He went inside to find that the place was almost unrecognisable, it was so tidy and looked more organised than he ever remembered seeing it before.

'Hello?' Maggie tentatively called out, appearing from her tiny partitioned office. 'Oh, hi Charlie,' she smiled. 'Early start today?'

'Morning,' he said, ignoring her question, 'I'm going to start coppicing on the west side of the island today. Is that cool?' His American accent accentuated the question and he inwardly cursed himself for sounding like a teenager, especially when he saw Maggie's eyebrows rise slightly with barely suppressed amusement.

'That probably is cool.' She paused as if to quietly mock him and he instantly loved that about her. It was so long since he'd had a good laugh with anyone and today of all days when he'd been dreading having to ask her permission for the coppicing, it was a welcome sign for Charlie that she had a sense of humour.

'Shall I come with you and you can explain your plans?'

Brilliant. No sooner had he warmed to her, now she was going to pick apart every tiny thing he wanted to do.

They walked to the west side of the island, Charlie purposely taking long strides that forced Maggie to work hard to keep up with him although he noticed she didn't seem to be struggling too badly for an office dweller.

'So, you're working full-time here but you don't live on the island?' she asked.

'No, I have a place across the harbour. It's only a few minutes by motorboat.'

'I saw you docking this morning. It's a cute boat but I wouldn't fancy it in choppy water.'

'The harbour is pretty sheltered so it's not often the weather gets the better of her.'

They carried on in silence for a couple of minutes, then Maggie said, 'I don't know how things work around here yet but did my predecessor check up on things with you, you know like today. What would have happened before?'

Charlie breathed a heavy sigh. 'It depends which predecessor. Everyone comes in with their own ideas and I just have to go along with it. I'm sure you'll be no different.' He hadn't meant to sound judgemental, but he'd been worn down by constant interference and just wanted to get on with his work.

'Right,' said Maggie, negotiating the increasingly dense undergrowth with silent determination, he noticed. At least she'd stopped asking him questions, personal questions. What did it matter to her where he lived? That was why he didn't live on the island. He needed distance, solitude and peace. The need for that was what had brought him here in the first place and it frightened him to think about what could happen if he let anything undermine it. Even Paul, the first manager he'd had and got on with, really knew nothing of Charlie's life. Or his past.

'I'm going to start here,' Charlie said, standing in the middle of the wood where it was so dense you couldn't see through the trees to the sea, even though it wasn't far away. The early morning sun had lost the fight to penetrate this part of the wood, despite the relatively small amount of leaf growth on the trees. 'I'll clear most of the smaller stuff that's rooted, it's mainly sycamore and hazel, and then I'll start thinning out the younger trees and go from there.'

They walked around together, Charlie picking trees of various sizes and species and explaining to Maggie his rationale for keeping or thinning or even removing them. She listened carefully, sometimes nodding but never interrupting him and he found himself wanting to explain and share his ideas with her to the point that he ended up forgetting to feel annoyed with her for checking up on him.

'Thanks, Charlie,' she said once he'd finished. 'That's exactly the kind of woodland management approach I would take as well. Obviously, you completely understand how important it is to take a long-term view.'

Charlie was stunned. That was exactly what he aimed to do and she totally got it. He wanted to allow the woodland to mature and regenerate naturally while managing any elements which would threaten that because of the delicate balance of native and non-native trees they had on Bramble Island.

'Thanks, I appreciate your support.' He knew he sounded formal but he wanted her to know that he was capable of a bit more than 'cool'.

'Okay, so I'll head back. Maybe see you later?'

'Yeah, okay.' He watched her walk away, again noticing how she was constantly looking around her as she walked as if she was trying to see every inch of the island.

He set off in the opposite direction to fetch his tools and buggy with its trailer which he could fill up with wood and debris for the woodpile or the compost heap. For the first time in months, he felt a sense of relief wash over him, knowing that he could work doing what he loved without being scrutinised. Perhaps Maggie Cassidy actually was different to the others.

Before dusk, Charlie untied his boat and clambered in, setting off towards home. Feeling compelled to look back at the island, he saw Maggie standing on the beach outside her cottage watching him, her hair blowing across her face forcing her to turn briefly so that the wind blew it away instead. She waved at him enthusiastically, then stopped and just stood there. It was as if Charlie hadn't realised she could see him, as if he was watching her through a one-way mirror, but seeing her face fall as she stopped waving he snapped out of the trance he was in and raised his hand. Her face lit up, making him do the same. It was a long time since he'd felt like this, since he'd allowed himself to consider his emotions but the brief euphoria he felt faded quickly as Maggie disappeared from sight and he tried not to think about what any of it meant.

5

Maggie stood on the quay shuffling from foot to foot with her arms folded, trying to keep herself warm as a strong, biting wind came off the harbour spoiling what would otherwise have been a perfect spring day. She was waiting for the four volunteers she had recruited who were arriving on the midday ferry.

She had spent the previous day cleaning and clearing out the volunteers' chalet, having to sweep it out at least three times before it looked reasonable. The windows were wiped over inside and out, the bathroom and kitchen scrubbed and she even cleaned out the wood-burning stove and laid a bunch of kindling twigs ready for the next fire. The chalet was on the opposite side of the island to the office and Maggie's cottage, in a less wooded area, closer to where visitors tended to head. Having been a volunteer herself for a couple of years after she left university, she had first-hand experience of how bad some of the free accommodation could be and wanted to make it as nice as possible for them. She had lived in places that were no more than glorified sheds with terrible kitchen and bathroom facilities. Admittedly, because she had just left university, her standards had been quite low and when you were volunteering, anywhere you could live for free tended to be acceptable, which would possibly be the case today, but Maggie wanted it to be a little bit better than their expectations.

As the ferry docked, she could see the volunteers on the top deck, hoicking their rucksacks onto their backs. There were two women and two men, all in their early twenties. Maggie waved as they disembarked, standing to one side to allow the day visitors to stream past her into the reception.

'Hi there, I'm Maggie Cassidy, park manager here at Bramble Island. Welcome to the island!' She shook hands with each of them as they introduced themselves as Eric, Josh, Megan and Alice before suggesting that they go straight to the chalet so that they could get themselves settled in.

'Wow, it's lovely,' exclaimed Alice as they walked in.

'Yeah, much nicer than the place in Cumbria where I was last summer,' said Josh, nodding appreciatively.

'Great,' said Maggie, really pleased that she'd managed to give them a good first impression. 'Take the afternoon to settle in and explore then come to my house for dinner around seven? It's the last cottage in the row down by the quay.'

Before she headed back to the office, Maggie went to find Charlie in the west woods. She wanted to see if he'd like to join them all for dinner. It was a good opportunity for everyone to get to know one another and would give Charlie a good idea of who he might like as his woodland sidekick for the summer.

She found him with a pair of loppers in his hands considering the fate of a hazel tree that looked particularly vigorous.

'You're going to need a bigger boat.'

Charlie turned around and grinned. 'I think you're right. I'll come back to it with the chainsaw.'

She'd never seen him smile before and it lit his eyes up.

'How's it going?'

'Pretty slow but y'know, okay. At least the weather's on

my side at the moment.'

'So, I don't know if you saw my note on the memo board in the office?'

Charlie looked sheepish for a second which Maggie took to be a 'no'.

'The volunteers arrived today so I wondered if you'd like to come to dinner, give us all a chance to get to know each other.'

The easy smile disappeared and he looked like a cat caught in the headlights so she was surprised when he accepted.

'Thanks, that sounds great. What time?'

'They're all coming round to mine at seven but whenever you're ready.'

'Okay, see you later.'

It was as if he'd never had a dinner invitation before, Maggie thought as she strolled back to the office along the wide path which formed part of the circular walk which took in the whole of the island. Was it just that she had caught him by surprise? His apparent feelings towards previous managers were perhaps an indication that there hadn't been much in the way of team spirit before. Perhaps it was slightly unorthodox to invite everyone round to hers and admittedly Maggie couldn't think of a time when she'd been invited to something like that as a volunteer, but she was really glad he'd said yes. It would be reassuring to have a relatively familiar face there and would hopefully make Charlie realise how important he was to her team.

Maggie had put in a grocery order with the café who had a delivery from the mainland most days. In fact, she had been doing her shopping via them since she arrived with the only other option being to use the Bramble Bay Ferry and then get a bus somewhere. It was working out okay but soon enough she'd need to stock up on toiletries and other things which she wouldn't feel comfortable asking them for.

As she wasn't the best cook in the world, especially when

it came to catering for more than two people, she'd opted for burgers and salad with fruit for dessert. The couple of bottles of wine and small crate of beers she'd asked for would hopefully help with the team bonding as well.

'Hi Jan, I've just come to pick up my shopping for tonight.'

Jan was in charge of the café and had been a mine of information about anything Maggie had needed to know since she'd arrived.

'Oh, Maggie love, hang on a minute,' Jan said, wiping her hands on a tea towel which was tucked into her apron ties and hurrying into the kitchen. 'Come through!' she called.

Jan pulled a carrier bag from the fridge and checked inside. 'Ooh, you're having a do?'

'The volunteers arrived today,' explained Maggie. 'I thought it'd be nice to have a get-together, saves them cooking tonight as well.'

'Is Charlie joining you?'

'Yes, he is.'

'Oh, good. I do worry about him, such a lovely lad. Between you and me, he's a bit of a loner. I think he lives on his own and he works here nearly every day, even in the winter. Very unusual behaviour if you ask me. It's about time he had a bit of fun.'

'Well, hopefully, it will be fun. Have you got the booze as well?'

'Yes, it's in the storeroom but you won't manage all of that on your own. Let me fetch the sack truck for you. Why don't you get the bread rolls out of the larder?'

At least she wasn't imagining Charlie's aloofness, and she was slightly relieved that it wasn't just her that brought out that side of him, from what Jan had alluded to. Perhaps he just wasn't used to being around people. Maybe tonight would help him feel more relaxed around everyone.

Jan went back to serving in the café, while Maggie loaded the sack truck and began manoeuvring it inexpertly across the quay, pausing to decide what to do next when the concrete turned to shingle and the wheels sank into it. She'd either have to drag it the rest of the way or take everything off and carry it bit by bit.

'Hey, need a hand?' Charlie came up behind her, assessing the sack truck with a serious expression on his face.

'Oh, yes, please. It's probably easiest to carry it the rest of the way.'

Charlie nodded and handed her the bag of groceries and the bread rolls before he picked up the beer and wine. 'Lead the way.'

While Maggie began preparing the salad, Charlie took the sack truck back to the café and by the time he came back the others were arriving too. Introductions were made and drinks were dished out before they all went out to the patio to enjoy the last of the sunshine while the burgers cooked.

'It's a gorgeous spot,' said Alice. 'How long have you lived here, Maggie?'

'Only a few weeks so I'm still astounded every morning when I wake up next to the sea. I moved from land-locked Worcestershire.'

'One of my mates is volunteering at Croftwood Court,' said Eric.

'Oh yes, that's where I was based before. Then I worked all over the place for a while...' Maggie managed to stop herself before she said too much. 'And now here.' They didn't need to know how she came to be on Bramble Island, or why. Tonight wasn't the time.

'I totally get why you'd want to move here, it's amazing,' said Megan. 'The variety of species we saw today is like, unbelievable.'

Maggie noticed Charlie suppress a tiny smirk.

'How about you, Charlie, do you live on the island?' asked Alice, her wide brown eyes and eager face giving away the fact that she clearly thought Charlie was a prospect, despite the fact he was at least ten years older than her.

'No, I live across the harbour.'

'In Studland?'

'That way, yeah.' His American drawl seemed more pronounced after a couple of beers, Maggie noticed. Alice obviously noticed that too and seemed to swoon slightly as he spoke.

'So, you take the ferry every day?'

Maggie could see Charlie slump slightly under the pressure of Alice's persistent questions.

'He has a little motorboat,' Maggie explained. 'You need to get the chain ferry from Studland to get to the Bramble Bay Ferry quay or drive all the way around through Poole. There are a couple of people who volunteer in the visitor centre who come that way but not every day, it would be a bit much. Charlie, could you give me a hand with the burgers?'

Maggie didn't think she'd ever seen anyone look as grateful as Charlie did then. He leapt up and was in the kitchen before she was.

'Thanks.'

'It's okay. It's a bit much when you haven't seen anyone except me and Jan for a few months.' Maggie didn't know who Charlie saw or anything else about his life away from the island, but she had a feeling it was quite solitary.

'I guess I'm out of practice with small-talk.'

'Well, she's a little bit pushy. She probably fancies you.' Maggie glanced sideways at Charlie who rolled his eyes as he began turning the burgers.

By the time they'd eaten, the temperature had plummeted along with the sun so they all squeezed into Maggie's tiny lounge where Josh took charge of lighting a fire that soon had everyone pinned against the wall. Alice, Megan and Eric were on the sofa leaving Charlie to perch on the windowsill and Maggie sat cross-legged next to the fire with Josh who couldn't seem to stop poking and tending to it.

'How about a game, or is that too cheesy?' asked Maggie, thinking about her team-building agenda.

'Not cheesy at all!' shouted Megan amidst good-natured groans from Josh and Eric and an eye-roll from Charlie, closely observed by Alice.

'Okay. So, it's woodland-themed, obviously,' Maggie said as she rummaged in the cupboard next to the chimney breast. 'It's Tree Trivia!' She flourished the pack of cards like a game show host. 'Right, so shall we have two teams? I'll be the question master so there'll be a team of three and a team of two. Charlie probably has an advantage here so maybe he should be on the team of two. Hey, Josh —'

'I'll go with Charlie!' squealed Alice leaping off the sofa and squeezing herself next to him on the windowsill whereby he promptly leapt up and stood awkwardly next to her instead. Maggie felt bad for a second and then thought that really, Charlie was a grown man who should easily be able to cope with a mooning twenty-year-old. She fleetingly hoped it would be a brush-off rather than anything else and then thought it really wasn't any of her business and got back to the matter in hand.

After Charlie and Alice had won and then Charlie and Josh had won the second game, they called it a night and the four volunteers headed back to their chalet with the aid of Eric's head torch, having planned to meet at the office at 9 am the next morning.

Charlie had been in the kitchen the whole time Maggie had been seeing them off and she went in there to find him washing and drying the glasses.

'You don't need to do that. Thank you, though.'

'You're welcome.'

'Are you going to be okay going home in the dark?'

He shrugged. 'Never done it in the dark before, I guess so.'

Probably never after a few bottles of beer either, thought Maggie.

'Because if you wanted to stay on the sofa…'

He looked at her for what seemed like minutes, to the point where she started to wonder whether she'd actually spoken the words or just thought she had.

'Thanks. That might be a good idea.'

She exhaled, having inadvertently been holding her breath as she'd waited for an answer. 'Great. Let me grab some blankets.'

When she came back downstairs, Charlie was in the kitchen making tea.

'I do have some English habits,' he said smiling.

'The most important one, luckily.' Maggie rummaged in the cupboard and found a packet of ginger nuts.

They sat at opposite ends of the sofa watching the fire as they sipped their tea. Charlie saying nothing, but raising his eyebrows when Maggie dunked a biscuit.

'So where did you do your training?' Maggie had wanted to ask him ever since she arrived but he always seemed so closed off, it had never seemed like the right time. She felt that he could easily take it as criticism in some way, but now that they had both had a few drinks, maybe he would be less guarded.

'I apprenticed with a guy in Tahoe, I haven't had any formal training but spent a year in the woods there. You come across pretty much everything over the course of a year. And you know, it's really about looking at the woodland and feeling how it's behaving, what it needs to thrive in each little part of itself and you can't learn that from a book.' He spoke gently but passionately. Clearly, he loved what he did.

'I can tell you have a flair for it by the way you're coppicing. I've seen lots of foresters just walk through tagging each tree without a second thought as if they're following some plan which they apply to every woodland.'

'Yeah, the guy I worked with lived in the woods and worked them, you know? Really old-fashioned nowadays and the area he managed was a drop in the ocean. But it was beautiful and magical somehow.' He smiled and shook his head. 'Too much beer. How about you, how did you make it here?'

She could have told him then about how she had needed to leave her old life because she'd alienated everything that had mattered, partly with careless disregard but partly because the person that had meant most to her didn't want to see her achieving more than him. But explaining that she had been blinded by success and charmed too easily by people who had flattered her inflated ego wasn't something she planned to do. Instead, she had a brief version of the truth prepared.

'I started off as a volunteer and eventually got a job at a Trust property in Worcestershire. I started organising bat walks and things like that which is how the Trust Treks started. So, then I worked for head office, travelling around helping set up the Trust Treks in other places.'

'That was your idea? Man, we did one last summer with a red squirrel trail.'

He pronounced it 'squorl' which Maggie inexplicably loved.

'I wanted to do one this summer looking for signs of animals that are living in trees, you know like woodpecker holes and stuff like that,' he said.

'That's a good one. I think some kind of tree treasure hunt would be great too. We could get the volunteers to help set it up. Speaking of them, did you get a feel for who might be a good sidekick for you over the summer?' *Please don't say Alice, please don't say Alice.*

'I think Josh is probably the most interested in the woods but maybe I should have each of them for a day and see which one works out? Though a day with Alice might be a bit of a challenge if you know what I mean.'

'If you keep her busy, she'll soon realise you're not interested in…you know.'

'Yeah. That's the last thing I'm interested in.' But then he paused and looked at Maggie as if he was about to clarify what he'd said. He exhaled, 'I mean…'

'Same for me,' she interrupted. 'Too complicated. Right, let's see if we can turn the sofa into a bed, shall we?'

The next morning when she came downstairs, all the blankets were neatly folded on the sofa, and looking out of the window Maggie could see that Charlie's boat had gone from the quay.

6

Charlie sat on the deck at the back of his house, freshly showered and enjoying a foamy espresso. He looked across the harbour towards Studland, a view that you didn't see from Bramble Island and a view that no one else had.

His back ached from his night on Maggie's sofa and the minute that dawn had broken and he could safely leave, he did, collapsing into his own bed for a couple of hours of more comfortable sleep.

He had to admit that he'd had a great evening, apart from Alice seeming to have a thing for him. The best part of the night had been once the volunteers had left because Maggie was really good company, their shared interest in nature gave them plenty to talk about. He couldn't help but find her engaging and they'd bonded a little over being the older ones in the group. And despite his comment about not being interested in women, he was beginning to think that he wanted to be friends with her and hoped he hadn't sounded as if that was off-limits too. She was a world away from the women he used to date where everything had been contrived, fake and over-done whereas Maggie didn't seem to worry about her appearance, wearing little or no make-up and not bothering about her hair being windswept or her clothes being mud-spattered. It was refreshing and Charlie felt as if maybe, one day, a woman like Maggie could make him happy.

He got to his feet and stretched his arms over his head, arching his back to try and get rid of the stiffness. After putting his cup into the dishwasher, he grabbed his bag and headed for the boat.

When he'd bought the island, which was tiny compared to Bramble Island, he'd intended it to be a secluded bolt-hole from his life in Silicon Valley. The island had been his sanctuary for the past two years. It had helped him heal when he had thought all was lost.

He'd had an architect re-design the uninspiring 1930s house which was now an open-plan space with a subterranean living area that opened out at the back of the house onto an expansive deck and lawns but where it was visible from the water it still looked like a normal house. He'd also had a traditional boathouse built to house his yacht which he hardly ever sailed but which he loved because it reminded him of summers spent on Lake Tahoe and that was where his little motorboat lived too.

He walked through the garden following the path of inlaid railway sleepers which dropped gradually towards the sea. Jumping into the boat, he pressed the remote control to open the door of the boathouse, started the motor and headed for Bramble Island. He narrowed his eyes against the wind and smiled. He was looking forward to the day ahead. Working with the volunteers would be fun if he could just get the Alice thing sorted out. This wasn't the first day he'd looked forward to recently, but he noted that it had only started happening since Maggie arrived. Before that, every day had begun with a slight feeling of dread; a hangover from his previous life which he'd not managed to shake off until now.

Before he went to collect the buggy and his tools, Charlie called in to the office to see if Maggie was there. She was busy pinning pieces of paper onto one of the notice boards.

'Morning,' he said, slightly surprised at how happy he was to find her there.

'Hi,' she said, spinning around and smiling at him, her hair mostly caught in a messy bun which had clearly been an afterthought rather than a style decision. 'Did you sleep alright? You must have left early this morning.'

'I slept great, thanks,' he lied. 'I thought I should head home and freshen up. I didn't want to wake you.'

'It's probably just as well. If you'd been there for breakfast I could only have offered you a piece of toast. I haven't really got used to not being able to nip to the shops.' She fiddled with a drawing pin as she spoke.

'I take the boat over to Poole every week or so to get groceries. You're welcome to come with me anytime you like.' The invitation was out of his mouth before he realised. Don't overthink it, he told himself. It's just a ride to the store.

'Oh brilliant, thank you. When are you going next?'

'How about tomorrow after work, around four? Unless it's raining,' he added. 'It's not a great trip in the rain.'

Maggie grinned at him. 'I think even that would be better than starvation, plus I'm almost out of deodorant so it'll be to your benefit too.' She blushed.

'You smell just fine to me.'

Her blush deepened. 'Are you still coppicing on the west side today?'

Charlie snapped out of the slight trance he'd gone into as he gazed at Maggie. 'Oh yeah. Probably got another week or so over there. I have some wood ready to stack if you want some in your wood store? It'll need a few weeks to dry out but you're probably a little low after last night.'

'That would be great, thanks. Oh, and we had a meeting this morning, me and the volunteers. I've sent them over to work around the churchyard today then tomorrow we'll start on this rota.' She indicated the notice board. 'So, you and Josh tomorrow, if that's okay.'

'Great. I guess I'll see you tomorrow? Down by the quay at four?'

'Perfect. See you then.'

He turned and left, already looking forward to the trip the following day. For the first time in a long time, Charlie felt the fog of loneliness and anxiety begin to lift from him. He had something he was looking forward to and it felt good. For the first time in almost two years, he could allow himself to think about tomorrow without worrying about whether it would be a good day or one he would struggle to get through. *This* tomorrow was going to be good; he just knew it.

7

At four o'clock the next day Maggie was waiting down at the quay next to Charlie's boat. After a couple of minutes, he emerged through a crowd of day-trippers who were waiting for the ferry, grinning a lopsided grin that automatically made Maggie smile. He really didn't smile very often at all, so she felt a little bit special that he did for her and she took it as a sign that he seemed to have started to relax around her.

'Ready?' he asked, gesturing for her to board the boat. Maggie jumped in and shrieked as it wobbled dramatically, clinging to the sides as she sat down.

'Oh my god, I thought I was going to fall in then,' she said, immediately ruining the image she wanted to portray of someone who was used to boats. She'd never had much to do with boats before but supposed she ought to get used to them, living on an island.

'You're okay,' he said gently.

Maggie was touched that he hadn't laughed at her, because he could have done, and she felt embarrassed at over-reacting.

'Sorry, I just wasn't expecting it to rock like that when I got in.'

'Don't be sorry. Little boats are all over the place. It's scary if you're not used to it but unless you go crazy you

33

won't end up in the water. Sit over to that side,' he pointed, 'then we'll balance it out.'

Charlie sat at the back of the boat with his hand on the tiller. He turned the engine and it started first time. Despite his reassurances, Maggie gripped the side of the boat as he made what felt like a very tight turn, and they headed for Poole.

'Where do you live?' shouted Maggie, turning slightly towards Charlie so that her voice wouldn't be lost on the wind.

'Over there,' Charlie called back, pointing vaguely in the direction of Studland. Well, she already knew that.

'Where do you keep the boat?'

'There's a mooring I use close to the house.'

'So not right on the water then?'

'Have you seen the size of these places?' he said, gesturing to the houses lining the harbour.

They were passing the backs of huge houses in Sandbanks, the opposite side of the harbour to Studland. Maggie had no idea how much they were worth but some of them had swimming pools in their gardens, immense glass windows and private docks to moor their boats. So yes, obviously it looked like it would be expensive to live that close to the water.

The journey took about ten minutes before Charlie pulled the boat alongside the harbour wall in Poole and tied it off. He pulled a folded sack truck and some bags out from under the front seat and laid them on the quayside before he leapt up there himself in one easy motion and then reached out his hand to Maggie.

'Just reach for my hand once you've put your foot on the side of the boat, and kind of bounce up.'

This was going to end badly, thought Maggie. Bounce up? She steeled herself for the inevitable humiliation, stared at his hand to be sure she knew where she was grabbing, trying not to be distracted by the thought of touching him, and bounced. As her hand came into contact with Charlie's he pulled her up and, along with the motion of the boat bobbing upwards from her bounce, she was surprised to find herself standing on the quay. Right in front of Charlie, close enough to be staring straight at his stubbly, beardy chin. Her gaze lifted to meet his eyes which were the deepest brown and looking intently back at her with a smile to them.

'It's this way,' he said, pointing with his free hand and then dropping hers so that he could pick up the sack truck and bags.

As she followed him along the narrow pavement, Maggie could still feel the warmth from his hand on her skin and she pressed her fingers into her palm to try and preserve it. She'd never felt like this about holding Ben's hand. Perhaps that had been too familiar in the end, nothing out of the ordinary to the point where she couldn't immediately bring to mind one memory of holding hands with him. Obviously, they had held hands, of course they had, but it had never made her heart swell so that the memory had imprinted on her forever. She knew this was altogether different.

Trying to be rational about it, Maggie reasoned that it was probably a combination of Charlie being the only man in quite a wide vicinity — Josh and Eric didn't count, the fact that she always fancied men who wore harnesses to climb trees — something to do with the straps around their thighs, and that he was lovely. Also, they had a lot in common, mainly work but it was a start and she could tell that they were both beginning to realise that they were on the same wavelength. Another massive plus was that Charlie had no problem with her being his sort-of boss and that was a wild improvement on how things had been with Ben in the end, if she was comparing.

They went their separate ways in the supermarket, meeting at the checkouts where Charlie was already packing his shopping. Maggie purposely picked a till away from him so that he wouldn't see her huge stockpile of tampons and she tried to bag them up quickly before he came over to help her.

'Got plenty of toiletries?' he asked.

Maggie blushed, maybe he'd seen after all.

'That's almost the only stuff Jan can't get for you if you're desperate.' No, thankfully it wasn't a reference to her shopping.

'Yep, and plenty of cereal and chocolate. Absolute essentials.'

While Maggie paid, Charlie strapped her bags to his truck leaving her to carry a couple of light bags which wouldn't fit on and they walked back to the boat in the sunshine.

Maggie felt more confident on the boat ride back. The weight of the shopping seemed to bed the boat down in the water making it feel more secure than it had before. Charlie pulled up to the quay on Bramble Island and left his own shopping in the boat while he helped Maggie carry hers to the cottage.

'Thanks for the lift.'

'Hey, anytime. It was nice to have some company.'

'So, will I see you in the morning?'

'Sure, I'll come by the office to meet Eric. I think it's his turn tomorrow.'

'Okay. Bye then.'

Charlie stuffed his hands in his pockets and smiled. 'Bye, Maggie.' He turned and walked back to the boat.

It was the first time she'd heard him say her name. He made it sound different to the way anyone else said it and she liked it. She went into the cottage and watched from the window as he got back in his boat and eventually disappeared from sight.

8

Charlie headed home feeling light-hearted. He was starting to notice that he often felt like that after spending time with Maggie. He enjoyed the ease of her company; the fact that she didn't ask him a lot of personal questions and didn't offer any information about herself either. Although as time went by, he was beginning to develop a curiosity about Maggie's life. Apart from masterminding the Trust Treks, what had she done before? Where did she come from? What were her dreams for the future? It seemed easier and safer not to know or ask at the moment but he couldn't help but wonder, which was only natural when you were friends with someone, wasn't it?

He thought back to the moment he'd helped her out of the boat in Poole. They had been so close to each other. Her hair had smelt of the wind and her eyes had sparkled when she looked up at him. He'd wanted to keep hold of her hand after that but couldn't bring himself to, it would have been too much of a leap. He could almost feel the rush again now, that feeling, whatever it was, when they had touched. It was really for the best that they were just friends. He wasn't ready for a relationship. On paper, it had been over three years since Jessica, but he knew it was only very recently that he'd begun to feel that he was over her. Over everything.

He put his groceries away and sat down at his computer to check his emails. These days there was rarely anything of any interest but he always checked anyway, out of habit. Today there was an email that almost made his heart stop when he saw who it was from.

Jared Kolowsky was the CEO of the company Charlie used to work for in the US. More than that, they had been roommates in college and had founded High 5 together. They'd written the code for the highly successful social networking site through long nights in their dorm room and launched it a couple of years after they'd graduated. They'd been together through everything right up until Charlie left.

Until this moment, Charlie had done his best to ignore his past life. He hadn't kept up at all with news, colleagues or friends from Silicon Valley. It had helped that no one really knew where he was, apart from his family. The email from Jared was the first contact he'd had with the company for three years.

Charlie sat, his fingers hovering over the mouse, building himself up to read the email, all the time wondering what it could be about for Jared to have gone to the trouble of tracking him down. He clicked.

From: jared@high5.com
To: charlie.mac@techmail.com
Subject: Hi (5) from the Valley
Hey Charlie,
I can't believe it's been so long. Too long. Things have never been the same without you. I know I promised not to contact you, especially about the company but you must have heard what's going down, even from over there on your island! Your mom told me how to get you, don't be mad with her.
So, Cumulus.com want to buy High 5 and man, their offer is out of this world. You need to be involved in this. Not just

because legally you still own 40% and as majority shareholders we both need to sign off on the sale, but it was ours, Charlie. Don't forget how it was in the beginning. I feel bad about how we left things. I could have done more, I know that now and you'll never know how sorry I am about what happened but this could be great for both of us.

I can't wait to hear what you think.

Best, Jared

Charlie stared at the email for a few minutes, slowly taking in what it meant. It had been so long since he'd had anything to do with the business that he had no idea of the implications of considering a sale. He trusted Jared to make the right decision for the business but knew that even if he went along with it all at arm's length, the time would come when he would have to physically go to the States to sign on the dotted line. He'd known deep down that eventually something would force him to return. Thinking back to how he'd felt back then was still hard. He hadn't come far enough to feel that things would be different, that he'd be okay if he had to return.

Maybe selling the company would be the best way of putting it all behind him and moving on. Since he'd left, the money had still been paid into his bank account every month despite him having no contact with them but that was Jared's guilt talking. He had kept High 5 going on his own for almost three years so perhaps Charlie owed him the chance to have all the hard work come to fruition. It had been their dream to have someone with the stature of Cumulus.com want to buy them, as if it was the ultimate validation of their success. But these days Charlie preferred not to think about it, not to dream about it because it was lost to him forever, whatever happened to it next.

He would put off the decision until another day, until he knew what he wanted to do.

9

Bramble Castle, the corporate retreat which was so tantalisingly off-limits to the rest of Bramble Island was finally about to be discovered by Maggie. As it was owned by the Trust and leased out, they were able to use it for meetings when necessary as there wasn't anywhere else suitable on the island for hosting Trust VIPs.

Maggie's visitors were the head of marketing, Verity Chase, the head of special projects, Rob Tanner and the area manager, David Simons. Maggie had met David before when she'd been interviewed for her job. He was a friendly, easy-going man who had been overseeing Dorset for years. He knew every property like the back of his hand and regularly visited them all.

The Trust's plans for Bramble Island had been made clear to Maggie when they approached her to be park manager on the island. She'd made a strong impression on the Trust's management with her Trust Treks initiative and they wanted her on board for a special project on Bramble Island. She'd been sworn to secrecy and this meeting was the first time it had been mentioned since she'd arrived.

Maggie waited on the quay as she watched the ferry approach. She wasn't sure whether Verity and Rob had been to Bramble Island before, so she was thinking about where she ought to take them to give them the best impression of the island. Maybe she should wait until after the meeting to decide in case it became obvious that there was an area that would be of particular interest to them.

William waved at her from the gangway as her visitors disembarked. It wasn't the nicest day, quite cloudy and threatening rain so there were only a handful of day-trippers. David made a beeline for her.

'Maggie, wonderful to see you here on Bramble Island.' He looked genuinely thrilled to bits and was beaming at her in the manner of a very proud parent, which was quite amusing if a little odd. 'May I introduce Verity Chase and Rob Tanner from Trust HQ. Verity, Rob, this is Maggie Cassidy, park manager on Bramble Island.'

They all shook hands and said hello. Maggie thought Verity and Rob seemed a little out of place with their attempts at dressed-down corporate outfits but welcomed them to the island and then led the way to the gatehouse of the Castle, trying to contain her excitement at finally being able to go inside.

The hallway was heavily panelled with dark, highly polished wood and a wonderful sweeping wooden staircase that demanded your attention. Maggie breathed in the smell of the place, the old wood fighting against the fresh modern scents of a hotel and winning. She gazed upwards and saw ornate plasterwork on the ceiling and beautiful light fittings which probably weren't original but were certainly inkeeping with the style of the old house.

They were led by the hotel manager into a large room that functioned as a lounge for guests. It had high ceilings with arched pillars and big windows which sucked in the light from outside even on this cloudy day. They walked through and were seated in armchairs around a low coffee table next to a huge window with glorious views of the lawns which led down to the harbour. David ordered tea and coffee for them all and then began the meeting.

'As you all know there is a proposal, still in its very early stages, to build a number of holiday lodges on Bramble Island. Today's meeting is to discuss and possibly view potential sites as well as being an opportunity for us to iron out preliminary details of the project so that when the time comes, we are well equipped to answer questions from other stakeholders.'

Maggie began to feel a little duplicitous. She had known that this was coming, that it was the main reason she had been chosen for the job on Bramble Island. Her enthusiasm for being involved in the project had been tempered since she arrived on the island and saw how beautiful it was and she found herself wanting to be an advocate for the island to make sure that any development was sympathetic to the ecology. She had fallen under its spell and would much prefer that absolutely nothing happened which might change the charm and natural beauty of the island. Perhaps that put her in a better position to fight for the best way forward if she had to, but she now knew she would have other issues as well. Like explaining it to Charlie.

'The aim of the project,' began Rob, 'is to create more Trust holiday accommodation in this area. Log cabins are proving to be a popular choice for families and done well, it can be a very lucrative stream of income. Having Bramble Island as our first venture into this, aside from our traditional cottages is key to the success of the initiative as a whole.'

'The Bramble Island project would be our flagship holiday offer,' said Verity. 'It is a unique site which is in a highly sought-after area as regards holiday destinations. There is an awful lot of space there begging to be utilised.'

Maggie had to stop herself from rolling her eyes. 'Well, it is utilised, mainly by trees at the moment. Do you have any idea of where you plan to build?'

'The south side near the Scout campsite is the obvious choice, being less wooded it should be relatively easy to bring in materials and the large expanses of flat would be easier to negotiate but we think the west side will offer that feeling of being immersed in the woodland and each lodge will feel more secluded if it's not on open ground,' Rob said.

'That's true but it's also one of the most attractive areas for visitors,' said Maggie. 'We need to be careful not to detract from what we can offer day visitors.'

'Yes, we do need to be mindful of the impact on the island, especially because of the squirrels,' said David.

'Squirrels?' chirped Verity. 'What have they got to do with anything?'

'Bramble Island is one of the only places in the UK with a breeding population of red squirrels,' explained David patiently. 'They're a huge draw for visitors. Think a marketing person would know that,' he added under his breath.

The discussion continued through the serving of tea and coffee after which point Maggie was starting to feel as if actually, nothing she said would have any impact on any of it. Verity seemed wedded to the idea of nestling the lodges in the woods Rob and David were having difficulty trying to convince her of any other possibilities. Perhaps the time had come to show them around so that Verity could see the place they were talking about rather than relying on one of the rudimentary maps which were handed out to visitors.

Maggie led them across to the west side of the island which was one of the most heavily wooded areas and where Charlie was still coppicing. He had Josh working with him all the time now which annoyed Alice no end, but she seemed to have realised by now that Charlie wasn't interested in anything remotely romantic.

Maggie spotted the two of them before they saw her and managed to take a different route. The last thing she wanted was to have to explain to Charlie what was going on in front of anyone else. When the time came she'd have to be tactful and careful if she didn't want to ruin the tentative friendship they were building.

'This is the west side, heavily wooded as you can see, with traditional English species like this magnificent oak and the ash over here,' Maggie said, pointing out the trees which she hoped might inspire a bit of restraint about destroying the woodland.

'It's quite dense, isn't it? We'd have to get rid of quite a lot of trees just to be able to access the site.' Rob pointed out the obvious; exactly the approach needed with Verity.

'Not a problem. I wonder if we can use the wood for building the lodges?' Verity asked.

Maggie was about to launch into a monologue on the importance of native English woodlands when David did it for her.

'Steady on, Verity. There are over sixty species of tree on this island, it's really quite remarkable and as the Trust, we must bear in mind that we are not destroyers of nature, quite the contrary. Any development such as this must strive to enhance the environment while being sympathetic to the nature.'

'Shall we head to the south?' said Maggie, leading them across the heathland in the middle of the island to the flatter area near the historic site of the world's first Scout camp.

'Ah, yes,' said David. 'Wonderful views of the bay. Visitors would love that.'

'Easy access for construction, as we said,' conceded Rob. 'It could be the better option.'

'It's not what was intended though,' said Verity, exasperated. 'It's hardly a woodland retreat, the whole bloody harbour would be watching your every move.'

'Maybe that could be a draw? A sea view and the closest thing we have to a beach on the island is on your doorstep.'

Maggie attempted a sales pitch for the south side. 'And with the views of the Sandbanks properties, people might feel that they are sharing in a slice of that luxury.'

'That's a very good point, Maggie,' said Verity, surprising Maggie by being so agreeable. 'I could definitely work with that idea.'

'Well, it's certainly worth considering. There are options here, that's the main thing. We'll draw up proposals and go from there,' said Rob. 'Thanks for your time today, Maggie.'

They said goodbye and David led Rob and Verity back to the quay to catch the next ferry back to the mainland.

Maggie headed back to the office feeling as if she'd had a small victory on behalf of the island. Although she worked for the Trust and had landed the Bramble Island job because of her experience and success in launching and marketing the Trust Treks, she wanted to make sure that she was protecting the interests of not only the island and the trees but the interests of the people who loved and cared for the island. People like Clare, Jan and Charlie. Somehow, especially Charlie.

Megan was in the office, busy designing a bug-hunting leaflet. 'Hi Maggie,' she said without lifting her gaze from the computer screen. 'Charlie was looking for you earlier. There's a tree which he thinks may need to come down and he wants you to have a look at it.'

'Charlie left that message?' Maggie somehow couldn't imagine Charlie coming in and offering a lengthy explanation to Megan.

'No, Josh came to say. What have you been up to?'

'I had a meeting with the area manager. It was in the Castle, it's amazing in there.'

'Oh my god! You have not been in the Castle! It's like some kind of fortress where no one comes in or out. Seriously, Maggie, I live here and I've literally never seen anyone.'

Maggie smiled. 'I know, but it has its own dock so they go in that way and the gardens are pretty big so maybe they don't bother looking at the rest of the island.'

'That's just weird. It would be, like, beckoning you, wouldn't it?'

'Yes, it would,' Maggie agreed, 'but not everyone's into nature like we are.'

'Hmm, weird, like I said.'

'Okay, so I'll head over to Charlie and Josh and look at the tree. Back in an hour or so.'

It was so nice to have the volunteers on the island. They were such an enormous help and it was great to see them settling in. Megan had really come out of herself and Maggie had a suspicion that she and Josh had started something. Thrown together just in the same way that she and Ben had once been.

10

It had been an easy decision for Charlie to choose Josh as his sidekick. Josh was passionate about trees and hoped to be a forest or woodland manager in the future. Having the opportunity to work with someone like Charlie was invaluable for him; experience was everything because it was such a competitive field.

Charlie had quickly noticed that Josh was on the same wavelength as him when it came to decisions about coppicing. The other three were well-qualified but not as keen on trees and didn't have a feel for what the woodland needed like he did. Not having to explain every tiny detail also suited Charlie who preferred to work in peace and quiet, and Josh seemed happy to go along with that.

'Did you see Maggie?' asked Charlie, as Josh returned from his visit to the office.

'Nope, Megan was on her own there. I've left a message with her.'

'And how was Megan?' teased Charlie gently.

'Good.' Josh grinned and then laughed. 'Actually, I really like her.' By Josh's own admission, it had started as a bit of fun. With just the four of them on the island, sharing the chalet, something was bound to happen.

'Good for you, man.'

'You and Maggie ever… y'know?'

'Maggie? No, no…'

'I just thought, you two, same age, tiny island.'

'Yeah, I can see how you'd think that.' More than anything, it amused Charlie that the volunteers saw him and Maggie as so much older than them.

'I think you'd make a great couple.'

'Thought you were dealing with that sycamore over there?' said Charlie, pretending to be stern but then breaking into a smile as Josh turned away.

'Yeah, you don't want to talk about it, I get it.'

It was great to kid around with a guy again. Charlie hadn't realised how much he'd missed that part of working with other people. Not that there had been much kidding around at High 5 in the end, at least not for him. That had been part of the problem. A little more kidding around might have led to a little less of a nervous breakdown.

How had he gone from starting up his own company with his best friend to being the guy who broke down in the most important meeting of his life? Even now, he didn't know the answer and that was what frightened him so much about the thought of going back there.

Ever since he'd had the email from Jared, he'd been wondering what to do. What it would be like to go back. It'd be awful having to face everyone again because basically, no one had seen him since the day he'd been led out of the building by Tom and driven home.

After spending two days in bed sleeping almost solidly, he'd gone to Lake Tahoe and bought the first place he'd seen. No one had known where to find him, and he'd just walked endlessly in the woods, sailed on the lake and eventually met Clay who taught him about working a woodland. It had given him a focus and helped him to reset himself. Even once he'd started to feel better, he couldn't face the thought of going back and had written to Jared saying that he would be taking indefinite leave. At the time, he really hadn't cared whether the company would be okay without him — of course it would be, but the feeling of the success or failure of the company being down to him personally, was hard to shake.

A year after he'd left High 5, he'd decided to take a vacation to his tiny English island in Poole Harbour. He'd not visited since all the work had been done to extend the old house because that had happened just before he'd left the Valley and was something he hadn't cared too much about at the time. He'd sailed around Poole Harbour in his yacht and one day had docked on Bramble Island. The woodland there had been managed but not with a firm enough hand and Charlie could see exactly what could be done. He sought out Paul in the Trust office and offered himself as a volunteer, initially for three months and he'd just stayed.

Charlie loved his island. The house was a modern, minimalist space which gave him everything he needed. He'd decided on the renovations with his architect and had left the finer details to his partner, Jessica. To begin with, it had been hard to be in the house knowing that her touch was everywhere but that feeling had waned over time and now Charlie really felt like it was his.

'Charlie!' Maggie called out to him from the edge of the heavily wooded area they were working in. Clearly, she wasn't prepared to fight through the undergrowth today.

'Hey, Maggie! I'm coming out to you.' He picked his way to the cleared area where Maggie stood.

'Josh said you have a tree for me to look at?'

'Yeah, it's over here.' He led the way, taking the footpath until they got closer.

'I think Josh and Megan are seeing each other,' said Maggie.

'Dating you mean?'

Maggie nodded.

'Yeah, he said he likes her.'

'Well, Megan is in a constant love daydream so I'm glad he feels the same way.'

'Watch out because the next thing will be they want everyone else to be in love as well. Josh is already onto me.'

'Really? Not with Alice?'

'No, with you.' He looked at her briefly to gauge her reaction and noticed her eyes widen, though she was staring at the ground. ''Because you know we *are* the same age, Maggie.'

She looked up at him and grinned. 'It's so funny that they think we're a couple of no-hoper old fogeys.'

'What the hell's a fogey?'

'Not fogey, *old* fogey. I don't know the exact definition but some ancient decrepit person.'

'Like an old coot?'

'Okay, if you like.' Maggie looked at him, with one eyebrow raised. 'Anyway, there's more to it than being the same age, obviously.'

'Obviously.' And there was more to it than that, Charlie knew it and he would bet on the fact that Maggie knew it too and that was why they were holding back from each other. He knew why he was; he'd taken losing Jessica so hard that he had never wanted to put himself in that position again. And it wasn't that he was suddenly over everything and ready to fall in love again, it was purely Maggie. She was making him think about falling in love again and he had no control over it. He was starting to see that maybe he had to let it happen and that was terrifying but exhilarating and exciting at the same time. On the other hand, she was literally the first woman that had crossed his path in years, not counting Jan and Clare. Was he just having these feelings because she was there and they got on, rather than because she was someone he would pick out of a crowd of eligible women? Did that even matter? Being friends was a great start. He needed a friend, someone like Maggie who made him smile and if that turned into something else, well, he would worry about that later.

They reached the oak tree. It wasn't huge, probably around fifty years old but it wasn't thriving. Maggie bent down to collect some leaves from the ground.

'It's got bad leaf drop for this time of year.' She looked up at the tree, concern furrowing her brow.

'And there are signs of beetle infestation. I think it could be Acute Oak Decline.'

'Are there other oak trees of the same species around here?' Maggie rubbed her hand against the bark as if she was soothing the tree.

'Yeah, I've checked them and there are no signs of it having spread. You think we should fell?'

'Reluctantly, yes. Do you?'

'Yes, I hate felling trees in their prime but in this case, there's good reason. Josh and I will do it tomorrow.'

'Poor tree.'

'It was probably always a little weak to have succumbed to that. It's the best thing for the rest of the wood.'

Maggie looked so forlorn that Charlie wrapped his arms around her and pulled her into a hug, her head resting against his chest. It had been instinctive and now that he'd had a second to realise what had happened he felt a little panicked at not having thought it through.

'I know.' Maggie said, her voice muffled as she spoke into his flannel shirt. 'Thanks, Charlie.' He felt her arms squeeze him a little then she patted a hand on his back and pulled away. He let her go, so relieved that it hadn't been at all awkward that he didn't stop to think about how amazing it had felt to hold her in his arms. How she had fit there perfectly and naturally as if she had been made to match his embrace.

'Well, I should get back to Josh, make sure he hasn't gone too easy on the sycamore. Thanks for coming to check out the tree.'

'No problem. Let me know if you two need a hand with the felling, Eric or Megan could help you.'

'Okay, thanks. See you tomorrow, I guess.'

Maggie walked away from him towards the main path. He took a deep breath. Something was happening. He felt it coursing through him like a bolt of energy and any reservations he'd had about getting close to someone again had evaporated. He just hoped she felt the same way.

As if she could hear his thoughts she turned back, briefly. Their eyes met and he could tell in that couple of seconds that he wasn't alone in wondering whether something was happening between them.

11

Maggie woke up to the sound of heavy rain blowing against the bedroom window. She wrapped a blanket around her and opened the curtains to see rain lashing the island and the sea looking grey and as choppy as it was likely to get in the harbour. She pulled on some woolly socks and still huddled in the blanket, went downstairs to make a cup of tea.

Sat on the windowsill in the lounge, warming her hands on the mug, she thought about how she'd sat there last night, feeling slightly stalkery, watching Charlie untie his boat from the dock, knowing now how his body felt against hers.

Since he'd taken her in his arms, she hadn't been able to stop thinking about him. That moment of kindness from him had made Maggie feel protected and loved more than she'd ever felt before and she'd had to force herself to pull away sooner than she'd wanted to for fear that she'd stay there forever and then Charlie would have realised that something had changed for her. But after she'd walked away from him in the wood, all she'd wanted to do was to run back to him and have him hold her tight, sweep her into his arms, swing her around and tell her that he loved her and then kiss her, deep and slow.

She smiled at how far-fetched the whole idea was, even for

a daydream, finished her tea and went to get dressed. There was nothing to be done because Charlie, she felt sure, didn't feel the same way.

The morning disappeared in a frenzy of work for the Trust Treks as Maggie had to review all of the leaflets Megan had produced before they were sent to the printers, then meet with Clare over at the visitor centre so she could approve it all from her side as it was a collaboration between them, particularly given that Clare would be providing most of the staff to run the Treks.

The heavy rain had turned into a drizzle that had settled a low cloud over the island and the harbour. As Maggie made her way from the visitor centre back to the office, she marvelled at how different the island felt in this kind of weather and how bleak it must be in the winter when there were fewer visitors. Charlie must be a hardy soul, she thought.

'Have you seen Charlie and Josh today?' asked Maggie, pulling off her waterproof coat and hanging it on the back of the door to dry.

'I saw Josh this morning when he went off with Eric to clear a drainage ditch over by the Scout campsite but I haven't seen Charlie today,' Megan said not looking up from the website she was scrolling through.

'I thought Josh was felling the oak with Charlie today?'

'He was but then the ditch needed clearing and Eric needed a hand. I think Charlie was getting on with the oak.'

Maggie stopped and looked at Megan. 'Not by himself? In this weather?'

Megan finally looked up. 'Well, Charlie would know if he should wait for Josh, wouldn't he?'

'I don't know. I'll be back.' Maggie grabbed her coat, pulling it on as she strode along the path towards the woods where she'd met Charlie the day before. She really hoped he wouldn't be felling that oak tree by himself. Aside from the sheer size of the tree, the weather conditions weren't ideal for felling. The wood would be slippery and difficult to handle even with two people. She was sure he would be getting on with something else as Josh wasn't able to help. But she knew that for all Charlie's intuition about the woodland, he probably lacked any formal training on health and safety issues. Maybe she was wrong, but whatever happened, she would be calling a health and safety briefing for everyone the next day and was berating herself for being remiss in not doing that as soon as she'd arrived on Bramble Island.

Maggie headed into the woods, away from the main path and towards where she hoped she remembered the oak being from the day before. She couldn't hear a chainsaw which was a good sign. The ground was slippery with wet leaves and huge drips occasionally landed on her head even though she was protected from the persistent drizzle by the tree canopy.

She saw the canopy of the oak tree which was easy to spot with its depleted leaf cover once she was in the right area. And she could see Charlie sitting at the base of the tree, leaning against it.

'Hi, Charlie!' she called, losing sight of him temporarily as she weaved in between the trees towards him.

'Hey, Maggie…I was just going to call you.'

As she got closer to him, she could see that his right arm was covered in blood, his left hand clasped around his forearm. He looked pale but managed a small smile.

'Christ Charlie, what happened? I knew you'd be trying to fell the bloody tree by yourself. Why didn't you wait for Josh?' She crouched down next to him, took her coat off and pulled her long-sleeved t-shirt over her head. She took her penknife from her pocket and used it to rip one of the sleeves off which she then wrapped around Charlie's arm over the place his hand was gripping.

'I wasn't felling… just roping it up ready for tomorrow,' he said weakly.

'Okay, it doesn't matter now,' said Maggie, softening slightly now that she knew he hadn't been completely gung-ho about the tree felling. 'I'm going to wrap this tighter. Take your hand away on three. One, two, three.'

Charlie took his hand away and groaned as Maggie tightened the makeshift bandage around his arm after having a quick look at the extent of the injury. It was a nasty gash; long, deep and jagged. She took her penknife to the rest of her t-shirt and made another couple of strips of bandage which seemed to do the job of stemming the bleeding and then she made a sling to keep his forearm high up across his chest.

'You're pretty good at this,' Charlie said breathlessly, leaning his head back against the trunk of the tree.

'I'd prefer not to be showing off my skills to you, but thanks.' Maggie smiled at him, then brushed his wet hair away from his eyes with a gentle stroke across his forehead.

'Shit Maggie, it really hurts,' he said, scrunching his eyes closed in pain.

'I know, we're going to get you sorted, don't worry.' Maggie pulled out her phone only to find it had no signal. 'I'm just going to call the office, I won't be a sec.' She made her way towards a clearer area of the wood and hoped for a couple of bars. Nothing. She had to go all the way back to the main path before she saw any sign of life. She rang Megan and asked her to call an ambulance to the quayside in Sandbanks and to see if she could hold the ferry to get them across there.

Maggie went back to Charlie who was exactly where she'd left him, though he'd fallen asleep and the blood was already seeping through the sling.

'Charlie! Wake up!' She rubbed his cheeks to try and revive him until he opened his eyes with some effort. 'Okay, we're going to get up and walk now. It's not far, ready?' She stood in front of him and pulled on his good arm to try and help him up. Once he was standing, she wrapped his good arm across her shoulders and held him around his waist as they started to walk.

It was tricky to walk through the wood two abreast, the trees were so close together and Maggie was constantly looking ahead to decide on the best route while trying to avoid any ground that was too uneven underfoot.

'I need to stop for a sec…'

'No, we're nearly there now, let's carry on.' Maggie could feel the full weight of him as he struggled to keep going, both of them struggling and soaking wet. Maggie kept glancing at Charlie's forearm which was bleeding profusely again and wondered whether they ought to stop to try and stem the bleeding properly or whether it was better to just get to the quay quickly. She felt like if they stopped, she'd never get him going again. It was a definite possibility that Charlie might pass out as he had become so drowsy. They just had to get there.

Finally, just as the visitor centre came into view, Megan came running towards them. The strength fled from Maggie's body as the relief that they had made it overwhelmed her and she struggled to support Charlie's weight.

'Oh my god!' cried Megan, trying to support the injured side of Charlie without hurting him. She managed to take some of his weight from Maggie by holding onto Maggie's arm where she was gripping around Charlie's waist. It was enough to enable them to walk faster, and they managed to get to the quayside before he passed out.

'Where's the ferry?' gasped Maggie.

'It hasn't come back yet. I tried to call them but I couldn't get through.'

Because of the low cloud, the Sandbanks quay was completely obscured from view and there was no sign of the ferry as far as they could see. For a minute, Maggie felt completely helpless. She had got Charlie this far and now they couldn't get him off the island. Then down to their right,

Maggie caught sight of Charlie's boat bobbing next to them.

'Help me get him into the boat!'

Between them, they hauled Charlie to his feet again, causing him to cry out.

'Charlie! We're going to take your boat. Where are the keys?'

'Pocket,' he mumbled as he stumbled into the boat. 'Maggie, you can't...' he began, then passed out again.

Maggie checked his trouser pockets and found the keys. She was so glad she'd gone on that shopping trip with him, otherwise, she'd have no idea where to start with turning on the engine, or anything.

'Shall I come with you?' asked Megan.

Maggie agreed without hesitation. It seemed sensible to have someone to keep an eye on Charlie while Maggie was driving the boat.

'Do you want me to take the tiller? My dad's got a boat with a similar motor.'

'Oh god, yes!' Maggie handed the keys to Megan and sat in the bottom of the boat, with Charlie's head resting in her lap, stroking his forehead and feeling for his breath with her other hand, relieved to feel it, warm and regular.

As she sat there, looking down at him, his forehead knotted in pain despite being unconscious, all she wanted at that moment was for him to be okay. This man, he meant everything to her.

12

Charlie was awake, although his eyes were still closed. It was too much effort to open them. He knew he wasn't at home, in his own bed. Someone was holding his hand and after a couple of minutes, curiosity won the battle he was having with his eyelids.

'Maggie,' he whispered.

She was sitting next to him, holding his hand, her hair looked crazy and she was pale but smiling.

'Hey, how are you feeling?'

'I'm good…I don't know…what are we, in the hospital or something?'

'Yes, remember…'

He followed her gaze to his arm which was heavily bandaged, resting on a pillow at his side.

He went to lift his arm, to take a look and winced when it hurt. 'Oh god.' He looked back at Maggie who tried to reassure him.

'You've got quite a few stitches so it'll be sore. Can you remember what happened?' She kept hold of his hand as if that was completely normal.

He remembered deciding not to fell the oak tree. And he remembered deciding to rope it up ready to fell, even though it was raining and he should have known better. He had climbed up a little way so he could throw a strap around one of the main branches to give them a head start when the weather cleared.

'I guess I slipped and fell out of the tree. I think there was a broken branch that caught me on the way down. Did I pass out?'

'Not until we got to the boat. We managed to walk to the quay but the ferry wasn't there so we had to take your boat, I hope that's okay.'

'Of course. How did you find me?'

She shrugged. 'I just had a feeling so I came to look for you. I knew you wanted to fell the tree and I was worried you'd have tried doing it on your own. Sorry, I should have known you wouldn't.'

'Don't be sorry, Maggie. If you hadn't come to find me I might still be there.' He squeezed her hand. 'Thanks.'

She moved her other hand on top of his and stroked it, blinking as her eyes filled with tears.

'Charlie, I...' She drew her hand away and wiped it across her eyes quickly.

'It's okay, honey,' he said tenderly, 'we're okay now.' He thought Maggie had never looked more beautiful than she did now. He knew just what she was trying to say because he wanted to say it too. And actually, neither of them needed to worry about finding the right words, they just knew.

A nurse came in and suggested that as it was the middle of the night, Maggie may want to go home and get some sleep. They were going to keep Charlie in for observation because he'd lost consciousness and was still on a drip.

'I can't really go home,' Maggie said after the nurse had taken Charlie's blood pressure and left. 'I told Megan she could take the boat back to Bramble Island and the ferry won't be running now.'

'Do you have any money?'

'No, I don't have anything. I left in a hurry.'

He smiled. 'Well, I appreciate that. Are my clothes here somewhere? My wallet's in my pants.'

Maggie rummaged under the bed and pulled out a plastic bag that contained all of Charlie's things, most of which were only fit for the bin now. She found his wallet, opened it and handed it to him. He pulled out a black Amex credit card and handed it to Maggie. She raised her eyebrows as if it needed an explanation.

'They're all like that in the States.' It was a metal rather than a plastic card, a hangover from his corporate life.

'Oh, really?'

'Really. Come here.' He whispered his PIN into her ear. With his hand gently resting on her hair he said, 'Go and find a hotel close by, don't worry about how much it costs, I mean it. Sleep and come back tomorrow.' He pulled her towards him and gave her the lightest kiss on the lips. He tried not to think about the fact that it was their first kiss because he wanted it to be so much more, but not now. Maggie stroked her fingers across his forehead and he suddenly felt that that had happened before but couldn't remember it properly. He closed his eyes and was almost instantly asleep.

Maggie came back the next morning looking refreshed and wearing clean clothes. She put an M&S bag on the bed before kissing Charlie on the cheek and perching next to him on the bed.

'I thought we ought to have some clean clothes, I used your credit card, I hope that was okay.'

'It's great, thank you. As long as you haven't got me slacks or anything too preppy.'

'I took a risk with a checked shirt, t-shirt and jeans,' she said.

He laughed and peeked in the bag.

'How are you feeling?'

'Better, sore but better. Did you find somewhere good to stay?'

'Yes, a very nice Premier Inn around the corner from here.'

She could have stayed anywhere. He had wanted her to sleep in the lap of luxury after what she did for him yesterday and yet she picked somewhere completely normal. Yet again she surprised him at how different she was from the girls he'd been out with before.

'A Premier Inn? You should have treated yourself.'

'That was a treat. As much as I love my cottage, a night in a huge bed with a hot, powerful shower was amazing. I slept like a log.'

'Me too.' Although he had slept well, Charlie had been woken up early to have his temperature and blood pressure taken and had been waiting impatiently for Maggie ever since, all the time mulling over what he could remember from the day before. Especially the part where they had been sat together holding hands. He thought they'd had an understanding but the more he thought about it, the more worried he became that he'd got it wrong. After all, he'd had some good painkillers and been unconscious. It could be that he'd mistaken Maggie's concern for something more.

'So, you know yesterday,' he cringed inwardly, unable to decide how to phrase it even though he was already talking. 'I don't know what you think but something was different with us yesterday.' He couldn't read Maggie's expression and she didn't say anything, so he felt he had to carry on. 'I mean, not just yesterday. The oak tree, that was when.'

Maggie was smiling now. 'For me, it was when you helped me out of the boat in Poole. And then the oak tree and then yesterday in the boat.'

'I don't remember that.'

'I know.' She reached over and took his hand. 'The thing is, I didn't expect this to happen. I thought I'd come to Bramble Island to start again. I had a lot I needed to leave behind.' She looked into his eyes, hers full of worry.

'I have plenty of stuff I've left behind. I just know that with you, none of that matters like it did before. You matter and that's kind of it.'

'That sounds too easy. It's easy to think we can leave the world behind, being on Bramble Island, but —'

'But we could see how it goes.' He looked up to the ceiling to take a second to gather his thoughts. 'I think we have something but it's so long since I've felt anything like that, it scares me in case... in case it ends up like before.' He wasn't ready or thinking clearly enough to explain to Maggie why he felt the need to hold back even when she was right here, wanting to be with him and even when he thought he wanted that too, more than anything. 'Let's just start off together and see what happens.'

She nodded and he let go of her hand to gently pull her towards him, unable to wait for a better moment to kiss her properly. As their lips met, it was as if tiny sparklers were brushing between them, the tingling so intense that all Charlie wanted was to take her in his arms and carry her right back to the hotel she had just come from.

13

Outside the hospital, Maggie found them a taxi and helped Charlie in, fastening his seatbelt. His arm was in a sling and although he hadn't said anything, she could tell from the expression on his face that he was in pain.

'Are you alright?' She stroked his good hand absentmindedly with her fingers as if she could smooth away the hurt for him. The nurse had said he would be weak for a few days because he'd lost a lot of blood and had been sedated for them to stitch him up, but he seemed to have faded gradually since he'd left the ward.

'Yeah, I'm good.'

'Will you be alright to get the Bramble Bay Ferry and then I can take you home on your boat? Or we could take the taxi round to Studland, but it'll cost quite a lot.' She wondered whether that kind of thing mattered to Charlie, armed as he was with a high-end credit card. Even she knew that card must have a hefty credit limit and that, coupled with the fact that he worked for the Trust, well it didn't add up.

'I don't live in Studland.' He offered no further explanation and Maggie didn't feel it was the time to press him as he was starting to look almost as bad as he did when she'd found him at the bottom of the oak tree. She half wondered whether she ought to take him back to the hospital.

'Okay...so Bramble Island?' He nodded, then laid his head back and closed his eyes. Perhaps he was expecting to stay with her. After all, the nurse had said he should have someone with him for twenty-four hours. She'd have to sleep on the sofa but that was okay.

The taxi pulled up at the Sandbanks quay and Maggie could see that the ferry was on its way back from the island so they wouldn't have to wait long. They walked slowly to a bench where they waited, Charlie once again sat with his eyes closed as if he was trying to shut himself off from the world. Once the ferry docked, William came and helped Charlie on board. They sat in silence which Maggie found increasingly worrying until Charlie placed his hand on her leg and gave it a gentle rub.

'Sorry, Maggie. I'm not feeling so good.'

'It's okay, we're almost there.'

When they disembarked, William gave Charlie a hand again. 'Your house, Maggie?'

'Yes, I think that's a good idea, thanks.'

'No, I need to go home, my boat's just there.'

'C'mon mate,' said William, 'you're in no state to pilot that.'

While entirely agreeing with William, Maggie knew that all Charlie wanted was his own bed, his own space.

'It's okay, I can take him,' said Maggie. William looked unconvinced. 'I can, it'll be fine.'

'Thanks, William, we'll be okay from here.' Charlie's voice said he was in no mood to argue. William shrugged and helped Charlie into the boat.

'You be careful, Maggie love. The wind's still strong today.'

'Did you drive the boat yesterday?' Charlie asked her.

'No, Megan did, it turns out she knows her way around a boat so I was off the hook. But I was paying attention when we went shopping. How hard can it be?'

Charlie managed a weak grin. 'Okay, you start it off but I'll take the tiller once we get close.'

Maggie started the engine having found the keys in the cubby under the seat. Good old Megan for thinking of that. She went slowly until she felt confident that she was in control, then wanting to get Charlie home as soon as she could, she let the throttle out and headed in the direction she had seen Charlie go many times before.

Before they approached Studland, Maggie needed to skirt around a small island but at that point, Charlie took the tiller and steered in the opposite direction, towards the far side of the little island. Maggie could see a clapboard boathouse come into view and Charlie was heading for it.

'You live on this island?'

'Uh-huh.' He smiled sheepishly.

The door to the boathouse opened at the push of a button on a remote control which Charlie had asked Maggie to dig out of the cubby. Maggie secured the boat, next to another, much bigger boat, feeling that while she and Charlie might have finally admitted their feelings to one another, there was an awful lot she didn't know about him.

He led her very slowly, seemingly finding it hard to catch his breath, up the shallow steps, through the garden, where eventually Maggie saw his house appear through the trees. It was white with huge bi-fold doors on the ground floor which led out to a deck with several levels. There were two storeys above with huge windows and Juliet balconies which would have a view of the open sea.

'God, Charlie. Seriously, I can't believe you live here.' She knew by now what a private person he was, so it was no surprise to her that she hadn't known, and that indeed no one seemed to know that Charlie lived on his own island.

'I will explain, but not now. I just need to sleep.' He let them into the house and headed straight for the stairs. 'Make yourself at home,' he said and left Maggie standing in the huge open-plan living area.

The whole place was painted white and had beautiful oak floors. There wasn't much furniture, just a huge navy blue corner sofa which was crying out for some scatter cushions, and an oak dining table surrounded by eight chairs. Maggie smiled because she didn't think for one minute that Charlie would ever entertain that many people at once but maybe she just didn't know him that well. Clearly not, after all she had found out today that he must either have been born into a fortune, won the lottery or something else that meant he could live like this *and* afford to do a job he loved. And apparently own an island.

She walked slowly around, trying to be quiet, almost feeling like an intruder. Although it was open-plan, there was a separate room off to one side which Maggie peeked into and discovered was an office with the most immense computer screen she'd ever seen. Back in the main room, there was a huge wood-burning stove in the fireplace and a large television hung on the chimney breast.

Opening a few cupboards in the kitchen, Maggie managed to find a mug and some teabags. Most of the cupboards were empty or just had a few items in them. There weren't any of Charlie's possessions, nothing personal at all. How had he ended up living in this amazing house with nothing in it?

Since they'd arrived on the island, barely half an hour earlier, Maggie had gone from feeling a huge connection to Charlie after they'd finally acknowledged their feelings for each other to now, feeling as if he was a total stranger. It didn't matter to her where he lived but for the past few weeks she'd been imagining him living in a little cottage in Studland. This place opened up so many questions for her about where he had been before, what his life was before. That was all part of what made him, and she wanted to understand everything, know everything about him.

If he hadn't had the accident, she still wouldn't know any of this. Maggie had been surprised at how seeing him injured had affected her and made her realise the depth of her feelings. Now that the adrenalin of the day before had worn off, she still felt the same way, of course, but she needed some reassurance from Charlie that everything she thought he felt too was still there. After all, he'd probably been high on drugs or something and today hadn't been that great with him struggling so much with the journey home.

She settled onto the sofa, turned the television on and sipped her tea. It wasn't long before she fell asleep.

14

It was dark when Charlie woke up, thankfully in his own bed although he was fully dressed having been too tired to care about taking his clothes off earlier. He sat up and winced; not only did his arm hurt but he felt stiff and bruised all over from the fall. He headed downstairs in search of painkillers and found Maggie asleep on the couch and the television playing quietly to itself.

He perched on the sofa next to her. 'Hey, Maggie, honey,' he whispered, stroking her cheek gently with his hand.

'Hmm,' she said sleepily, opening her eyes after a few seconds. 'Charlie, are you okay?' She sat up and rubbed her eyes with her fingertips. 'What time is it?'

'It's ten-thirty. You could have had a bed too, you know.'

'Well, I wasn't planning to fall asleep, I'm looking after you.'

'Oh, okay.' He smiled and kissed her softly on the forehead.

'Do you want a cup of tea or something?' she asked, sitting up.

'I could do with some of the pain meds we got from the hospital.'

'Oh god, I should have woken you up, you haven't had any

all day.'

'It's fine, I'm fine. We should fix some dinner too. Have you eaten?'

'No, I think I've been asleep almost as long as you.'

Charlie led the way to the kitchen, surprised by how much he loved the feeling of having Maggie in his house. She insisted that he sit down at the breakfast bar while she rummaged in the fridge and cupboards looking for something she could make while he sipped a glass of water and took some pills.

'How does pasta sound?'

'Perfect.' He watched her every move as she pottered around his kitchen finding pans and spoons, as she chopped garlic and picked fresh, slightly neglected, basil from the pot on the windowsill. He felt contented, as if this was how it was meant to be. Not Maggie cooking for them, but Maggie being here in his house, doing normal coupley things, looking after him. He couldn't imagine that Jessica would have done the same. She'd probably have hired someone to help instead.

'So Charlie, as much as I would love to stay here with you,' she said, as she began cooking the onions, 'I should probably go back to Bramble Island in the morning if you're okay to be by yourself by then. I was wondering if I could take the boat and then when you're ready to come back to work, I can come and fetch you?'

'The only problem with that is that I really don't want to wait until then to see you again, so if I say no, you'll have to stay,' he teased.

'That is true and a tempting thought, but I think we'd starve to death. If you let me leave, I can bring supplies.' Maggie turned down the pan of pasta, stood beside Charlie and wrapped her arms around his neck. 'Don't worry, now that I know where you live, I'll be hard to get rid of.' She kissed him and it felt amazing, still new and unexpected.

'I get it, the house has won you over.'

'I don't give a shit about the house.' She smothered anything else he had to say with another kiss. 'But I do love that you have your own island,' she said with a grin.

They ate in the kitchen, neither of them having realised how hungry they were. Then Maggie made them steaming hot mugs of tea and they sat on the sofa looking out at the blackness of the island and the sea beyond.

'So how, Charlie? How is all this yours?'

'Really? Tonight?' He felt beaten down by the question. Did he tell her everything or the edited highlights? He didn't want to tarnish her view of him by telling her about what was basically the worst time of his life, but at the same time he understood that she wanted to know.

'The curiosity is killing me, to be honest. I mean, an island of your own. It's crazy.'

It was crazy. When he'd lived in his Silicon Valley bubble as a tech millionaire, it had seemed perfectly normal to buy an island in England as a holiday retreat. After all, many friends of his were doing the same thing in the Caribbean or Dubai but England had always been his spiritual home ever since he'd holidayed at his grandparents as a kid. Everyone he knew had money to spend and just being part of that world had demanded a certain lifestyle. And that had attracted certain kinds of friends, certain types of women who at the time also seemed perfectly normal but if you plonked that world down here, in England, it would instantly seem absolutely insane.

'I started a company with my friend while we were in college. We developed an app and at the time, social media was just Facebook and the beginnings of Twitter. Our High 5 app revolutionised social media use amongst young people.'

'You invented High 5? That app where you can only message with five words? Oh my god, that's insane.'

Charlie laughed; Maggie's face was a picture of incredulity. 'Yeah, insane. We were just lucky, it took off and

I bought an island.'

'So why aren't you doing that now? If it's your company, are you still involved in between coppicing jobs?'

'Not really. I left a few years ago and haven't had much to do with it since.' That was the truth, the briefest version of it but he couldn't tell Maggie what had happened, not tonight. He would let her see the glossy topcoat of his previous life to start with and see what happened.

'But it's completely different to being a forester. Don't you miss all of that? I mean, we're so cut off here, it must be weird after having a high-tech life.'

'This is better, believe me. I'd rather be here with you than anything else I could be doing back in the Valley.' He could see Maggie's eyes sparkling even in the low light. He took her hand. 'I could do with going back to bed. Want to come?'

Her face lit up momentarily and then she said, 'I do... but I'm worried I might bump into your arm or something.'

'It's a huge bed, Maggie, we could both starfish like crazy and still not touch each other.' Charlie stood up and pulled at her hand. 'It's okay, I'll take the risk,' he said gently. Maggie stood up and followed him upstairs.

If his bed hadn't been so big, Charlie would have worried about inviting Maggie to join him but now he was more worried about the fact that he'd not changed the sheets for a week and that the bed looked so dishevelled from earlier on that he was starting to regret his suggestion. He wasn't planning on anything other than talking and sleeping as he was still feeling so sore, but it would have been nice to be able to offer Maggie something a little more romantic than a slept-in, slightly unsavoury man's bed.

'Okay, it's a huge bed.'

Charlie stopped himself laughing at Maggie in case it gave her a complex, but he genuinely loved seeing her reaction to everything. She was so open and unconcerned about trying to seem cool about it all and he loved that. He loved being able to share all of it with someone, knowing that it wasn't the main reason they were there. It was a relief.

They got into bed, Maggie having helped Charlie to undress properly this time, just down to his boxers. She let him get comfortable before she climbed in next to him and lay on her side, facing him. She was wearing white cotton panties and a white stretchy crop top which inexplicably he found far sexier than fancy lingerie. Maggie was slim and toned and although he wanted to caress every single piece of her, explore this part of her he had never seen before, tonight he had to settle for reaching for her hand.

'I can't believe you're here,' he said. 'It seems like it's happened so quickly and at the same time I felt like I had wanted to tell you for so long.'

'Why didn't you?'

Because the past had smothered him in a mist of self-doubt and mistrust that had only lifted when he had known that Maggie felt the same way, that was why, but instead he said, 'It's complicated.'

'Complicated is just a polite way of saying you don't want to talk about it, and that's okay. Another time.' She leaned over him, her hair brushing his cheek, the look on her face reassuring him that she didn't mind. 'Night Charlie, sleep well.' She kissed him tenderly and slowly, then snuggled down next to him.

'Night Maggie.' I love you.

15

Despite having been away from Bramble Island for less than two days, it felt like longer. Maggie had called Megan when she had got to the hospital with Charlie to let her know what was going on with him, but the volunteers were more than capable of holding the fort so she hadn't worried about work. Charlie had phoned Josh that morning to let him know he could carry on with the coppicing although there was plenty of other work for him if he wanted to wait until Charlie was back.

Maggie had a backlog of emails to go through. The busy season was approaching and the island was flourishing. There was plenty to do anyway but there were lots of requests coming through from the visitor team that needed dealing with, from footpaths that needed overhanging bushes cutting back to questions about where the most reliable red squirrel sightings were.

Among her emails was one from Rob Tanner, the project manager for the holiday lodges. Maggie felt anxious as soon as she saw it. She'd managed to put it out of her mind for the past couple of weeks but the whole thing felt even worse now that she was involved with Charlie. She knew she had to tell him because he was probably more invested in the wellbeing of the island, especially the woodland, than anyone else but she told herself it was better to be armed with concrete facts before she said anything. After all, it may be that they chose the flat, south of the island which would have hardly any impact on the woodland and it could all come to nothing anyway. That would make things a lot easier.

Maggie opened the email and breathed a sigh of relief. It was a document laying out the pros and cons for each site and asking Maggie to add her comments about to the ecological impact of each. Well, she could easily do that for them and if they had only got this far at least it meant that the whole thing was proceeding at a glacial pace.

At around lunchtime, Maggie was still glued to her emails when the volunteers piled in through the office door.

'Maggie, how's Charlie?' Alice was the first to ask. Obviously, she was still carrying a torch for him, which Maggie felt slightly alarmed about now that she and Charlie were together.

'He's doing okay, he's got a lot of stitches in his arm and he's sore from falling out of the tree, but he's up and around.'

'I still can't believe he didn't wait for me to help him rig the tree,' said Josh, shaking his head.

'I know and what if you hadn't found him, Maggie. It doesn't bear thinking about.' Alice closed her eyes and pressed her hand to her chest in such a dramatic fashion that Maggie had to try not to laugh.

'Well, yes, it could have been worse, but he really is okay. He's not going to be back at work for a couple of weeks but I'm sure we can cope without him. You've spoken to him, haven't you Josh? Are you okay to keep the foresting side of things going until Charlie's back?'

'Course. Happy to do whatever you need.'

'Thanks, Josh. As we're all here shall we just have a quick catch up on what we're all up to and then we'll get on.'

After Josh, Eric and Alice had left, Maggie and Megan

were alone in the office.

'Megan, thanks for everything you did the other day for Charlie, you were brilliant.'

'That's okay. I'm glad he's alright. How have you been?' It was the first time that anyone had expressed any concern for her for such a long time that Maggie was touched and had to blink away a few tears that had sprung from nowhere.

'Oh, I'm fine,' she smiled.

'I know how you feel about Charlie.' Megan looked at Maggie who had blushed right to her toes, her face full of understanding. 'I could tell on the boat. Don't worry, I haven't said anything to anyone. But if you need anything, even if it's someone to talk to, just say.'

'Thanks, Megan, I appreciate that.' And she really did. Maggie missed having a close friend she could talk to. She had friends from university and school and it was brilliant when they got around to seeing each other but they weren't there to call on for day-to-day chats and Maggie had missed that. In her previous jobs with the Trust she had always had colleagues that were her peers, and because of the nature of the work, they established close friendships very quickly and could be alienated just as quickly, it had turned out. Here, it had seemed different until now. Maggie hadn't expected to find a friend amongst the younger volunteers but Megan's calm involvement in helping to get Charlie to hospital and now asking Maggie if *she* was okay was very touching.

She was happy to keep her relationship with Charlie quiet for now. It would be easier to tell everyone or let them figure it out for themselves once he was back. She could do with the time herself to get used to the idea of being involved with someone she was working with having sworn that would never happen again after Ben.

Over the next two weeks, Maggie tried to visit Charlie every couple of days. The initial euphoria over their new relationship had dissipated somewhat as Charlie became frustrated once he started to feel better. All he wanted was to get back to work and the hard part for Maggie being his boss as well as his girlfriend was that she had to be objective about whether he was well enough to return to work. But she knew that the doctor had said he should wait until the stitches were out, so with medical advice on her side she stuck to her guns.

She wasn't sure what Charlie had been doing while he was off work but every time she'd visited he was on his computer, looking at the screen with a deep frown across his brow and a gradually flourishing beard. Given that computers had been his livelihood not so long ago, Maggie wasn't surprised that he had turned back to that in the absence of anything else to do. She was just relieved that he wasn't trying to fell his own trees or something when he should be recovering.

She had been using Charlie's boat to visit him so he'd been stranded on his island for most of the time. He needed to go to the mainland for a check-up so Maggie had arranged the morning off so that she could take him. She left Bramble Island early so that the harbour would be quiet and headed to Charlie's island.

She had become relatively skilled at driving in and out of his boathouse over the past two weeks and had begun to enjoy the short journeys across the harbour to visit him. When she arrived that morning, the yacht which was always moored in the boathouse was gone which could only mean one thing: Charlie had taken it out.

16

Charlie stood on the deck of his yacht, *Idlewild*, named after one of his favourite places in Lake Tahoe, with the wind and sea spray whipping against his face feeling freer than he had for a long time. He needed this, needed to feel in charge of something again. At one with the elements instead of stuck inside, waiting for his body to repair itself. Well, today the doctor was going to tell him he was as good as new, the stitches would be taken out and he could get back to normal.

All he had thought about over the last couple of weeks was the email he'd had from Jared. Unfortunately, he hadn't wanted to spend that kind of time thinking about it but with nothing else to do, it had taken over his thoughts and dominated almost every waking minute. Today, he thought he had finally come to a decision about what to do but he knew that sailing would help him clarify his thoughts and he needed to do that before he saw Maggie. When he'd woken early and seen the beginnings of a glorious day he hadn't hesitated.

Maggie had been like a spark of light in the gloom that had been part of him since he'd left High 5 behind. He hadn't realised how insular he'd become until he'd begun noticing that he was looking forward to seeing her every day. His heart would leap when he saw her which was a total surprise to him at first. It still worried him a little that he was throwing himself at the first woman, the first friend, he'd had since he left the States. But it felt right.

The past couple of weeks had been strange because although they both knew how they felt about each other and had tentatively embarked on a relationship, it didn't feel like that yet. Charlie had been stuck at home not able to see Maggie apart from when she came to visit and they'd both decided, without saying it to each other, that nothing physical was going to happen until he was back to normal. Because of that, she hadn't stayed over since the first night he'd been home. It was a big step for both of them, not that he knew too much about Maggie's past, he just got the feeling that something was holding her back as well.

Being in a better place emotionally had meant that Charlie felt ready to address the question of what to do about the High 5 sale and he knew he didn't have any option other than going back to the States. He'd done plenty of research on the current state of his company and it seemed like the prime time to consider a sale. It was profitable, which was more than could be said for many of other companies in the same sector, and it had solid growth and profit forecasts. Standing in the way of a sale wasn't fair on all the people who had worked hard to get the company to that point and whatever his feelings about Jared, Charlie felt he owed it to the rest of them to do whatever he could to facilitate the sale. Back in the days when they had struggled to recruit, they had given share capital away as an incentive to their employees so there was a lot at stake for a lot of people.

A gust of wind caught the mainsail and jerked the wheel out of Charlie's hand, causing him to bang his arm as he tried to catch it.

'Christ!' he pulled his sleeve up to check that he'd not damaged the wound which had healed but was still livid and full of stitches that had become uncomfortable. It was okay but it hurt, serving to remind him that he ought to be heading back to meet Maggie. He tacked into the wind and took the boat about, heading back to his island.

It was the first time he'd been out on the yacht in almost a year. Why had he waited so long? He could blame it on working too hard when the weather was favourable and only having time when the weather was no good for working in the woods, which meant it was also challenging sailing weather or he could be honest with himself and admit that he hadn't felt spirited enough before now. It gave him such a sense of euphoria when he sailed that he almost knew it would have been too much for him until now. He had been concentrating on building himself up from the inside and although he hadn't felt like sailing, he knew now that he should have gone out before. He knew it would have helped him because now, racing across the waves, he felt invincible.

The little motorboat was moored in the boathouse when he got back to the island. He instantly felt bad that Maggie had arrived before he was back and worried that she might be mad with him, used as he had been to Jessica's high expectations of him and the almost constant look of disappointment on her face.

He headed towards the house and could see Maggie lying on a lounger on the deck. Her eyes were closed and she didn't stir even when he was crouched next to her, about to take her hand.

'Are you sleeping?' he said softly. Maggie smiled, her eyes still closed, looking so beautiful that all he could do was lower his lips to hers and kiss her. As soon as he saw her, he realised that she didn't mind that he hadn't been there and a wave of relief washed over him.

'I was just snoozing,' she replied between kisses. 'Where've you been?'

'I sailed out to Old Harry. It's the perfect day. I wish I'd waited and taken you with me.' He would next time, he could just picture Maggie on the deck of his boat, the wind whipping her hair. 'You could have gone inside, the door was open.'

'Well, it feels a bit weird when you're not here.'

'*Mi casa e tu casa*, as they say.' Their kisses became more urgent. 'Have we got time to go inside?'

Maggie pulled away and swept his hair from his forehead as she gazed into his eyes.

'It depends whether you want to be late because then you might miss your turn with the doctor and I hear your boss won't let you back to work until the stitches are out.'

'Okay, let's take a rain check on going inside and just get going. Do you want me to drop you back at Bramble Island on the way?' He was hoping she'd say no. He wanted her to go with him to the doctor but he didn't want to have to ask her.

'I don't mind coming to keep you company, I mean, I have the morning off.'

Perfect.

17

There was enough of the morning left for a stop at Maggie's cottage before she had to go back to work. They both knew what was going to happen; they'd been waiting for weeks, and it was an unspoken understanding between them that it would be their first port of call after Charlie's visit to the doctor.

Maggie led the way upstairs. She felt nervous even though it was all she'd been thinking about since the first night she'd spent at Charlie's house and she had spent most of the time since then imagining what it would be like.

They stood in Maggie's tiny bedroom, just inches apart. Charlie grinned at her then leaned in and kissed her. She was used to his kisses by now, but this one was full of intent and passion that conveyed exactly how he was feeling. Maggie gave herself up to him, the feelings that had been brewing within her finally able to soar. The firmness of his body, the way he was holding her, with his hands on her back. His thumb moved inside her bra, rubbing the side of her breast as his mouth explored hers, moving to nip at her neck, his stubble scratching her skin in an oddly erotic way. He undid her bra then lay her down on the bed and began kissing her breasts as she lost her fingers in his hair, torn between pleasure and pain as he gently pulled on her nipples with his teeth. She grabbed at the back of his t-shirt and pulled it over his head, forcing him to stop for a second so he could discard it. As he knelt above her, she popped the top button on his jeans, wanting him, all of him. She couldn't wait another second to feel him inside her. Without breaking eye contact, they both pulled off their jeans and underwear and she finally saw him at his glorious best. He leant her back down, pinned her arms above her head with a tanned, toned forearm while his other hand instinctively knew exactly what she wanted from him. His thumb was a very good second best to what she had been waiting for and drove her to the limits of ecstasy. She felt for his erection and took it firmly in her hand, eliciting a low moan of pleasure from him, until he finally gave himself to her, just in time for them both to reach a heady orgasm together, clinging to each other as they both experienced something amazing that cemented everything they felt for each other.

Afterwards, Maggie couldn't help but have a huge grin on her face. She was lying next to Charlie in her normal-sized bed in her tiny cottage in the middle of the day. She turned to look at him, his features were relaxed and his mouth turned up at the corners; the hint of a smile even though he was dozing. The moment they had been waiting for had been worth every second of the past two weeks of that wait.

She didn't think she'd ever felt such an attraction to anyone before, certainly not with Ben. She thought now that it had been too easy to fall into a relationship with him, convenient rather than anything else and that was no reason to be with someone. With Charlie, it seemed as if they had always been part of each other. Yes, they were still getting to know each other but at the same time, Maggie felt so comfortable with him that it was as if they'd been together for years. She wondered, worried perhaps, whether that feeling would fade and they'd end up too familiar with no excitement left at all.

Like it had been with her and Ben.

Maggie concentrated on Charlie's eyes, wondering if she could get him to wake up by the power of her mind.

He opened one eye and Maggie had to stifle a shriek – it had worked.

'I'm not asleep, I can feel you looking at me. It's weird.'

'It's not weird, it's loving.' She snuggled into his side and he wrapped his arm around her and pulled her to him. 'I need to go to work.'

'You don't, I thought you had the day off.'

'I had the morning off and it's the afternoon now.' She reluctantly pulled herself up, leaning on her elbow. 'You can stay here if you want.'

'No way,' he said, springing into life and jumping out of bed. 'I've waited two weeks to get back to Bramble Island and now you're leaving, I can get back to my trees.' He grinned and leaned down to kiss her.

'Fair enough but remember what the doctor said.'

'Don't worry, I can get Josh to do all the heavy stuff.' He winked as he pulled his jeans on. 'Man, I am so glad to be back. And not just because of the trees.'

She sat back and watched him dress even though she should have been doing the same thing, she just couldn't take her eyes off his body. His muscles were well-defined and Maggie watched them rippling across his arms and shoulders wishing there was time for her to drag him back into bed but instead she waited until he was dressed before she got up herself. There wasn't quite enough room for both of them to do that at the same time.

'Will you call into the office before you leave?'

'Of course. Then we'll come back here so you can get ready because I'm cooking dinner tonight. And you'll need an overnight bag.' He pushed his hair off his forehead and took Maggie, still naked, in his arms and kissed her again. 'Maggie, honey, I just can't get enough of you.'

It was a bright spring day and was surprisingly warm as there was hardly any wind. As Maggie walked from the cottage to the office she noticed many more birds and even a red squirrel out of the corner of her eye, as if the island was coming alive now that it was spring. She had arranged to walk around the island with the volunteers ahead of the May bank holiday which heralded the beginning of the busy season. Now that the Trust Treks had been confirmed, they were going to make sure that what people would expect to see in the way of wildlife was actually there, or traces of it at least.

Megan had made a map for each of them with the location of each Trek marked in a different colour. She had really thrown herself into the project which Maggie was grateful for as she'd had a lot less time to spend on it than she'd hoped.

'Okay, so we'll start with the Squirrel Spotter Trek,' began Megan. 'The area I've marked is where they had the most sightings last season so we'll start from there but we can be fluid about it as we find more successful spots.'

'I've seen a few over at the Scout camp,' said Eric 'but it's not the best area to send visitors when there's an actual camp going on.'

'Agreed,' Maggie said. 'We'll try and stick to the woodland for that one. I think visitors would prefer that to hanging around the campsite toilet block.'

They strolled through the woods to the next location, at the same time all keeping a look-out for red squirrels. They had a quick look for some insects in a couple of hollow trees and a rotting woodpile for the Bug Hunting Trek and then Josh suggested leading the way to the area they'd been coppicing for the Tree Detective Trek.

Maggie's heart leapt at the thought of maybe seeing Charlie even though it was barely an hour since they'd parted at the cottage. Maybe he wouldn't be coppicing, she thought, trying to manage her expectations. And besides, part of her wanted to preserve the sense of anticipation that had been building for their date that evening.

Megan's leaflet had some detailed pictures of leaves that needed to be matched to trees and then children could write the name of the tree or collect a leaf to show they'd found it. Josh had already scoped out a trail that he thought would take in all the examples in the leaflet and led them all along it.

Maggie could hear Charlie; he was sawing, the rhythmic sound telling of his absorption and measured approach to what he was doing.

The sound had also alerted Alice to the fact he was there and she stopped and perked up like a meerkat. 'Is that Charlie? He's back at work?' she asked looking at Maggie.

'Yes, his first day back.'

Alice hurried along the path calling his name. Megan rolled her eyes at Maggie as they all followed Alice through the wood. 'You should tell her.'

'I know. It's hard to find the right time.'

Alice had already begun interrogating Charlie when they caught up with her. She was busy examining his scar. 'It still looks so sore. Are you sure it's healed properly?' Her face was full of concern.

'It's absolutely fine, thank you,' he said extracting his arm. 'Hey guys, good to see you all.'

'Good to see you too, mate,' said Josh.

'Hi, Maggie, honey.' Charlie walked over to Maggie and kissed her gently on the lips. Everyone apart from Megan gasped and Maggie heard Josh say, 'Nice one,' under his breath. Despite loving Charlie's public display of affection, Maggie immediately felt terrible for Alice but when she glanced over at her she didn't look devastated thankfully, just surprised.

'Where are we headed next, Megan?' She squeezed Charlie's hand and whispered, 'See you later.'

'Bird spotting on the north headland!'

18

When Charlie arrived at the office to meet Maggie she was ready to leave, only needing to lock the door. They walked to the cottage together, hand in hand for the first time. Charlie kept glancing at Maggie just to see her look back at him with her eyes sparkling. He'd never had a woman look at him that way before and he knew he'd never get tired of seeing it and hoped she'd never tire of feeling that way about him.

After calling into the cottage to pick up Maggie's bag, he carried it to the boat for her and helped her in before heading for his island. Although she had visited him while he'd been recovering, he didn't count those visits as part of their fledgling relationship as he hadn't been able to treat her the way he wanted to or be with her the way he wanted to. Tonight was the start of it, for him at least.

'Is it alright if I have a shower and change?' she asked, blushing a little.

'Of course, make yourself at home. You know where it is?'

'Yep. Do you need a hand with anything first?'

'No, thanks. I'll get started on dinner and then freshen up myself.'

Jan from the café had managed to get him a couple of beautiful fillet steaks which he planned to serve with peppercorn sauce, mushrooms, asparagus tips and French fries. It was so long since he'd cooked for anyone apart from himself, that he was a little nervous that he wouldn't be able to pull it off but heck, it was just steak. Simple.

Maggie came downstairs, her damp hair twisted into a loose bun, wearing jeans and a pretty blouse. Charlie took her in his arms and kissed her, pushing a stray hair tendril behind her ear. She wore no make-up and he loved that she felt that she didn't need to; that she was confident enough with herself and with him to be natural and relaxed.

'You look beautiful and you smell amazing,' he said.

'I think that's probably the dinner, but thanks.'

'There's a glass of wine for you on the counter.'

She sipped the wine, watching him prepare the dinner.

'Go and relax,' he said, nodding to the couch. 'I'll just get the veg prepped and I'll join you.'

Maggie sat on the couch, flipping through one of his tech magazines.

'It says here that your company is up for sale?'

'Uh-huh.' He poured himself a glass of wine and sat down next to her. 'It's kind of a take-over more than a sale. So, this other company, Cumulus.com want to acquire High 5 and have made an offer which the CEO wants to accept.'

'Does that affect you anymore?'

'Yes, it does.' Now seemed as good a time as any to explain. 'I still own forty per cent of the company so they can't do anything without me. Jared wants me to go over... I kind of have to. He's kept it going without me for a few years so it seems only fair to go along with his decision to sell.'

'Do you want to go back?' Maggie looked at him, her eyes full of concern and uncertainty.

'No, I don't. I left under... difficult circumstances.' Why couldn't he just tell her? He knew by now that she wouldn't think any less of him if she knew what had happened and he couldn't ask her to go with him unless she knew the whole story.

'I had a breakdown.' He looked down at the floor, not wanting to see what she thought of his revelation. It was the first time he'd ever said it out loud to anyone and while he couldn't shake the overwhelming embarrassment that was always there when he allowed himself to think back on what had happened, at this moment, it felt strangely freeing.

'Oh, Charlie.' She took his hand and squeezed it.

Remarkably he found it easy to carry on explaining. 'It was tough, the pressure of the work, you know. I had this terrible kind of panic attack in a really important meeting and that was it, I just never went back.' Again, he had skimmed the surface of the truth; it was too much to explain everything now. It seemed too soon for them to be talking about such intense, personal stuff. That would come in time. If Maggie could go with him, he'd make sure she knew then.

'So it'll be hard to go back.'

'Yeah. I've been putting off making the decision but I don't really have a choice, I have to go.' He took a deep breath. 'Will you go with me?'

Maggie's face lit up. 'I'd love to go with you! Oh my god, I've never been to America before.'

Charlie wrapped her in his arms. He was thrilled that she wanted to go with him. He hoped that having Maggie with him would take the edge off the anxiety he felt about going back. And he couldn't wait to show her where he was from. San Francisco was still one of his favourite places in the world and Maggie would love it.

'Maybe we could get this work stuff out of the way and then I can show you around.'

'Take me to your old haunts.'

'Well, some of them,' he winced slightly at the thought of some of the places he and Jared had ended up in the days when High 5 had just started to take off. When they'd thought the partying was a harmless reward for all their hard work.

No, Charlie was going to show Maggie where he came from before all of that had happened.

19

America! Maggie couldn't believe it. She had always wanted to go but never had a good enough reason before or anyone who wanted to go with her, which was the bigger problem. Going with Charlie would be perfect.

But the timing wasn't great. The busy season for Bramble Island was about to start and she really shouldn't be taking any holiday in the summer. But she desperately wanted to go; Charlie needed her. She'd been taken aback by his admission of having a breakdown and having to face the place where it happened for the first time since, well, who knew how he'd react?

When Maggie had first met him, he was so reticent, hard to connect with and now, she could understand that it was because he'd been through a massive crisis, a crisis that had led him to leave everything and start a completely different life. Hopefully, the distance would have given him perspective on what had happened but it could equally be that a new place would have made it easy for him to shut out everything that had happened instead of facing up to it. Maggie knew only too well that it was easier not to let yourself think about these things that had almost broken you. Keeping all of that somewhere else, hidden from yourself as well as from anyone else felt easier to deal with. There was probably more to Charlie's story than 'a breakdown' but she would wait for him to tell her when he felt the time was right. After all, she had plenty to tell him; things that were starting to press on her because she felt he had a right to know about her past now that they were together. The holiday lodge project could come between them, she knew that. It had happened to her before. She had let a project come between her and Ben and yet somehow even that didn't urge her to find the right time to tell Charlie.

'That steak was amazing,' said Maggie, dabbing at her mouth with a cloth napkin. If they'd been dining at her house it would have been a piece of kitchen roll but Charlie seemed to like to do things properly. He didn't have much in his house but he did have what he thought were the bare essentials and apparently napkins were one of them.

'Thanks.' He poured some more wine for them both.

'When do you think you'll need to go?'

'I don't know. I guess I need to tell Jared and take it from there. There's probably a lot of legal stuff that needs to happen before they need me to sign anything, so not right away.' He took her fingers and twined them into his. 'It means everything to me that you would come.'

'It's not a difficult decision, a trip to America with you. It won't be that bad.'

'Where do you usually go on vacation?'

'We used to go to Cornwall every year when I was a kid. I loved it and it never occurred to me to wish I was going somewhere else. Lately, I've been to Greece a couple of times but I still love exploring Britain, especially the coast. I still can't believe I actually live by the seaside.'

'And what brought you to the seaside?' He raised his eyebrows as he said 'seaside' and Maggie wondered if she'd ever get tired of him thinking that her accent and colloquialisms were amusing.

'I got offered the job, you know, and it seemed like the right time...'

'Right time for...?'

Perhaps now was the time to impart just a little bit of her story. But it was technically their first date and she didn't want it to be the last.

'Well, I'd set up the Trust Treks and was working away from home more and more and things sort of fell apart. I was away so much that I drove a wedge between everything that was at home and the comparatively glitzy life I had while I was working for head office. Some of the people treated me like a VIP, I suppose, and it was quite flattering.'

One person had done that. One person who seemed to be everything Maggie had thought she'd needed in her life but who had turned out to be using her to his advantage and before she'd realised, everything was ruined. The regret crept across her. She pulled her hand away from Charlie's.

'Hey, it's okay. You don't have to talk about it, honey.' He reached out and stroked her cheek but she couldn't let him be kind to her and she leaned back to avoid his touch. He looked surprised but she was relieved to see there was no hurt in his eyes. Maybe he understood, somehow. She couldn't bear to see hurt in anyone's eyes again after how she'd treated Ben.

'Sorry. Bad combination of wine and reminiscing.' She tried to smile.

'How about some fresh air?'

They walked across the deck and down the steps onto the lawn. The moon was bright enough to see by until they went into the woods at the edge of the garden. The trees weren't too dense and there was a path of sorts for them to follow. Charlie was leading the way and they held hands but didn't talk. He seemed to know that the evening had taken a nosedive and was trying to pull it back.

Being in the wood at night lifted her mood. The smells were heightened and she could hear the sounds of the nocturnal animals. The feelings that had been briefly resurrected sank back to their proper place — hidden.

When the trees thinned, they emerged onto a small beach. There was nothing to see apart from the sea which faded into the dark and to the uninhabited Studland nature reserve beyond.

'I knew you lived on an island but I'm still impressed that you have your own beach.'

Charlie stood behind her, his arms around her waist as they looked out over the moonlit sea together.

'You're easily impressed. Beaches are a dime a dozen around here.'

'Not if you want one to yourself. This is amazing.' She turned to face him, wrapping her arms around him and burying her head in his warm chest. 'I'm sorry,' she murmured into him. He replied with a squeeze, then touched his fingers to her chin and lifted her mouth to his.

His kiss was tender but almost immediately filled Maggie with an intense physical desire. She pushed her hands up under his shirt, caressing his back and sides, beginning with featherlight touches and then as she lost control, pressing her fingers into his skin, kneading it, rubbing it, conveying without words how much she wanted him.

They both fell to their knees, pulling each other's clothes over their heads then pressing their naked torsos together, kissing each other everywhere, until they fell onto the sand where Charlie made his kisses gentler, teasing her until she was writhing, begging him to take her.

They lay in each other's arms, still naked, with the heat from their lovemaking keeping them warm.

'Do you think that's ever happened on this beach before?' Maggie asked.

'It's never happened anywhere on the island, at least not involving me,' said Charlie.

'We just christened the island.'

'Uh-huh, I guess we did. That's pretty special.'

'You're pretty special, Charlie. I just can't believe I found you on Bramble Island.'

20

From: charlie.mac@techmail.com
To: jared@high5.com
Subject: Re: Hi (5) from the Valley
Jared,

I've done some research and agree, it's a good time to exit. I appreciate you keeping everything going while I've been gone and let me tell you, I have no intention of coming back. I'll go along with whatever you want to do and if that means coming over to sign on the dotted line, I can do that for old times' sake. Whatever our differences might be, you've always had good judgement when it came to the business and I guess whatever else changed that didn't, as it looks to be in better shape than ever.

Let me know when you're ready for me and I'll make arrangements.
Charlie

Charlie's mouse hovered over the send button. He had already re-written the email countless times, trying to strike the right balance. Most of what he'd deleted had been more personal, about how he felt Jared had let him down and at one point he had even made reference to Jessica. As cathartic as that was, he decided to keep it purely about the business. He certainly didn't want to come across as not having moved on; even though that had only just happened, Jared didn't need to know.

He pressed 'send' and heaved a sigh of relief, running his hands through his hair as he leaned back in his chair. He could forget about it now, for a while at least.

Maggie had a meeting over on the mainland for something or other so he'd taken her over to Sandbanks in his boat to save her waiting for the ferry and then as it was still early, he'd gone home to sort out the email. It was the first chance he'd had since Maggie had agreed to go with him to the States; up until that point, he still hadn't completely decided. He didn't want to go alone and turning it into a vacation with her would make it just that, rather than a solitary business trip. An hour or two out to sign the papers and that would be the end of it.

There was other stuff to sort out too, as he was there. All the stuff from the apartment he'd shared with Jessica, the stuff that was his, she'd sent to his house in Lake Tahoe. He needed to organise moving that over to the UK so that he could rent the place out. It was in a beautiful spot, close to the lake for the summer and near the ski slopes for the winter. He wasn't going to use it right now but he wanted to keep it because who knew, he might change his mind one day. Besides, he wanted to show it to Maggie so it could be part of their trip. Perhaps he wouldn't mention the sorting out he had to do, although he had a feeling she wouldn't mind.

He took the boat over to Bramble Island and went straight to the area of woodland which he and Josh had almost finished coppicing. Josh was leaning on a rake chatting to some official-looking guy in a high vis vest with a clipboard and a case of equipment.

'Hey, Josh!' he called.

'Hi, Charlie. This is Gareth, he's a surveyor for the Trust.

Gareth, this is Charlie, the forester.'

'Ah, come to count our trees have you?' said Charlie with a grin.

'Actually, I'm carrying out a ground survey for the proposed development.'

'Development?' Charlie frowned. No way would there be any development on an island like this, it was protected.

'Yes, the holiday lodge development.'

'Oh, okay. Yes, the holiday lodges.' Josh was staring at him as if he was insane but Charlie avoided his eye until Gareth had walked off with his case.

'Have you heard about that?' asked Josh incredulously. 'No way will they be allowed to build on the island. No way.'

'Nope, no idea but I didn't want him to know that. I don't think Maggie can know, she would have said something. I can't believe they would be doing something like that without involving her and Clare, you know? It's underhand.'

'It can't be true. The Trust is like the protector of the island.'

Maggie was due back after lunch and had planned to catch the ferry back to Bramble Island. Charlie sat and waited on the quay, his legs dangling over the edge as he watched the activity in the harbour. It was about time he took Maggie out on the yacht. He was longing to go out again, perhaps they would sail towards the Isle of Wight on Sunday if the weather was fine. They could anchor off the west side somewhere and have a picnic lunch on the deck.

The ferry was approaching and Charlie could just make out Maggie sat on the top deck just as she had been the very first time he'd seen her, the wind blowing her hair everywhere. He smiled, she was funny and gorgeous and he could barely be apart from her for a couple of hours without looking forward to the next time he would see her.

She waited until everyone had disembarked, chatting to William, making him wait for her, flashing him a teasing smile. Then when she finally made to come onshore, Charlie grabbed her around the waist with his hands and lifted her from the boat onto the quay, pulling her straight into a hug.

'Missed me?'

'I should say he has by the looks of him!' said William. 'Can't keep his hands to hi' self!'

Maggie laughed and waved as Charlie carried her over to the harbour wall and sat her on there so that she was just a little taller than him.

'Good meeting?'

'Boring meeting. Much more interesting things going on here.' She grinned at him, her eyes sparkling.

'Well, there have been interesting things. There's a surveyor in the woods reckons he's looking into a holiday lodge development.'

The colour drained from Maggie's face.

'You know about that.' Charlie spoke quietly. She didn't need to answer for him to know that she did. 'Seriously? You know and didn't say anything?' He tried to stay calm. This was Maggie, after all. There would be an explanation. He raised his eyebrows to try and extract one but Maggie seemed to have been struck dumb. 'Okay, you don't know what to say. So you knew about it and didn't tell me, despite everything because... well, I don't even know why. I guess it's a secret?'

'It is a secret,' she began, 'but that's not why I didn't tell you, it's just that nothing's been decided yet. It might not even happen. I didn't know they were sending a surveyor, they said this morning they were preparing for a consultation so I was going to tell you today.'

'Oh, of course, you were going to tell me *today*. Not because I met the surveyor, of course you were going to tell me anyway. Well, guess what Maggie, now I know. Everyone knows.'

He could see the tears spring into her eyes at his harsh

words but he felt equally wounded. After everything that had happened to him, he'd managed to get involved with someone else who was doing things behind his back. It had been a mistake to open himself up and allow the same thing to happen again. How was he such a poor judge of character?

'Charlie…' Maggie jumped down from the wall and tried to take his hand. He pulled away from her and took a step back.

'No,' he said, his hands in front of him stopping her from coming any closer. 'I have to go.'

21

Maggie watched Charlie walk across the quay, heading back into the woods. He was striding and despite him having his back to her, there was no mistaking how angry he was. She wiped her eyes with the back of her hand and walked slowly to her cottage.

She completely understood how he felt. She'd known that would be his reaction which was why she hadn't said anything. She couldn't believe that the Trust had sent the surveyor onto the island without warning; they hadn't even mentioned it at the meeting she'd been to that morning. In fact, they had said that they were preparing the options for the public consultation and wouldn't be releasing any details until after that. Maggie had thought she'd have more time.

Pulling off her smartest clothes, the ones she'd worn for the meeting, Maggie stopped and looked at the bed thinking that the last time she'd slept in it had been with Charlie and now she'd ruined everything by deceiving him. She sat on the edge and cried. She'd come to Bramble Island for a fresh start, to try and be a better person than she'd been before. Not knowing anyone had been an easy way to ensure she wouldn't hurt people she cared about and falling for Charlie had ruined that and yet again she'd managed to hurt someone she loved by putting herself and her career first.

Maggie blew her nose and then washed her face and changed into her usual work clothes. Having a good cry had made her feel better and she realised there was no need to feel sorry for herself. Yes, she was sorry that she'd not been honest with Charlie but her reasons had been solid. She didn't know for sure that anything was going to happen and there was a professional expectation that she would not share the project with anyone yet. The only thing she'd done wrong was to create a conflict between her personal and professional life by embarking on a relationship with Charlie. She suddenly felt indignant about his reaction because surely he should understand that she was in a difficult position?

This time was different. She hadn't blithely disregarded Charlie's feelings at all, it was *because* she was worried about hurting him that she hadn't been honest with him. And it would have been fine if the Trust hadn't thrown a spanner in the works with their surveyor.

When she'd been working on the Trust Treks, she had left Ben behind. They'd grown apart partly because almost overnight she had been elevated to the kind of position he'd been working towards for years and partly because she'd started to think she was better than him. She inwardly cringed at how awful that was when she looked back on it but she was glad that she was able to be honest with herself about how she had behaved.

Allowing work to come between them, well, she couldn't let that happen again. She had to tell Charlie what had happened with Ben so that he would know how important it was to her that she wouldn't do that to him. She needed to explain that she was on his side about the lodges, that it wasn't a done deal and that she had only kept it from him until she knew what was actually happening. The truth was that since they'd been together nothing had happened on the project and she had put it to the back of her mind.

Instead of heading to the office, she headed to the woods. She needed to make sure Charlie knew the facts.

'Josh! This hazel is a mess, man. You can go much harder on it.' Maggie could hear Charlie's voice before she could see them. Poor Josh.

'Sorry Charlie, I didn't think there was much more to do without chopping it down altogether.'

'Well, I'm telling you—'

'It's fine, Josh,' said Maggie.

Charlie flipped around, anger etched on his face.

'Can you give us a couple of minutes?' she said to Josh.

'Sure.' Josh grabbed a saw and headed off into the wood.

'Charlie, don't take it out on him. It's not fair.'

He raised his eyes to the sky and breathed out heavily. 'Maggie, I don't know what to think. One minute we're having the time of our lives and the next minute I feel like I don't know you.'

'I need to explain. I really wasn't trying to hide anything from you.'

He rolled his eyes and turned away from her.

'Charlie! Give me a chance to explain, I deserve that.'

He stood for a moment, then turned around, thankfully with a less frightening expression on his face. They sat down on the trunk of a felled tree and Maggie began.

'When I was offered this job, I knew it was because they wanted me to be involved in a big project. I'd been working on the Trust Treks with head office and they came to see me as a valuable link between the Trust on the ground, if you like, and the head office. So when that project was up and running they wanted to use that relationship again on another project. I did know about the holiday lodge proposals but believe me, I didn't know what it involved or how it would impact the island until I had my first meeting after I came to Bramble Island.'

'So you came here purely because of the project?'

'No, I came here to be the park manager of Bramble Island but then to be part of the project. I wanted to get back to a job where I could be working outside again instead of being stuck in an office. But the work I did on Trust Treks, well, I loved being involved in that so this gave me the chance to have the best of both worlds.'

Maggie paused to gauge whether her explanation was having any impact on Charlie. After a minute or so, he turned to look at her, his expression softened.

'You could have told me, Maggie, when you found out. It's just the secrecy… I can't be in a relationship where there are secrets.'

'No, I know, Charlie. But you and I, well we hadn't really broken the ice when I found out and then by the time we were together, nothing else had happened so I just hadn't thought to tell you. Honestly, I know how important it is to be straight with each other. I promise you, I was going to tell you today once I got back from the meeting.'

Maggie waited to see whether Charlie was going to forgive her. If he wasn't ready to, she thought it was probably more to do with something that was going on with him rather than that he had an actual issue with her not telling him about the lodges. Now that she'd explained, Maggie didn't think Charlie had any reason to hold a grudge. Saying it all out loud had clarified her feelings and she knew she hadn't deliberately deceived Charlie. As far as she could remember they'd never had a conversation where she'd had the opportunity to tell him and then omitted to.

'Okay,' he sighed, 'So what is actually going on?'

'The Trust want to build some holiday lodges on Bramble Island. At the moment that's all it is, an idea. They have picked out two areas, one around here in the wood and the other on the south side, around from the Scout campsite.'

'And you don't know anything else?' He had shifted so that he was facing her, a positive move, Maggie thought. A sign that he was thawing.

'At the meeting this morning, they reviewed the pros and cons of each area and went through what needs to be covered by the environmental study which I'm doing part of.'

'So it kind of depends on your study?'

'It'll be part of a bigger study but it gives us a chance to highlight anything we feel needs treating sensitively so anything you can add to that, about any stand-out tree specimens in this part of the wood would be great.'

Charlie took her hand in his. 'Honey, I'm so sorry.' He brought her hand to his lips and peered at her over the top of it with a puppy-dog expression. 'Are we okay?'

'Yes, we're okay.' But could she be in a relationship that was already sending her on an emotional rollercoaster?

22

Charlie felt wretched. Although he'd felt wronged by Maggie, he realised that actually he had been the one in the wrong. He should have allowed her to explain instead of storming off like a complete idiot. If she hadn't come to find him, he'd still be in the middle of the wood taking it all out on Josh. And she shouldn't have had to justify herself to him over something that had happened before they were together.

His reaction was more to do with what had happened with Jessica than anything else, and recognising that only made him feel worse about being so awful to Maggie. He needed to tell Maggie everything, what had happened with Jessica and High 5, but it was hard to think of those as things that had happened to him. It seemed so long ago and — because he'd broken all ties, he knew very little about how things had ended up once he'd left. The first contact he'd had from anyone in the Valley was from Jared, thanks to his parents keeping schtum about where he was.

Maggie had left to go back to the office and he headed back to where he'd been working with Josh.

'Hey, Josh. I'm sorry I gave you a hard time earlier. I had something going on and I shouldn't have taken it out on you.' He held his hand out to shake Josh's.

'Don't worry about it, mate. Trouble with Maggie?'

Charlie smirked, 'More like she was having trouble with me.'

Even though they had made up, Charlie still worried that things wouldn't be back to normal between them and that he should try explaining to Maggie why he was so screwed up about people lying to him. It was the least she deserved.

After he and Josh had cleared up and packed the tools away, it was after 6 pm. Charlie headed to Maggie's cottage knowing that she would have left the office already. They hadn't made any plans to see each other but he didn't want to go home without seeing her, just to make sure she was okay.

Having knocked on the front door and there being no answer, he poked his head around the side of the cottage and saw Maggie sitting on a garden chair which she'd dragged down near the water's edge where she was sipping a glass of wine. She was looking out to the harbour, lost in her thoughts, her chestnut hair being gently tugged by the breeze every so often. It took Charlie's breath away to think that she was his; how had he managed that?

He strolled down to where she was sitting, hands in his pockets, feeling a little awkward. The crunching of the shingle under his feet gave him away and she turned, smiling when she saw it was him. Thank goodness.

'That looks like the perfect end to the day,' he said, trying to be light-hearted and feeling suddenly optimistic given that she looked pleased to see him.

'It is, grab a glass from the kitchen and join me.'

He headed back to the cottage and picked up a chair for himself on his way back.

'Maggie,' he began, 'I know we started to talk about this earlier but I need for you to know some things. Stuff which might go some way to explaining why I overreacted.'

'Okay, but there is stuff I could tell you too about why I hadn't been that forthcoming in the first place. We're probably both as bad as each other.' She smiled and leaned across to give him a quick kiss. 'You go first, then.'

'It's hard. It seems like someone else's life now.'

'Maybe that makes it easier, like telling a story about someone else,' she said gently.

He told her everything.

'High 5 began to be successful and Jared and I started to be invited to all kinds of events, we were treated like celebrities. It was fun in the beginning to have a glimpse into the world of the rich and famous. And we became very rich very quickly.

'Jared lost sight of the business. He got caught up in the partying and could barely drag himself into the office most days so I was picking up the slack and it was too much. But around the same time, I guess a little before, when I was still kinda enjoying the partying, I met Jessica. In hindsight, I should have realised what kind of girl she was but in that world, she fitted in, seemed normal. I mean, she was normal for Silicon Valley, after a guy who had money and status. And she did a good job of making me think she loved me rather than my money or the lifestyle we had.' He paused. It was so hard to talk to Maggie about Jessica. It made him feel like a fool, to admit to her that he'd been taken in by someone like that. That he hadn't been able to tell whether a relationship was based on love or not. It seemed so obvious now.

'That's not your fault. You must have been under so much pressure to keep the business going.' She slipped out of her chair and knelt next to him, holding his hand.

'There was a meeting where we had VC's we were pitching to for second-round funding, really important and Jared hadn't turned up. We were partners, we'd been working towards it for months and I couldn't do it by myself. I bombed it. I just froze and had a panic attack right in front of everyone. Tom, our CFO, sent everyone away and drove me straight home. Then when I walked in the apartment and went to the bedroom, Jessica was in bed with Jared.'

'Oh Charlie.' Maggie had tears in her eyes and when she reached up to touch his face, he realised she was wiping a tear from his cheek. 'I can't believe anyone could do that to you.'

'Even now I don't know how I missed it. I was just so caught up with work, I knew she'd been tagging along with him and his girlfriend, to some premieres and stuff. I was so preoccupied, it never occurred to me that she'd started seeing him. Or that he would do that to me either.'

'You should be able to trust your best friend.'

'Yeah. Anyway, I guess what I'm trying to say is that I have trust issues.' He smiled at her. 'And I know it doesn't excuse how I behaved but I wanted you to know.'

'I'd already forgiven you, you do know that?' Maggie squeezed his hand tight and then pulled herself up off the shingle and sat gingerly on his lap. Wrapping his arms around her waist, he nestled her into him.

'I know. But you know, if we're gonna do this, I need you to know everything.'

Maggie leant in and kissed him slowly. 'And I love that you told me.'

23

Maggie had gone back to the cottage to fetch some snacks, leaving Charlie sitting on the beach. They hadn't eaten and she hadn't had an appetite until Charlie had called round. After their talk in the woods, she'd known that everything would be okay but there had still been an edge of awkwardness between them when they'd parted.

Hearing Charlie's story had restored Maggie's faith in him. Even though she'd had no problem forgiving his treatment of her following the holiday lodge revelation, knowing what he'd been through before he'd left America did help her to understand.

But now she felt that everything was one-sided; he'd told her his deepest personal story and she had told him barely anything about herself. It felt wrong to tell him now when he had just shared his deepest secrets with her. Tonight had to be about his story, not hers. One thing she was sure of was that she was definitely going to go with him when he had to go back to America to sign the papers for the business. There was no way she was going to let him face that alone. She wasn't even sure whether he had ever spoken to Jared or Jessica since. Were they still together? Did Charlie even know?

Maggie managed to find a bag of tortilla chips, some houmous and a couple of carrots which she chopped into sticks. She also tucked the bottle of wine under her arm before she went back to Charlie.

He'd moved the chairs back from the water's edge and had laid some bigger stones in a small circle which he'd filled with odd bits of driftwood.

'Got a light?'

'Yes, next to the fire in the lounge.' How lovely to have a fire on the beach. It was one of those things which Maggie had romantic notions about doing once she'd moved to the coast. At the time she hadn't considered that it might happen with a handsome man right outside her back door.

She watched him as he lay on his side, leaning on one elbow while he poked and prodded the fire into life, the flames lighting his face up as he watched it. He glanced over to her and smiled when he saw her watching him.

'It's a good fire, huh?' he said lazily.

'I've always wanted to have a fire on a beach.'

'Back home, we used to have bake-outs on the beach. Have a few beers, cook a lobster or something. It was really cool.'

'I've got absolutely nothing we could cook on a fire. Not even a marshmallow.'

'We should do that sometime, not marshmallows but actual food. Maybe with Josh and Meg and the others?'

'God, Charlie, I never thought I'd hear you suggest anything as sociable as that.'

He grinned and pointed a charred stick at Maggie, 'Clearly you're rubbing off on me.' She moved to sit behind him and he put the stick down and twisted until he was lying in front of her. 'Thank you, Maggie. For understanding.' He put his hand at the nape of her neck and pulled her in for a kiss. Wanting to drink in the moment, Maggie lay down in front of him, between him and the fire and they lay together, watching the flames dance, Charlie's arms wrapped around her, his whole body warming her through.

'I want to come with you when you go back. You can't do that by yourself after everything that happened. I know I said I'd come before but I just want you to know that I'm going to be there for you.'

He nuzzled a kiss into the back of her neck in answer.

They retreated into the house when the fire had died down leaving them chilly.

'I love you, Maggie.' Charlie said softly. Words which others had said before but which had never meant as much as they did coming from Charlie, the man that bizarrely, she also loved. Something she would have said was impossible after such a short time but had happened nevertheless.

After what they'd been through that day Maggie knew that this love wasn't going to be straightforward. Charlie clearly had plenty of baggage to go with her own but she also had the feeling that it would be worth it. Every time she looked at him, except maybe when he was so angry earlier, she couldn't believe that they were together, that he had chosen her.

But she needed to make them even, to let him know what kind of person he was getting involved with. At the very next opportunity.

24

Sunday dawned and looked to be a perfect spring day but Charlie checked the weather forecast thoroughly, just to be sure. The last thing he wanted was to have anything go wrong the first time he was going to take Maggie sailing. He wanted it to be perfect.

Jan from the café had come up trumps and prepared him a picnic which luckily he remembered to retrieve from the fridge just before he left the house. He went down to the boathouse, stowed the picnic in the small galley of *Idlewild* and checked that everything was ready to go before he bounded back up to the house to wake Maggie.

She was still sound asleep; it was early, especially for a Sunday and he had come to learn that Maggie was not a morning person. Placing a cup of tea on the nightstand next to her, he kissed her cheek and watched her as she slowly woke up. He found it amusing, the very few times he'd seen her wake up, that opening her eyes seemed to be such a struggle.

'Hey, honey, it's time to wake up. We're going sailing.' He hoped that might make her excited enough to leap out of bed, but no.

'Mmm. Sailing. Is it sunny?'

'It's glorious. Cup of tea for you here.'

She exhaled heavily and propped herself up on her elbow, eyes barely open, feeling for the cup of tea which Charlie shifted towards her wandering hand. He sighed quietly. It would be a miracle if they were on the water before lunchtime.

Almost an hour later, they had finally made it onto the boat. Charlie carefully manoeuvred her out of the boathouse while Maggie sat on the nearest seat to him looking a little worried.

'Will I have to do anything?' she asked nervously.

'No, this boat will mostly do everything for us if we want. It's a little boring that way but great if I want to sail alone. We can do stuff if you want though?' he shrugged, smiling at her.

'No, that suits me fine, I just want to sit back and try to enjoy it.'

'Well, you're good for now but when we leave the harbour we'll get the sails up and once we get into the wind you'll need to move around the boat depending on which way she's leaning.'

Maggie looked panic-stricken. He thought back to how scared she'd been in his little motorboat the first time he'd taken her shopping. 'If you don't like it we'll switch back to the motor and take it steadier.' But he had a feeling that once she felt the wind in her face, she'd love it.

They passed over the path of the chain ferry which crossed the entrance to the harbour and once they were in open water, Charlie hoisted the sail and set their course for the west coast of the Isle of Wight.

Maggie seemed okay. She was sitting at the stern, just behind him and had been quiet while he was sorting out the boat. Once Charlie was happy that the conditions were as he'd expected, he turned on the digital steering and joined her.

'Have you let it sail itself before?'

'Yeah, a couple times. Don't worry, you're safe and it's only for a few minutes while I show you what's what 'cause believe me, I want to sail this boat today.'

He carefully explained to her what she should do when he tacked, and the boat would lean. He told her what to watch out for and what she should do if he called certain commands to her, which although unlikely, he wanted to prepare her for just in case.

He went back to the wheel and took control of the boat while Maggie sat on the edge of the boat, looking braver than she had only a few minutes before. She was starting to find her sea legs, he thought.

When he prepared to tack, he shouted 'Starboard' to Maggie in plenty of time, which was just as well as she looked to him to check she was doing the right thing before she moved. He gave her a thumbs up and then let the sail flip as he tacked into the wind. The boat tilted and Maggie shrieked as she was sprinkled with spray but she had a huge grin on her face when she turned to look at him. She was beautiful.

Once they had passed the Needles, the trickiest part of their short voyage, Charlie sailed closer to the island and dropped anchor off the coast near a sandy bay that looked as if it would be difficult to access from the land. Being slightly sheltered, the sea was calm so Charlie was able to relax and enjoy their picnic lunch. Maggie went into the cabin to find some glasses, plates and cutlery while he tied off the ropes and then they sat on the deck which spanned the bow of the boat, in the sunshine.

'Do you feel like a sailor yet?' Charlie asked, between bites of his sandwich.

'God, not really. I don't know how you would begin to learn how to do that. But I do love being on the boat with you.' She smiled at him, her cheeks still rosy from the wind and her hair a tousled, yet attractive mess. 'Where did you learn?'

'I joined the sailing club at college and spent many *many* hours on Lake Tahoe. It's not like the ocean but I loved it. Then I did a course on sailing on the ocean before I got the boat, I guess just after I bought the island.'

Maggie rolled her eyes. 'It still sounds bizarre when you drop it into conversation. You bought an island!'

He laughed. 'I know, now that I live here all the time it seems like a very fancy thing to own, for a forester.'

'Well, it is. And so's the boat actually.'

'But that's part of my seduction technique, so you know, essential.' He leaned across and kissed her, a twinkle in his eye. 'Want to see my cabin?' he asked, standing up and offering his hand to Maggie.

'Thought you'd never ask,' she said, taking his hand as he swept up their glasses of prosecco and led the way inside.

He'd barely ever been in the cabin having only really sailed alone and for short periods so it was immaculate and aside from some basic kitchen equipment was devoid of any trace of anyone. But the bed was made.

'Where else could we go?' Maggie asked him as they lay on the bed facing each other, the sunlight streaming through the small windows above them.

'I guess we could go to most places in Europe, she'd probably make it across the Atlantic but I don't know if I'd be up to that.'

Maggie looked horrified. 'Neither would I.' Her face softened and began to look dreamy. 'Imagine anchoring off a little Greek island where nobody else goes and just diving off the boat into the warm Ionian Sea. And then pottering around to the next cove and doing it all over again. That's a pretty good reason to have a boat.'

'It is. We could do that.'

Maggie raised an eyebrow.

'What's stopping us?'

'Work? Although I know that's no issue for you,' she teased.

'Well, your issues are my issues.' He traced his hand across her forehead, gently pushing a stray hair away. 'But know this, Maggie Cassidy, wherever you want to go, I'll take you.'

25

They'd left the delights of the cabin in favour of sunning themselves back on deck. And it seemed as good a time as any. They were having the most incredible day and at least it wasn't going to lead to the first hurdle their relationship would have to face because that had already happened.

'I came to Bramble Island for a fresh start,' Maggie began. 'I'd been working at a Trust property, Croftwood Court in Worcestershire. In the middle, near Birmingham,' she added in response to Charlie's vacant look as she'd mentioned a place other than London or Poole. 'And I started the Trust Trek idea at Croftwood. It took off straight away and visitors started putting it on social media and other properties started contacting me about setting it up at their places too. Anyway, head office picked up on it and invited me to go and talk to them about rolling it out properly across all the Trust properties.'

'And the rest is history,' said Charlie with a grin.

If that was the whole story it would be easy to tell. Maggie managed a tight-lipped smile and carried on.

'I was living with Ben, we'd been together for a few years, we met when we were volunteers after Uni. I was seconded onto a team at head office to roll out the Treks. It was so different to what I'd done before and so kind of fancy, you know working indoors with smart people for a change.'

'Instead of slumming it outside whatever the weather with people so heavily layered in waterproofs that you can't tell who they are. I can understand your excitement.'

Maggie smiled, grateful to Charlie for trying to be light-hearted about it. 'There was this man, Nick, who was from a marketing agency and we started seeing each other.' She looked at Charlie, wanting to gauge the level of his disgust with her. 'It started with a group of us going out for drinks and he paid so much attention to me…and well, you know.'

Charlie took a deep breath and raised his eyebrows, clearly taken aback. 'Wow, I didn't see that coming. So what happened? Did you tell Ben?'

'Not straight away and I will always regret that. He deserved better but he was pissed off that I'd fallen into the kind of job he'd wanted which made things between us even worse. I was really enjoying this taste of a different life and tried to keep everything separate for a while but he confronted me, saying I'd become distant and caught up in a world that wasn't mine. Now, when I look back, I know it only happened because we'd already grown apart. We were more like friends than partners by then. Not that that's an excuse. I couldn't believe a guy like Nick would look twice at someone like me, I was flattered and… stupid, as it turned out. As soon as the campaign was finished he wasn't interested and I realised that I'd been such a fool.'

'Oh, Maggie. You can't blame yourself for that. The guy sounds like a sleazeball.'

'God, Charlie. I cheated on Ben and Jessica cheated on you. Don't you think that's terrible? I did to him just what she did to you.' She put her head in her hands, not able to look him in the eye now that she'd pointed out the obvious.

She felt Charlie's hands on hers and he gently took them away from her face. 'Honey, it's not the same. Jess cheated on me with my best friend. As far as I was concerned, we were doing great. I was stressed out at work but she seemed supportive and I loved her for it when actually, they were having a great time together while I was working myself into a breakdown. You said you'd grown apart from Ben, was it really a huge surprise to him? And he was jealous of you when he should have been proud which is even worse.'

'I suppose it was inevitable that we wouldn't be able to weather it,' she admitted. 'To be honest he was more annoyed by what he thought was me getting too up myself to be happy when I went back to Croftwood.'

'Up yourself? Doesn't sound like he *does* know you that well.' He smiled and shifted across the deck so that he could hug Maggie. 'And you've been worried that I'd think you were like Jessica?'

'I've been worried about telling you that I ruined my life over a few flattering comments. That I'd been shallow and disloyal. I *am* like Jessica. Whatever excuse you want to make for me, Charlie, I cheated on Ben.' She pulled away from him so that she could look him in the eye. 'But you know now.'

'Yeah, I know now. And *you* should know that it doesn't change the way I feel about you. At all. It's kind of cute how worried you were about that.'

Maggie didn't know whether to hit him or hug him. She was glad he'd not taken it as seriously as she'd thought he would but at the same time, it had been a huge thing in her life. It had led to her leaving Croftwood. The Trust wanted her back there as the park manager but she couldn't have gone back there and been Ben's boss, and he'd been adamant it should be her to leave rather than him. She had felt so guilty that she'd agreed and that was when the Trust offered her the Bramble Island job instead.

'And if all of that hadn't happened you'd still be somewhere in the middle of England with Ben instead of sunning yourself on my boat. How can that be a bad thing?' He let go of her and started to take his trousers off.

'What are you doing?'

'Celebrating!' He pulled his t-shirt over his head and dived off the boat into the sea. Maggie couldn't help but shriek, she was so taken aback. It did look inviting, especially after they'd been sat in the midday sun picnicking for a while but when Charlie surfaced, shaking his head to flick the water out of his hair, trying to pretend that it wasn't freezing cold, she made her mind up not to join him.

'Oh my god, you're a lunatic! It's not even June yet, it's freezing!'

'Nah, it's beautiful, come on!' It took a couple of minutes of him treading water before he realised he had no chance of persuading her to take the leap but he was good-natured about it, climbed back onto the boat via a ladder at the stern and then spent a couple of minutes threatening to give Maggie a cold, wet bear hug before he went down into the cabin to dry off.

Once he was dressed again, he thought they should cast off and head back to Bramble Bay. Maggie was quite looking forward to the journey back. She loved the feeling of whipping across the sea at such a pace that the wind and spray were in her face. It felt amazing and she knew she was safe with Charlie. It was quite a turn on to see him in control of the boat, knowing exactly what he was doing.

She was so immensely relieved that everything was out in the open now, for both of them. Now, it really did feel like she had a fresh start and telling Charlie made her realise that the whole sorry episode with Ben had got so much worse in her mind since it had happened. She would always regret the dalliance with Nick but it would have ended with Ben anyway. She knew that now.

26

Charlie checked his bag for the hundredth time that morning. Passport, tickets, wallet, phone, laptop. He had everything. Except Maggie. She had insisted on spending the night at her cottage alone so that she could pack in peace.

The only downside to living on an island was that there was no easy way to get off in style. If they'd been on the mainland, he'd have sent a car to fetch her but as it was, he was taking his little boat to Bramble Island to collect her, in his fancy clothes and with his luggage — at least it wasn't raining — and then they'd leave the boat there and get the Bramble Bay Ferry to Sandbanks where a car was meeting them to take them to the airport.

Jared had emailed him the week before, saying that everything was ready for him to sign so he'd put the wheels in motion to travel over to the States. Luckily Maggie had got the launch of the Trust Treks over with as well as the busy late May bank holiday weekend so she had felt happy about coming away now before the summer really kicked off on the island.

When he arrived at the quay, Maggie was already there waiting for him, her suitcase next to her. She looked amazing. Her hair was loose, falling in glorious chestnut waves around her shoulders and she was wearing dark jeans with ballet flats, a white sleeveless shirt and a red cardigan around her shoulders which made him notice the hints of red in her hair all the more. They'd hardly seen each other out of their work clothes so it took Charlie by surprise to see her looking comparatively sleek.

For his part, he was wearing dark jeans with his favourite brown brogue boots. He'd put them on that morning for the first time in so long and he felt great; smart and confident. His shirt sleeves were already rolled halfway up his forearms to make sure he didn't get covered in dirt from the boat engine and he had a tweed jacket with him, another forgotten but loved item of clothing from his old life. He wondered whether Maggie was thinking the same thing about him as he watched her face spread into a grin while he docked.

'Wow, what's happened to my woodland friend?'

'He took a really long shower and smartened himself up. I smell pretty good you know.' He stepped onto the quay and gave her a lingering kiss.

'God, you do smell good.'

He could see in her eyes that she thought he smelled so good she might want to break the journey with a quick detour back to her cottage.

'Okay, you got everything? Passport? Panties?'

'Really? That's your last-minute checklist?' she laughed.

'Not for me, but I have the tickets and the money so, you know. Passport?' he persisted, having heard too many stories of people leaving their passport behind, and living on an island made it much worse if you needed to come back for anything you'd forgotten.

They made their way with their luggage over to where the Bramble Bay Ferry would pick them up.

'I'm so excited,' Maggie said. 'I can't believe we're going to America.'

'Neither can I,' said Charlie, with a slight grimace. He

knew there would be more to the visit than just a signature required. That was all he wanted to do but he suspected there would be a fair amount of press attention about the sale and probably about his return to the Valley after stepping away for so long. He hadn't shared that worry with Maggie because he was hoping for the best; that it would be an amazing holiday with her and just a quick meeting to sign the papers.

Charlie was in his element at seeing Maggie get excited about everything from the airport lounge – she'd never been in one before – to the beds on the plane. He was going all out to make it an unforgettable experience for her. He could still remember the first time he'd flown first class, the first time people had treated him differently because he'd had money. Arrogance was something he'd frequently seen go hand in hand with coming into money through friends he'd known who had made it big and he'd always been conscious not to let that happen to him. He'd tried to keep himself grounded, so didn't often flaunt his wealth but today, he just wanted to make the most of being able to give Maggie everything.

After they'd polished off a bottle of champagne between them and had a pretty good meal for airline food, they'd settled down to sleep on the lie-flat beds. Maggie was spark out straight away but the closer they got to the US, the more anxious he became. Knowing he wouldn't be able to sleep, he pulled his laptop out of his bag and did a little work.

The aftermath of his accident a couple of months earlier had nearly sent him insane. At first, he hadn't known how he was going to fill his days without being able to work in the woods, so he'd gone back to his first love, writing software. That was where it had all started and as soon as he picked it up again, he'd realised how much he'd missed it. He'd started contributing to some open-source software projects and had found it hugely satisfying. It had ticked along in the background ever since.

They landed in San Francisco in the early evening. It was

warm but raining and they were both exhausted. Charlie had arranged a car to pick them up from the airport and take them to the hotel. Maggie fell asleep on his shoulder in the car. He looked out at the streets which still looked so familiar and wondered what she would think of the place that used to be his home.

The plan was to have a couple of days in San Francisco before heading to San Jose for the signing of the papers. Charlie had wanted it out of the way at the start so that they could enjoy the rest of the trip without it hanging over him. He had sent a brief email to Jared outlining his itinerary up to the point of the meeting and then, Charlie thought, he need never see him again.

Now that he was with Maggie, he had started to move on after being stuck in limbo since he'd left the States and it felt good to be about to put this chapter of his life behind him once and for all.

27

Maggie stirred and lay with her eyes shut for a while, deciding whether to try and go back to sleep or whether to get up. She could feel Charlie next to her and could hear his even breathing; he was still fast asleep. But she was wide awake and excited to explore San Francisco.

When they'd arrived the evening before, she had been exhausted, despite having slept for a few hours on the plane. She hadn't paid much attention to anything on the journey to the hotel but what had looked like a run-of-the-mill brick building turned out to be the most spectacular hotel she'd ever set foot in. Charlie had explained that it was a members' club as well as a hotel and that he was still a member even though he'd not even been in the country for a couple of years. It was just another thing that made Maggie wonder just how much money Charlie must have. She checked every single penny that went out of her bank account every month. For Charlie to have kept up his membership for three years, knowing that he wouldn't use it, seemed incredible.

She turned and switched her bedside light on and despite being wide awake, was appalled to find that it was only 6 am. It seemed unnatural to be awake this early in the morning. Creeping out of the bedroom into the lounge of their suite, she opened the curtains to find a spectacular view of the city. The sun was low in the sky and glinting off the windows of the many buildings that surrounded the hotel and she could just about see the water of the bay beyond.

Torn between not wanting to wake Charlie as she knew he hadn't slept on the flight and yet wanting to share her excitement, she eventually went back and sat on the bed next to him and began giving him gentle kisses. It didn't take long for him to wake up.

He smiled sleepily and wrapped one arm around her waist, pulling her towards him.

'Morning,' he said as he opened his eyes, kissing her. 'I guess the jetlag has kicked in for you to be up before me.'

She grinned. 'Yep and I'm starving.'

'Okay, well we could get breakfast in bed or we could go out.'

'I do want to go out but it's only 6 am. Do you think there will be anywhere we can eat this early?'

Charlie laughed. 'Maggie, we're in San Francisco. You can eat anytime you want.'

They were ready in ten minutes and set out from the hotel hand in hand. Maggie's heart was bursting with love for Charlie. Despite him having been reluctant to return to America, he seemed confident and happy to be there. He looked the part too, in his smart jeans, boots and jacket. His hair was swept back and tidy and he'd trimmed his beard into cool stubble. It was a smart, well-groomed Charlie that she hadn't realised existed before.

A stroll down to the water led them to a wonderful place where they ate breakfast overlooking the bay and the Golden Gate bridge. Until now, any time they'd spent together had been confined to Bramble Island or Charlie's island and it felt wonderful to be exploring somewhere different.

They spent the day walking for miles, interspersed with frequent stops for coffee and food. Charlie couldn't get enough of the coffee because as good as his machine at home was, he insisted that it simply wasn't as good as fresh coffee drunk in a stylish coffee house in his home city.

Charlie insisted on doing all the very touristy things for Maggie. They went on a tram to Fisherman's Wharf, visited Union Square and then walked along the edge of the bay along the Embarcadero. Maggie loved the vibe of the city. It was more laid back than London, felt more spacious and less hurried and she couldn't imagine how Charlie had ever wanted to leave.

It turned out that Charlie hadn't lived in the city itself for very long. He went to university at Berkeley, moved to the city and shared a flat with some friends. Then once High 5 started, he and Jared moved to Palo Alto in Silicon Valley. But the city wasn't far, and from what Maggie gathered, a lot of the socialising that they'd done in the year or so before Charlie had left, had been in San Francisco itself. That was how he came to be a member at The Battery so that he could stay there when he was in the city.

Charlie's phone pinged with a notification while they were sitting in the Pier 23 café having a beer and sharing some fries.

'It's an email from Jared,' he said, paling slightly. 'He wants to meet up tomorrow night before the signing on Friday.'

'Maybe it's a good idea to see him beforehand, to clear the air?'

'Mmm.'

Maggie was surprised at how thrown and uncertain Charlie was. It was a big deal having to face Jared, she knew that, but she had expected Charlie to take it in his stride and perhaps hadn't realised how worried he was about the initial encounter.

'I can come if you want me to, even if it's just to help break the ice at the start. But if you want to go alone, that's okay too.'

'I suppose I'd thought we might be able to avoid being alone and having to talk. You know, we could have just signed the papers in an office with a load of lawyers and not had to speak to each other.' He rubbed his face with his hands. 'I guess I have to do it.'

Maggie reached for his hand across the table. 'I think you might be surprised. It could help to clear the air.

She watched as Charlie tapped out a brief reply arranging to meet Jared at a bar near their hotel the following evening. She had to admit, she was quite curious to meet Jared and to hear what had happened after Charlie had left. She wondered if he wanted to try and renew his friendship with Charlie. He probably felt like it was a long time ago whereas for Charlie, well, he'd only just begun to get over it all. And a lot probably depended on what had happened to Jessica.

28

Half an hour before they were due to meet Jared, Charlie suggested going to the hotel bar. He needed some Dutch courage. Maggie wasn't quite ready which he didn't mind at all, he was quite happy with his own company for one drink.

The hotel bar was very comfortable with well-worn leather armchairs and a discreet, cosy atmosphere. Charlie sat on a stool at the bar and ordered a double Jack Daniels. The temptation to drink it in one gulp was overwhelming but Charlie forced himself to sip it until Maggie joined him, at least. There was a fine line between steadying one's nerves and rocking up wasted.

'Charlie?'

He swung round on the stool and was faced with Jared, right there in their hotel. He stood up, wondering whether he ought to offer his hand and deciding against it, which clearly Jared had too.

'Jared, I thought we were meeting down the street?'

Jared looked much the same as he had the last time Charlie had seen him. Maybe a little more relaxed in the way he was dressed and carrying a little more weight.

'I'm still a member,' he said shrugging. 'You're staying here?'

'Yeah, still a member too.'

A brief silence descended between them. It was always going to be awkward.

'Do you want to join me?' Jared asked, gesturing to a table next to the window which had what also looked like a Jack Daniels sitting on it.

'Sure. Another drink?'

Jared nodded.

'Still a JD man?'

Another nod and a half-smile. It was hard to entirely forget the years of friendship that had gone before. Charlie ordered two more doubles from the bar and followed Jared over to the table.

'How've you been?' Jared asked warily. His eyes kept flicking to look at Charlie but he seemed unable to make normal eye contact. He was just as nervous, Charlie realised, and he briefly felt a pang of sympathy for Jared having made the first move.

'Well, you know, not great for a while. But lately, really good. I've met someone…'

'That's great, Charlie, great man.' Jared looked visibly relieved as if what he'd done was less of an issue if Charlie was no longer pining for Jessica.

'How about you?' Charlie braced himself to hear not only about Jared but Jessica too. To know what had happened after all this time. Jared's eyes were looking elsewhere, at Maggie, Charlie saw as he turned to see, who was walking towards them, smiling, with her coat over her arm.

'Hey, honey,' said Charlie standing up and pecking her on the cheek. 'This is Jared. He came here for a pre-drink drink too. Jared, Maggie Cassidy.'

Jared stood up and offered his hand to Maggie which she took with a broad smile.

'Great to meet you, Maggie,' he said, shaking her hand and nodding his head politely before sitting down again.

'Nice to meet you, Jared.'

'Let me get you a drink,' said Charlie about to gesture for the barman.

'No, I won't stop. I just wanted to let you know that I'm nipping out to that bookshop we saw today. I'll see you later.' She reached up and kissed him on the cheek and gave his hand a squeeze of encouragement at the same time.

He and Jared watched her walk away before Jared said, 'She seems great, Charlie.' He looked sincere and sounded a little sad. 'You know it never came to anything... with Jess.'

Charlie sighed. 'I don't know if that's worse than if you were still with her. At least it would have been something if you'd loved each other.'

'After you left, I was working real hard, man, I'm not surprised you... y'know. There was a lot to pick up and she wasn't interested in being with anyone who didn't want to party all the time. And that's all we'd done. I'm so sorry for what happened. Really.'

So this was why he'd come. He needed forgiveness, thought Charlie. At least he knew what he'd done. The first email he'd had from Jared was almost flippant about what had gone on but now Charlie could see his old friend sat opposite him. The Jared who wouldn't have dreamed of taking the girl Charlie loved. The guy who wanted nothing more than to write code twenty-four-seven.

'I'm sorry I never got in touch after. It took me a long time to get myself together,' said Charlie. Every word was like a little piece of weight drifting off his shoulders and he realised how much sadness and regret he'd still been carrying with him.

'It wasn't your fault at all, any of it. I left you to it, at work, you were carrying the place alone. I want to make amends and I thought that selling the company would kind of draw a line under it. For you.'

'Is that what you want too?' Having just felt a sense of

relief, Charlie didn't need to replace that with guilt over Jared going along with the deal for Charlie's benefit. ''Cause I don't mind either way, Jared. If you want to carry on without me, buy me out. We don't have to exit.'

'I think it's the right time. The market's right and it's a good offer. I've taken a step back from the day-to-day stuff anyway so I know it'll be fine without us. Neither of us will need to work again.' He sounded like he was joking but he didn't smile. Charlie knew it was because neither of them could live with doing nothing.

'I've been doing a bit of open-source development lately. I had a couple of weeks off work and was bored. I'd forgotten how much I love coding and there wasn't enough of that once the business grew.'

'Yeah, I miss that too. Remember back at the start we'd wake up and code 'til we dropped in the middle of the night?'

'Those were the days, huh?' said Charlie managing a smile. 'What are you going to do?'

'Have some time out, do some travelling maybe.' He paused and looked Charlie right in the eye. 'Time out looks good on you, that's for sure.'

'Maggie did that. I was working just as hard before she came along but with trees instead of software.' He loved her even more for what she'd done tonight. Even though he knew she'd been curious about their meeting, she'd realised when she came to the bar to meet him that he was with Jared and had left them alone to talk. And she'd been right. Seeing Jared had helped. Over the past three years, mulling over what had happened had turned Jared into a monster that Charlie didn't recognise but tonight had shown him that it had been his friend all along. What had happened had been a mistake and while it was too soon for Charlie to forgive him, he was open to it happening at some point.

Jared got to his feet. 'Thanks for tonight. I wasn't sure you'd want to meet, I appreciate it. I guess I'll see you tomorrow.' He held his hand out, Charlie took it, then on impulse pulled Jared towards him and clapped him on the back.

'It's good to see you, man.'

29

Charlie and Maggie were sat in a coffee shop near the High 5 offices in San Jose. It was an hour before Charlie had to be there and he was so nervous that Maggie had suggested leaving the hotel early so that the journey was out of the way and at least being late was one less thing for him to worry about.

He looked amazing; he had been up and ready before Maggie was even awake and was the most well-groomed she'd ever seen him. He smelt gorgeous and was wearing a slim fitting navy blue suit with a subtle floral shirt. If it wasn't for the fact she'd have ruined all his hard work, she'd have dragged him back to bed. Also, it wasn't the time for joviality. He'd not felt able to eat breakfast and had been pacing the hotel room while she got ready which was when she'd suggested leaving early.

Thank goodness he'd met with Jared the night before, it would be even worse if that was yet to happen too. From the brief version of the evening that Charlie had recounted, it sounded like it had gone well and that they were both glad about having met. She also gleaned that Jared was not with Jessica. Charlie hadn't explicitly said as much but she didn't think he would have gone so far as to say it had gone well if that was the case. He'd tell her once all of this signing business was over.

When there were just fifteen minutes left, Maggie gently suggested to Charlie that they should make a move. He had been staring into his coffee cup, stirring it endlessly for the past half an hour and she didn't think she could take much more and wanted it to be over. He looked pale, like he might be sick.

'It'll be okay, the hard part was last night.' She put her hand on his, gently taking the spoon and putting it to one side. 'In an hour or so, that'll be it.'

He took a deep breath and then exhaled slowly. 'Come on then, let's do it.' He left a twenty-dollar bill on the table, took her by the hand and led the way outside.

It was a beautiful day, warm and sunny. Maggie was wearing a dress, which didn't happen very often at all but she felt it was a special occasion of sorts, so she'd made an effort. Besides, with Charlie so dressed up she needed to look like they were together. She wanted him to be proud to be with her, as she felt about him.

As they walked down the street, Maggie could see the building ahead of them. The sign on the front of the building was huge; you couldn't miss it. Charlie must have been so proud that his business had reached this point where everyone knew about it, she wanted to say as much but it wasn't the time. He was gripping her hand tightly and looking straight ahead with his jaw set. There were several reporters outside and as soon as the first one of them saw Charlie approaching, they surged towards them. Charlie gripped her hand even tighter and pulled her closer to him, bracing them against the onslaught of questions.

'Charlie, are you back to stay?'

'Comment on the rumour that Jared has forced you to sell!'

'Did you have a breakdown?'

He led the way into the building, both of them breathing an

audible sigh of relief at having run the gauntlet and emerged relatively unscathed. The reception area was full of Cumulus.com helium balloons weighted to the floor; there was no mistaking what was going on there today. The receptionist looked up and waited with one eyebrow raised for Charlie to announce himself.

'Charlie Mackenzie to see Jared.'

She leapt out of her seat. 'I'm sorry, sir, I should have recognised you.' She fumbled for a card which she handed over to him before looking at Maggie.

'And this is Maggie Cassidy. You should be expecting her too.' He looked at Maggie and winked while the receptionist tapped on the computer. At least he seemed more at ease, thought Maggie with relief. 'I know the way, are we okay to go through?'

'Um... um, okay. You need this,' she said, thrusting another card at Maggie.

Charlie tapped his card on a panel next to the door and they went through into a huge open-plan office that had so many desks, Maggie couldn't begin to guess how many. They were arranged in small groups and in between were scattered numerous beanbags, a couple of football tables, a few retro arcade games, tree-sized plants; all manner of things which you wouldn't associate with working in an office. Not in England, at least.

Charlie led the way through, still holding her hand, nodding and returning waves from some of the people who noticed them. She found it a huge turn-on to see this side of Charlie; it was obvious he was a big deal here, and she was relieved to see that he had begun to relax. Maggie wasn't sure what he had thought was going to happen but so far, so easy and at least there were no press inside.

As they approached the conference room, which being a trendy company was made entirely of glass, they could see that there were quite a few people in there already.

'Who are all those people?' she whispered to Charlie.

'Lawyers and more lawyers and some of the bigger minority shareholders. Jared and I need to sign the deal but it affects all the shareholders.'

'So does it feel okay to be here?'

'Yes.' They paused at the door to the conference room and he turned to face her. 'Thank you. I don't think I could have made it here today without you.' He smiled at her and squeezed her hand. She was so glad that he seemed to finally be taking it in his stride. This had been the right thing for him to do.

They walked into the room and Charlie stopped dead in his tracks. 'Jessica,' he whispered.

30

Despite feeling nauseous all morning, seeing Jessica made Charlie feel like he was actually going to puke. She was sitting at the conference table talking to someone, presumably a lawyer. Jared was stood across the room, looking at her nervously. As soon as he spotted Charlie and Maggie, he headed over to them and joined them in a huddle near the door.

'What's she doing here?' Charlie asked in a low voice.

'Christ,' said Jared, 'I didn't think she'd have the nerve to show.' He visibly slumped before saying, 'I gave her some shares when we were together. She was upset about what had happened and about you leaving, said she'd been left destitute or whatever. I was partying way too hard, I didn't think about what I was doing… '

Charlie couldn't believe she was there. In the same room. It was one thing having a drink with Jared to clear the air but the way she'd betrayed him was worse. She hadn't cared that he'd had a breakdown, she'd just carried on her affair with Jared as if nothing had happened. Charlie could no longer give her what she wanted so she had turned to Jared instead, as if they were interchangeable. And now she was here when he'd thought she was out of his life for good. The only link he had to her now should have been sorting out the stuff she'd sent to his house in Lake Tahoe.

Maggie hadn't said anything since they'd entered the conference room. She was staring at Jessica as if she were in a trance and there was no one else in the room. Jessica was dressed up to the nines in a red bodycon dress, her blonde hair in perfect waves down her back and wearing more make-up than Maggie had worn in the whole of her life, he thought grimly. What had he seen in her? She looked like a doll. There was nothing natural about her at all and if Charlie also found himself staring at her it was because it was incredible to him that he'd ever found her attractive.

Jessica looked up and fixed her gaze on him with a self-satisfied smile. He forced himself to nod in acknowledgement but that was as far as he was prepared to go. There weren't going to be any fake friendly greetings. He took Maggie's hand and steered her over to the far side of the room where there was a table set up for the signing. He just wanted it over now.

'You must be Charlie?' A slightly dishevelled guy in a suit was grinning at him.

'Yes. Charlie Mackenzie, nice to meet you,' he said, assuming that the man must be a lawyer.

'I'm Ed from Cumulus.com. I've heard a lot about you and seen a lot of your work. You've left an impressive legacy here.'

'Thanks,' said Charlie uncertainly.

'I'd love to talk to you today, after the signing. Are you staying in town?' He looked at Charlie and Maggie questioningly. His face was open and friendly. Charlie liked him.

'We're staying in San Francisco but we're leaving for Tahoe tomorrow.' He looked at Maggie who had raised her eyebrows and was half-smiling at him. 'I guess we could postpone that for a day or so?'

'We definitely could,' she said.

'Ed, this is Maggie Cassidy.' He felt awkward not knowing how to refer to her. He could say 'girlfriend' but they weren't kids and it wasn't a bit of fun. 'Partner' sounded too formal, so he was at a bit of a loss.

'You're British!' he said, stating the obvious. Charlie smiled. It wasn't the first time she'd had that reaction since they'd arrived.

'I am. Nice to meet you.'

'So you don't mind me stealing him away from you for a couple of hours?'

'Not at all.' Maggie smiled and squeezed Charlie's hand.

An expensively-suited lawyer shepherded Charlie and Jared over to the table along with a man and woman from Cumulus.com. Despite Jared looking like a rabbit caught in the headlights every time he caught Jessica's eye, he managed to remember to introduce them to Charlie. Ethan and Jacquie were clearly very excited about their acquisition and were a little solicitous which Charlie didn't take to but Jared seemed to like.

Luckily Jared had been through the contract with their lawyers and passed on the comments to Charlie which he'd reviewed on the first night they'd arrived after Maggie was asleep. The lawyers from Cumulus.com briefly outlined the main sales clause before they invited Charlie to sign first, then Jared followed by Ethan and Jacquie. There was one television camera from Bloomberg to capture the moment but thankfully no reporters. Then from nowhere, someone popped some champagne and the conference room erupted with cheers and congratulations on all sides.

'Charlie.'

He turned around to find Jessica standing next to him. He caught sight of Maggie talking to Ed out of the corner of his eye. She didn't appear to have noticed.

'Jessica. How are you?' He didn't care how she was, he

was just trying to avoid the conversation veering into anything personal. Formal was best.

'Really good, Charlie, and it's great to see you.' She stood in front of him, smiling as if nothing bad had ever happened between them. 'You're with her?' She moved her eyes briefly to glance at Maggie.

'Maggie, yes.'

She looked amused as she said, 'Interesting, Charlie. Not your usual type.'

'What do you want, Jessica,' said Charlie, unwilling to enter into a conversation on how she and Maggie compared with each other. 'Why did you come here?'

'I wanted to see you.' She touched his arm as if nothing had changed between them. Charlie drew away from her so quickly that he spilt the champagne he was holding.

'There's nothing to say. I think you should leave.'

'Well, I'll be seeing you then,' she smiled, appearing annoyingly unruffled, and swept out of the room. Charlie breathed a sigh of relief and hoped he never saw her again.

31

It had been a strange couple of hours. Maggie had left Charlie at the High 5 offices where he was catching up with some of his old colleagues and she'd gone back to the coffee shop they'd been to earlier that morning.

She was pleased that it seemed to have gone well; the signing itself was never going to be a problem, it was everything that went along with it, but Charlie had seemed fine once he'd walked in. She knew he'd convinced himself that going back to High 5 for the first time since his breakdown would have immediately brought everything he'd felt on that last day flooding back, but everyone had been so pleased to see him that he'd relaxed pretty quickly and she was glad for him that the worst was over and now he could enjoy their holiday.

After enjoying an hour or so drinking great coffee and watching people going about their business, she strolled back to the offices where this time the receptionist let her straight into the inner sanctum. There was hardly anyone in there and the conference room was empty save for the detritus from the signing party.

'Where is everyone?' she asked a young man, who was typing furiously and barely looked up to answer her.

'Out back.' He jerked his head towards the other side of the conference room. 'Follow that corridor past the kitchen and it'll take you outside.'

'Thanks,' said Maggie, heading towards the corridor. She emerged into the sunshine at the top of a metal fire escape at the bottom of which was a basketball court where a game was going on and being extremely well supported from the sidelines.

Charlie had taken his jacket off, rolled his shirt sleeves up and was bouncing the ball in front of him, contemplating his next move. His hair had escaped its grooming and was flopping across his forehead. Maggie found it inexplicably arousing to see him in this environment that was part of his old life that he had fallen back into so naturally. His forearms, tanned from working outside were rippling as he played and... absolutely perfect.

Charlie scored and the spectators erupted. His team were high-fiving each other, how appropriate, and clapping each other on the back. From her vantage point, Maggie looked to see whether Jessica was still there. She wasn't, which was good and she couldn't help but feel relieved.

'Hey, Maggie!' Charlie had spotted her and raised his hand in greeting. She waved back and walked over to stand on the sidelines. 'Time out, guys!' He gestured a T-shape with his hands and jogged over to her. 'Sorry, honey, I couldn't resist, for old times' sake,' he grinned, before planting a lingering kiss on her lips.

'It's fine, I'm glad it's gone so well.' She squeezed his hand. 'Look I'm going to head back to the hotel.' She could see he was in his element and didn't want to hang around making him feel like she needed entertaining or anything like that. She was quite capable of looking after herself for a few hours.

'Really? Are you sure because I'll only be an hour or so.'

'No, stay as long as you like. I bet you've not had a chance to catch up with everyone yet. Just relax and enjoy yourself, honestly. And maybe I should see if we can add a couple of days to our stay there?'

'I don't think I'll get to meet properly with Ed today so it might be good to stick around for a bit. Are you sure that's okay?' He looked concerned.

'Yes, of course it is.' She reached up and swept his hair back from his face. 'Love you.'

'I love you.' This day had probably been hugely cathartic for Charlie and it felt like the start of a new chapter for them now that he could put this behind him.

 Maggie got an Uber back to the hotel where she arranged to extend their stay by a couple of days. She sat in the room alone which felt odd after spending virtually every minute with Charlie since they'd left Bramble Island three days before. It felt like longer ago than that and this unplanned turn which the trip had taken had ruined the momentum, but Maggie was pleased that Charlie was enjoying himself now that the signing was out of the way. He'd clearly been taken with Ed and was excited to talk to him about whatever it was. Maggie knew she could have stayed but she didn't want to hang around like a spare part while Charlie was busy.

One thing that did bother her was Jessica. She had seen Charlie talking to her after the signing but Maggie hadn't had a chance to ask him anything about their conversation. And she felt a bit uncomfortable about asking him anyway. The whole 'Jessica' subject still seemed difficult for him to talk about. She knew Charlie wasn't going to be somehow enchanted by Jessica, she was just worried that she could somehow have a bad effect on him.

She made herself a coffee and sat flicking through the television channels for a while before quickly concluding that she hadn't come to America to sit in a hotel room watching daytime television. There must be more of San Francisco that she could explore on her own.

32

Charlie and Ed were sat on beanbags drinking beer out of the bottle in the now-empty offices of High 5.

'Today was a good day, huh,' said Ed, leaning back momentarily with his eyes closed. Maybe the early start with the champagne was catching up with him, thought Charlie, smiling.

'Yeah, it feels great to be back.' He gazed around the office where nothing much had changed. There was the odd new addition to the eclectic mix of furniture but it felt the same to Charlie. It was even nicer for him not being there actually working because when he had been, he'd barely had time to notice any of it.

'Good enough to stay?' asked Ed, sitting up and looking at Charlie as he swigged his beer. Charlie laughed off the question but Ed gave a pointed nod, clearly waiting for an answer.

'It's not my world anymore. That's probably why it feels good.'

'You know, it's no secret that you were the brains behind this place. The deal was practically contingent on you making the trip over here so we could try and recruit you back.'

This time, Charlie didn't laugh. He felt a wave of cold

wash over him. 'Okay… I didn't know that.'

'We had it on good authority that if you knew you probably wouldn't have been interested.'

'That's probably true,' conceded Charlie. 'I have a life and a job in the UK now. There's no chance.'

'Look, I know it's not about the money for you. If you didn't have enough before today, you do now, right? But don't you miss the thrill of the win? When your brilliant idea is coded up and works like a dream? You don't have that.'

Charlie looked at Ed. He wasn't trying to strong-arm him, he was a nice guy and he was right. If there was anything Charlie missed, it was that. The open-source project he was pitching in on was great but it wasn't the same; there wasn't as much at stake and that's what Charlie missed.

'What do you want, hypothetically?' he asked.

'Hypothetically, we want you back as Chief Tech Officer.' He held up his hands as Charlie went to speak. 'Hear me out.' Charlie nodded. 'You can have all the good bits with none of the crap. I know it sounds too good to be true but we can make that happen for you because you're the guy, Charlie. Cumulus.com want to launch a spin-off picture sharing app under the High 5 umbrella, think High 5 meets Instagram, only better.' He smiled. 'You know this software like no one else. There have been no major changes since you left, they spent two years tightening up what was already there. That tells me that you were this company.'

'I can't move back here.' Maybe he could have done a couple of months ago if he'd known that coming back wouldn't have sent him into the downward spiral he'd expected as soon as he set foot in the place. But now everything was different.

'Working remotely could be a possibility.'

That could be the best of both worlds, Charlie thought, but really, he knew that wasn't totally practical.

'Or perhaps some intensive periods spent here?' Ed was

clutching at straws now. Besides, intensive periods of time in this office were exactly what had caused the problem in the first place. Being here now was supposed to be a cathartic kind of ending to his old life, not the beginning of Groundhog Day.

'I don't know, Ed.' He shook his head and stared at his beer. This guy was gently persistent and Charlie could tell that he wouldn't let it go without a definitive reason why not. 'Do you know I had a breakdown? Right there in that conference room,' said Charlie, pointing his beer at the glass room where it had all come crashing down. 'Coming back here…'

Ed sat forward on his beanbag and put his beer on the floor. 'I know what happened, Charlie. And I can understand why that would make you reluctant to come back.'

'Believe me, it's not as simple as being reluctant. The thought of walking back into this building terrified me and a few weeks ago I wouldn't have done it. But—'

'But, Maggie?'

Charlie grinned. 'Yeah, Maggie. I wouldn't be here without her, literally.'

'It's not an option to relocate back here, with Maggie?'

'I don't honestly know what she'd think. She has a life back in the UK too, a job, family, I guess.' He laughed, feeling a little sheepish. 'We haven't really got as far as families yet.'

Ed laughed and lay back on his beanbag, his hands folded behind his head. 'Oh man, that is a new relationship!'

'Uh-huh,' agreed Charlie good-naturedly. 'And I need to get back to her.' He stood up and swayed fairly violently as he tried to gain control of his legs which had seemingly taken the brunt of all of the alcohol he'd drunk.

'No way, man, don't bail on me now. We need to catch up with the others.' Ed took his phone from his pocket, sliding it to and fro in front of him as if he were playing the trombone as he struggled to focus on the screen. 'They're at Haberdasher. Let's go.'

Charlie pulled out his phone too. He had a text from Maggie to let him know she'd extended their stay by a couple of nights. Would she mind if he stayed out tonight? It was kind of a special occasion and she knew he was talking to Ed about stuff. It was fine. He sent her a brief text saying that he'd stay in the Valley overnight.

33

Lake Tahoe was beautiful. Charlie's house was beautiful. It was less of a house and more a huge glazed wooden mansion on the shore of the lake. It was all beautiful. Yet somehow, Maggie wasn't feeling it. Their plan of retreating to the lake house after the signing had been disrupted by Charlie having agreed, she assumed in a drunken moment, to host a party for all of the High 5 staff at the house. Thankfully he'd employed an events company to organise everything from the catering to booking nearby hotels for most people to stay overnight but it meant that the house had been full of strangers since they'd arrived.

Charlie had spent the past couple of days rifling around in the boxes that had been unceremoniously dumped there by Jessica. Helping him made Maggie feel like she was intruding too much, so she'd left him to it and had spent her time walking, swimming and reading. Numerous decks stepped down from the house until the last one led to a jetty that reached out into the lake. Sat with her legs dangling in the water while she devoured the latest Marian Keyes book, Maggie was soaking up the wonder of being in a place like this and at the same time, couldn't help wondering just how much money Charlie must have to own a house like this which he hadn't even set foot in for over two years.

There was a niggling thought which wouldn't budge that maybe it had all been too perfect. Their relationship had blossomed in a cocoon where real life didn't exist. Bramble Island, Charlie's island, it was all so otherworldly compared to what they'd come to in America. And that special world they'd been in, well maybe it was no match for reality.

'Hey, Maggie!'

She turned to look at the house where Charlie was standing on the deck, barefooted with his jeans rolled up.

'Are you hungry?'

She turned the corner down on the page she was at, something she only did when there was nothing else at hand to mark the page and got to her feet. Charlie had already headed back into the house before she reached the end of the jetty.

He had made a salad and there was a jug of iced water on the table.

'Well, I think I've broken the back of it.'

'That didn't take long. I think it'd take me more than a couple of days to look through stuff I hadn't seen for three years.'

He shrugged, 'I hadn't missed most of it so I guess I don't need it. But there's some stuff which will be nice to have in the island house. Are you all set for the party tonight?' He looked a little sheepish. 'I'm sorry I sprang it on you. After tonight the vacation starts for real.'

'It's okay, it's what we came for. Well, not the party but it'll be fun. It's a great place to have a party.'

'It is. And I need to catch up with Ed again.'

Ever since Maggie had heard about the party she'd been panicking about what to wear. All she had was the dress that she'd worn to the signing which wasn't really a party dress as such and most of the people who were at the signing would be at the party so it would look really sad to wear it again.

Charlie had caught her rifling through her clothes trying to decide what to wear and had suggested that he could phone someone who would bring her some appropriate outfits to choose from. It seemed insane to Maggie but he insisted that people did that kind of thing all the time so she went along with it and someone called Claudia was due any minute to save her from fashion humiliation.

Just minutes after Maggie settled herself back on the jetty with her book someone shouted, 'Someone for you Miss Maggie!' from the back of the house.

A young woman wearing the most gorgeous fifties-style dress and a bright smile was waiting in the hallway with her hand on a clothing rail on wheels.

'Maggie? I'm Claudia, it's lovely to meet you.' She held her hand out and Maggie took it with huge relief that this woman seemed like she might be on the same wavelength as her.

'Thanks so much for coming, I've never done anything like this before but Charlie assures me it's completely normal.'

Claudia laughed and said, 'Maggie, you'll love it. You'll want to shop like this all the time.'

That was doubtful. Charlie had insisted she shouldn't worry about the money as he'd sprung the party on her but she'd never afford to pay for this kind of thing normally. Besides that, it was completely out of her comfort zone. She'd never even rung a bell for help in a changing room before.

Maggie helped Claudia wheel the rail through the house until they found one of the ground floor rooms which hadn't been taken over by party preparations.

'How did you choose what to bring?' asked Maggie. There weren't a huge number of things on the rail.

'I had Mr Mackenzie tell me your size, your colouring and what kind of clothes you normally wear,' she said. 'He told me you like relaxed clothes, not too close-fitting and that the most important thing was that you should feel comfortable at the party. So I'll let you look through the rail, pick anything that jumps out and then we'll go from there.'

'I have no idea what people would wear to this kind of party,' Maggie said, as she began to look through the clothes, overwhelmed by the pressure of choosing something that would look acceptable.

'No problem,' said Claudia gently. 'It's an upscale party but at a relaxed venue. You need to look sophisticated yet effortless and comfortable.' As she talked she pulled out a white jumpsuit with a fitted top and wide-leg trousers. Maggie would never have chosen it from the rail but she had no choice but to trust Claudia. She also pulled out a dark green seventies-style maxi dress in silk which had swirling deep pink flowers around the hem. Again, the top of it was fitted with the sleeves gently ballooning at the cuff.

'Okay, I know you're looking at these and already thinking no, but trust me. Try on the dress first.'

Maggie pulled her top off and dropped her jean shorts to the floor before sliding the dress over her head and letting Claudia zip her up. Claudia produced a full-length mirror from inside a garment bag and stood it in front of Maggie. Then she stood behind and swept Maggie's hair into a loose bun.

'Oh my god, the dress looks gorgeous!' said Maggie. It made her look slim, tall and although she would never have chosen it, it made her feel amazing. Claudia was clearly an expert.

'It's a good start. It looks great with your hair colour but I think maybe it's too dark for this event. Let's try the pants.'

The jumpsuit was made of the softest jersey which draped beautifully. The bodice crossed at the front, not too low, it was sleeveless and the high waist made Maggie look like she had the longest legs in the world. Claudia rummaged in a bag and pulled out some mustard coloured wedge sandals which

Maggie put on and loved straight away. She never wore heels but they were really comfortable.

'I think this is it,' she said with a questioning look at Claudia who smiled back at her.

'Great decision, Maggie. It's the perfect choice. Chic, comfortable and you look like you're the hostess of the party. That's important.'

'But I still love that other dress. Could I buy that as well only I'll pay for that myself.'

'The dress is yours but Mr Mackenzie wants to pick up the bill for anything you want. He was very insistent on that.'

'Thank you so much, Claudia. I don't know what I would have done without you. I was so nervous about tonight but I think it'll be okay now,' she said confidently.

'It's been my pleasure.' She handed Maggie a card. 'Here's my number, give me a call whenever you think I can help. Oh, and wear your hair down, it'll look better with that outfit. You'll kill it tonight.'

34

Handing over the party arrangements to a company had its benefits but it hadn't stopped Charlie from being nervous. It was a long time since he'd entertained on such a large scale and he worried about how it was going to go. He had gone along with Ed's suggestion that they celebrate the merger with the whole company but he had no idea why he'd thought it was a good idea to host it himself. The guys at High 5 worked hard and partied hard so they deserved it but did he want that in his house? Still, it was just one night.

He had wanted to talk to Maggie about the offer Ed had made him but he'd decided to wait until after the party when they were alone again and a line had been drawn under the whole business side of the trip. He had all but made the decision but wanted to talk it through with her, after all, they'd agreed not to keep anything from each other.

He went up to the bedroom to get changed for the party, expecting to find Maggie up there too but she wasn't. Maybe she was still with the stylist; he'd barely seen her today because when he wasn't answering questions from the party organisers he'd been on the phone to shipping companies trying to organise the removal of his stuff to England.

Once he'd changed into a fresh pair of jeans, a pale blue

shirt and a navy blue linen jacket he went to find Maggie. As he walked along the hallway, she came out of one of the other bedrooms, looking stunning. Her hair was shining in chestnut waves and she had a glow about her which could only come from her knowing that she looked amazing.

He walked up to her and placed his hands on her hips, kissing her gently and saying softly, 'You look beautiful.'

'Thanks, you look handsome,' she grinned, returning the compliment.

'You take my breath away.' He kissed her gently, wishing that they were alone and not about to host a huge party.

'It's going to be great tonight,' she said, taking his hands in hers and squeezing them reassuringly.

She was wearing make-up but rather than the thick, overdone look that Jessica favoured, Maggie's was subtle and only served to enhance what was already there. The fact wasn't lost on Charlie that it was a sign she was worried about the party, and he briefly took her into his arms and held her for a minute.

'You've got nothing to worry about. You're stunning and I love you.' He stood back, looking into her dark blue eyes.

'I love you too, Charlie.' She reached up to kiss him, holding his gaze for a few more seconds, letting the words settle between them.

'Let's do this.' He led her downstairs where a few guests had begun to arrive and took a glass of champagne from a tray for each of them as they made their way outside.

It was dusk and the decks were lit with thousands of fairy lights, twinkling all the way down to the water. There were beanbags, hammocks, sofas and tables spread around encouraging the party to be outdoors – there was only so much of an invasion Charlie could take.

'It looks brilliant, doesn't it?' said Maggie. 'Maybe we should get some fairy lights for your place? Your other place,' she added, giving him a look.

'Maybe we should. I think that's Ed arriving, we should go say hi.'

He led the way back into the house to where Ed and his wife were handing their coats to the cloakroom attendant.

'Charlie! It's quite a place you have here. I want you to meet my wife Rosemary. Honey, this is Charlie and his partner Maggie. She's British.'

'It's lovely to meet you both,' said Rosemary. 'I love coming out to the lake, it's a beautiful spot you have here.'

'Come through,' said Maggie, 'Grab a drink and we'll go down to the jetty.' She glanced at Charlie who loved that she understood he wanted to speak to Ed. He didn't want her to feel she had to behave like a corporate wife but he was grateful.

'Listen, Ed. I haven't talked to Maggie about staying yet, so if we could keep it to ourselves tonight I'd appreciate it.'

'No problem. We're not here to work tonight anyway. Shall we catch up with the girls?'

They all sat on the jetty, on a conveniently-placed pair of rattan sofas until Charlie saw that Jared had arrived and excused himself, bounding up to the back of the house.

'Hey, Charlie. Thanks for the invite. This place is awesome. I had no idea you'd got a place on the lake!'

'I got it just after I left. Lived here for about a year, I guess.'

'So, I talked to Ed. You're going to stick around for a while, huh?'

'It's a possibility. I need to talk to Maggie but I want to be involved. I really miss it.' Charlie grabbed a couple of beers from a big tub of ice and handed one to Jared. They both leant on the balustrade, looking down to the water, watching Maggie laughing with Ed and Rosemary.

'Is Maggie staying too?'

'I don't think so. I want her to but she has her job back home. It's more practical for me to base myself here for intensive periods, as Ed put it. I mean, it's not permanent, just to get the new product off the ground. I think we can make it work short term.' He hoped they could. 'Are you coming in on it?' he asked Jared.

'I'm still thinking about it, but it's tempting,' said Jared sincerely. 'It'll be like back in the day when we were proper partners.'

'Eat, sleep, code?' grinned Charlie.

'You know it.' They embraced briefly, clapping each other on the back, then as they pulled apart, Charlie saw Jared's face drop. 'Christ. It's Jessica,' he said.

Charlie turned around to see Jessica standing on the deck, just behind where they'd been talking. Although this time she wasn't alone. Her companion was a long-haired man who hadn't taken any notice of the party dress code and was wearing black jeans and a t-shirt with a software brand logo on it. The fact that Jessica was with someone should have been reassuring but a cold dread crept over Charlie.

'What are you doing here Jessica?' he asked, already knowing that he was paying the price for asking the event company to contact High 5 directly for a list of employees and 'relevant friends of the company', he remembered saying.

'Not pleased to see me guys?' she said smugly. 'This is Drew, he works with me,' she said leaning into Drew in a way that suggested they were more than colleagues.

'It's not appropriate for you to be here,' said Charlie while Jared looked like he wanted to be anywhere else.

Jessica took a glass of champagne from a passing waiter and said, 'I was invited,' before making her way down to join the crowds of people on the decks with Drew in her wake, leaving Charlie in no doubt that he'd have to physically remove her if he wanted her to leave.

35

Maggie saw Jessica making her way towards the jetty. She couldn't begin to imagine why Charlie had invited her. Then as she got closer, Maggie felt a coldness sweep over her.

Jessica was wearing the same jumpsuit as her.

'Would you excuse me for a minute?' she said to Rosemary and headed towards the house.

She could see Jessica talking in a group on the far left of her and kept far enough to the other side to avoid bumping into her. She felt like a child whose friend had worn the same dress to her birthday party. Maggie felt ridiculous for letting it bother her but the fact was that Jessica intimidated her. She had a past with Charlie, she had supermodel looks and the brazen confidence to go with them. Plus, whatever her reason for being there, it was probably to do with Charlie.

Managing to sneak into the house without running into any of the very few people she knew, Maggie ran upstairs and sat on the edge of the bed to gather herself and weigh up her options. What she wanted more than anything was to link her arm through Charlie's, go up to Jessica and throw off the horror of the matching outfits with a laugh and a shrug while leaving her in doubt at all that she was of no consequence to either of them.

But that wasn't her. She was wildly out of her comfort zone, among strangers in a place which seemed to exist on an entirely different plane to her own life and where Charlie seemed so at home that he suddenly seemed to have drifted away from her.

The simplest option was to get changed. The only people who'd notice would be Ed, Rosemary, Charlie and inevitably, Jessica. She had the dress which she'd bought from Claudia earlier. Claudia, who apparently was some kind of duplicitous spy for Jessica, because what other explanation was there? She tried not to be angry with Charlie for using Jessica's personal shopper but it hurt that he'd put her in this position, albeit unwittingly.

She felt better once she'd changed. It was a gorgeous dress which she paired with a pair of white canvas trainers as it clashed with the new mustard wedges she'd been wearing. She left her hair down as it had been and looked at herself in the mirror. She looked okay. The dress was great but she could see in her reflection that she looked weary, beaten and that made her angry. It wasn't right that she should be made to feel like this. Why couldn't Charlie have asked Jessica to leave? Why did it have to be her that came off worse from this encounter?

So maybe she wasn't going to confront Jessica but she was going to at least pretend that she wasn't there and try to have a good time. What did it matter to Charlie whether he networked with these people anymore? She would find a drink, find Charlie and enjoy what was left of the party with him.

Before Maggie managed to get a drink into her hand, she found herself face to face with Jessica.

She adopted what she hoped was a commanding expression and said, 'I love your jumpsuit.' It felt like the bravest thing she'd ever said to anyone.

Jessica gave a tinkling laugh, 'What a coincidence. You

didn't have to change, you looked fabulous before.'

'Thank you,' said Maggie, going to move past but finding Jessica deliberately blocking the way.

'So, I hear Charlie's decided to accept Ed's job offer.'

Maggie so nearly said, 'what job offer?' but managed to stop herself from walking into the trap that Jessica was goading her into.

'That's Charlie's business.'

'And yours?'

'Yes, but not yours, so please excuse me.'

Yet again, Jessica physically stopped Maggie from walking past her.

'I hear he's staying on alone. Maybe he will need a little company.' She gave a self-satisfied smile and swept through the front door leaving Maggie stunned.

Charlie was sitting on a beanbag chatting to a couple of younger men. He grinned at Maggie as he saw her approach and held out his arm, beckoning her to join him.

'Hey, Maggie, I was looking for you. This is Logan and Cal.'

She smiled with all the enthusiasm she could muster, which wasn't much and said, 'Can I talk to you for a minute?' She stood with her arms folded, waiting for him to see, to realise something was wrong.

'Back in a sec, guys.' He handed his beer to one of them and heaved himself out of the beanbag. 'You okay honey? Are you wearing something different to before?' He looked confused and pretty drunk.

She took his hand and led him towards the house. 'We need to talk.'

They went into the den which was off to one side of the main part of the house and so out of the party area.

Charlie leaned back on the sofa and closed his eyes. 'Man, I have had too much beer. And champagne, I guess.'

'Charlie. Are you planning to stay?'

'Um, I don't know, maybe we could go back to the city for a couple days if you want? Or somewhere else, you can choose, honey. Whatever you want to do.' He was sat there, looking slightly squiffy but still loving her, whereas Maggie had a dozen questions that might be better answered by a sober person.

'No, I mean are you coming back here to work? Staying here instead of coming home.'

Charlie's face told her the answer. He sobered up almost immediately, his eyes wide with surprise. He was surprised she knew. And it was true.

36

'When I talked to Ed the other day, he made me an offer. They want me to work for High 5 again. There's a new project and they want me to be their tech guy for it.'

'Okay... you're staying here... now?'

'To get things off the ground, consolidate things after the takeover, you know.'

Maggie looked devastated but said brightly, 'Well, that's great, isn't it? I mean, you got on well with Ed and going back there wasn't as bad as you thought it was going to be.'

'I'd need to work out of the Valley for a while.' He paused and felt wretched as he said it, 'I would love you to stay with me.'

'Really? I heard you were happy to stay alone.'

The beer and champagne mix had been a bad idea, he was so confused. Why did Maggie think that? How did she even know? Then it dawned on him that Jessica had been standing right next to him and Jared just after they'd spoken about it and she had told Maggie what she'd overheard to cause trouble.

'You talked to Jessica? Maggie, honey, all she wants to do is cause trouble.'

'Was she lying?' Maggie had tears in her eyes now and

Charlie reached out to take her hand but she snatched it away. 'Was she lying to me, Charlie?'

'Look, I was going to talk to you about staying but I thought you would want to go back to Bramble Island to work. It's just temporary. I can work from the UK too, this is just an intensive period to kick things off.' He reached for her hands and this time she let him take them in his. 'Would you think about staying with me?' He was looking deep into her eyes, desperately imploring her to stay.

'I can't, Charlie. I have a contract for another six months at least, longer if the holiday lodge project comes to anything. I can't leave Bramble Island. It was a new start... I need to see it through.'

Of course she did. 'It's bad timing, I know that. But know that I want to be with you, Maggie, more than anything. I wouldn't have come this far, literally or... any other way, without you. Just, this is a chance for me to leave the company the right way, finish up the way that I wanted to all along. I need that but I didn't realise it until I talked to Ed. I'm sorry.' His eyes had filled with tears and he hoped she could see that he meant what he said, more than that, he hoped she understood why he was saying it, but that didn't stop him from knowing her heart was breaking because his was too.

'I understand that Charlie, I really do. That's why I wanted to come with you, to support you, to help you while you got closure on it.' She stopped and looked at him, then lowered her eyes and shook her head very slightly. It suddenly felt like the end of the world. Whatever Maggie said to him next, he knew it was going to bring everything crashing down around him.

Still not looking at him, she squeezed his hands and said softly, 'I don't know who you are when you're here. You're not my Charlie anymore. Here you're someone who thinks it's okay to ask his ex-girlfriend's stylist to help out.'

Charlie paled. He'd been so busy worrying about Jessica that he hadn't even noticed that she'd turned up wearing the same outfit as Maggie. And now it made sense that Maggie was wearing something entirely different.

'Here, you're someone who lets his ex-girlfriend who cheated on him, and has a track record of being a bitch, stay at his party, which I really hope she wasn't invited to by the way, without making sure that his actual girlfriend has all the facts so that when the ex goes in for the kill, she has nothing.'

Charlie felt sick. He'd got caught up in all of this crap, all of this meaningless shit again without even noticing. And worse, he had let Maggie down by not noticing it was happening.

'Maggie, I am so sorry. You're right and, god, I just fucking hate that I did that to you.' He put his head in his hands. 'I should have known it would be like this, it's so fucked up and I never should have dragged you into it.'

'It's just turned out to be more than you thought. It was probably naïve to think that you could come back and sign the papers without getting involved. And now that you know you're okay being back, I get that there's a temptation to stay.'

'I never wanted it to be like this. Look, after tonight no more work until...' He didn't know what would happen now because he hadn't thought beyond talking to Maggie. If he did take the job what would he do about going back to Bramble Island? He couldn't let Maggie go back alone. But they could talk about that tomorrow. 'The vacation starts tomorrow.'

She leant her head onto his chest and he hugged her tight, stroking her hair and hoping to God that he wasn't going to lose her over this.

37

Late that night, after all the guests and all of the staff had left, they lay on a nest of beanbags and blankets on the deck, underneath the stars, so many more stars than Maggie had ever seen before and made love. It was more tender than it had been before, as if they were each trying to remember every moment of it to see them through the time they would be spending apart.

There was another week before they were due to fly back to the UK but Maggie knew she couldn't bear spending those days together in the state of melancholy which had come over her since Charlie had decided to stay. It was hard to believe that not long ago they were telling each other 'I love you,' for the first time and now they were about to be half a world apart.

Once she was sure Charlie was asleep, she crept into the house, called the airline and arranged to change her flight to the next available one back to London. There seemed little point in staying now and there was definitely no point in Charlie coming back with her to England. Better that she took the decision out of his hands, knowing that he would feel obliged to go back with her. At least she could go back to Bramble Island and get on with work. It was probably better to be going back a week earlier than planned because she still felt guilty at taking time off. However much she wanted to believe otherwise, it was sure to be hectic the minute she got back.

She called a taxi, thankful that in America it seemed that you could have anything you wanted at any time of the day or night, packed her things, her cheeks wet with silent tears and wrote a brief note to Charlie which she tucked carefully into the pocket of the jeans he'd been wearing so she could be sure he'd see it. She took one last look at him, sleeping soundly under the beautiful night sky and hoped it wouldn't be the end.

38

Charlie couldn't believe that Maggie had left, especially after the night they had spent together. He'd thought that she'd forgiven him, yet there was no note, no explanation but all of her things had gone.

He'd tried calling her, thinking that she couldn't have got a flight out that quickly, but there was no answer. It even occurred to him that she might still be at the airport if he followed her there. The only thing stopping him was that she obviously had thought about what she was doing.

He knew she'd been upset since she'd found out about his talk with Ed, maybe more about the way she'd found out. More than anything, he wished he'd just talked it over with Maggie right from the start, included her in his decision. That was probably why she'd left.

It had never been his intention to send her back on her own. He wanted to go back together, sort everything out and then come back to the States but now maybe it was just as easy to stay. All his stuff was here, at least. His plan to ship it all over to the UK could wait and he could always use the lake house as a bolt hole while he was in the Valley.

But the thought of Maggie travelling back to the UK without him was awful. They'd had such a great time on the

way out and he hated to think of her sitting alone without
having had the chance to say a proper goodbye. It was going
to drive him crazy. There was absolutely no reason why he
couldn't go too. Christ, if he'd learned anything from the past
three years — hell from the past twenty-four hours, it was to
make sure to know what was actually important rather than
getting caught up in the day-to-day shit that tended to blur
things.

He called the airline and established that Maggie had
changed her ticket and was booked onto a flight that left in
three hours. Luckily he was able to get himself booked onto
the same flight and because they were flying first class, the
airline was very happy to arrange for him to sit next to
Maggie and to organise expedited VIP access for him to
bypass check-in and security. It wasn't often that Charlie took
advantage of these things which were on offer to the
wealthiest people but if there was ever a time, it was today.

The next thing he did was call for a helicopter to take him
to the airport, the absolute only way he would have any
chance of making it in time.

When he landed at San Francisco International Airport a
guy was waiting for him.

'Good Morning, Mr Mackenzie, I hope you had a good
flight.' He held out his hand to shake Charlie's. 'My name's
Ryan, I'll be escorting you to your connection flight today.
Unfortunately, sir, the flight you were booked on has already
boarded so we've taken the liberty of changing your ticket to
the next flight later this afternoon. Would you like me to take
your bag?'

Charlie stopped in his tracks. 'Already boarded? There has
to be a way to get me on that plane,' he said desperately. 'I
just pulled a clip from a James Bond movie to get here.
Please, Ryan, tell me there's something I can do.'

'Follow me, sir.' They walked into the terminal building,
along a classy looking corridor to the VIP lounge where

Charlie was hoping against hope that Maggie would be waiting for him.

'Sir, would you like to give me your passport and I'll see what I can do,' said Ryan.

'Sure, thanks,' said Charlie, and he dug into his pocket for it. As he pulled it out, a piece of paper fell to the floor. It was folded, with his name written on it. He handed his passport to Ryan, then picked up the note and sat on a nearby chair to read it.

Charlie,

I think it's best if I leave. Waiting another week will just make it harder to say goodbye. I'm fine about last night, it's not because I'm angry or anything like that. I just think you're not ready for the High 5 stuff to be over and that's okay. Take the time you need and know that I will be waiting for you. Let yourself enjoy it and have all the fun you should have had before. I love you so much and I want you to come back to me with no regrets so that we can start our life together. Don't worry about me. I'll be waiting for you.

All my love, your Maggie

'Your passport, sir.'

Charlie wiped his eyes with the back of his hand before turning to Ryan. 'Thanks. My plans have changed. Any chance you could call that helicopter back for me?'

'Certainly, sir.'

Charlie pushed his passport back into his pocket along with the note from Maggie, wondering what to do. He hated that she'd left without him, that she was travelling back to the UK alone. And whatever she said in her note, he worried that she hadn't forgiven him for not looking out for her and he was angry with himself for letting that happen. The best thing he could do was throw himself into the project for Ed and get back to Dorset as soon as he could.

39

The plane journey home was the longest ten hours of Maggie's life. Being in first class at least meant she could cry without the whole plane watching her. She would cry, then be hit by a sudden panic that she'd made the wrong decision by leaving, then break her heart by realising that Charlie had got caught up in his old life and she wasn't part of that. And the cycle went on and on.

At Heathrow, she came through customs into the arrivals hall and immediately noticed a chauffeur standing there with her name on a placard. That meant that Charlie knew she'd left. Of course he did. And given that he'd been thoughtful enough to arrange a car for her, perhaps he understood why she'd left. She hoped he did. He had to understand that although she loved him, more than she'd ever loved anyone before, she couldn't risk her new future on someone she hadn't known for more than a handful of weeks. And even then, did she really know him? Before they went to America she never would have thought that they would end up here. She would have staked almost everything on the fact that Charlie would never be interested in that kind of life again. How could it compete with what he had here? She had thought he was in love with the woods. And in love with her.

But now, she felt like she hadn't known anything about him at all.

Thankfully the Bramble Bay Ferry was waiting, yet to embark on its first journey of the day when she arrived at the Sandbanks quay early in the morning. Though she was glad to be home she was exhausted and hoped that William was not in his usual exuberant mood.

'Morning, Maggie,' he said, grabbing her suitcase and hauling on board before she had chance to say anything.

'Morning, William. Thanks. I think I might sit upstairs today. Can I leave that with you?'

''Course,' he said as she disappeared up to the top deck before he could ask her why Charlie wasn't with her.

The weather promised a glorious early summer's day and although there was a breeze, it wasn't cold. Maggie thought back to the last time she'd sat on the top deck of the ferry, on her first day on Bramble Island. This felt much the same. Now that she was back, without Charlie, it felt like it was a new start of sorts. Not the new start she had wanted but it felt as if treating it like that was the only way she was going to be able to carry on. Carrying the heartache of how things had turned out with Charlie was natural but she wasn't going to let it define her. Otherwise she was back at the same point she'd been when she had first arrived here, carrying the heartache, albeit not as badly, of how things had turned out with Ben.

She closed her eyes and let the sun warm her face. This was what she needed. She needed to embrace the island, let it heal her as it had done before. And hope that it was the island that had done that and not just Charlie. Hope that she could live there without thinking of him every time she walked through the woods or saw a little motorboat like his in the harbour. Because although she'd promised him she would wait for him, she knew after ten hours of riding an emotional rollercoaster on the flight home, that she couldn't allow herself to be in limbo. She had to allow herself to move on and try to build a life without Charlie, just in case he never came back. And that was all very well to say but she loved him. That made everything harder.

After calling in at her cottage just long enough to enjoy a sporadically hot and cold shower and to change her clothes, Maggie headed to the office. Although she hadn't slept on the plane, she wasn't feeling tired and knew that staying in the cottage and dwelling any more on things wouldn't be helpful.

She walked in to find Megan holding the morning meeting.

'Maggie! We weren't expecting you back today were we? We've just boiled the kettle if you want a cup,' she added, helping Maggie avoid the need to answer the first question.

'Yes, that's just what I need,' she said with a smile.'

'I'll make it,' Josh said, standing up and gesturing for her to take his seat.

'Thanks, Josh. So how's it been going?'

They spent the next ten minutes filling her in on what they'd been doing. Almost nothing aside from the Trust Treks it seemed, and a bit of essential maintenance like keeping pathways clear of all the greenery which was making the most of the warm, sunny weather to have its major growth spurt of the year.

'Thanks for keeping everything going so brilliantly,' she said as they all stood up to leave, heading for whatever they had planned for the day.

'No problem, it's so much fun now that there are so many visitors,' said Alice. 'Is Charlie coming in today?'

It was inevitable.

'He's stayed behind to finish off some business in San Francisco.'

'Oh. I thought you were staying longer, anyway. Is everything alright?'

Maggie steeled herself against Alice's questions with a bright smile. 'Everything's fine, thanks Alice. I'll see you later,' she added firmly.

Megan stayed behind and sat down at the desk in Maggie's office. 'Do you want to talk?' she asked, leaning her elbow on the desk.

Maggie sighed and flopped down into the chair opposite. 'Charlie decided to stay and do some work for his old company.'

'Right... like indefinitely?'

'Yes. He asked me to stay but I can't just up sticks and leave Bramble Island. And I don't want to. I really didn't expect anything like that to happen.'

'So, he kind of got back into the swing of all of that?'

'Definitely. Almost straight away. I don't mind that, I was glad that he had faced his demons and come through it better than he expected to. I think that surprised him too and made him think that he could go back and it'd be different to how it was before. He's after some closure.'

'So were things different between you there?'

'Not to begin with but I think we've been in a bubble here and not had to deal with anyone outside of that. His ex is a nightmare, Megan. I just couldn't see how Charlie could ever have been with someone like her. He really must have been a different person back then, or she was.'

'Well, you probably did the right thing by coming home. Let him get it out of his system or whatever,' Megan said, standing up. 'I've got some rhododendrons to tame this morning. Do you want to help?'

'Yes. Anything other than a Trust Trek or having to wade through my emails sounds very appealing today.'

Megan hugged her before they left the office. 'You'll be okay, Maggie. You're strong. You're what keeps the team together and motivated. Just concentrate on that.'

Maggie felt understood and knew that Megan would tell Alice and the others enough of the story so that there would be no more questions.

'Thanks Megan. You're right. I'm going to focus on what I came here to do in the first place.'

40

Being back in the office was strange for Charlie. Given how things had gone the last time he was there, before his return to San Jose with Maggie, he'd been surprised to feel the old adrenaline buzz was still there when he'd walked back into High 5. And he'd kind of been hoping, expecting it to have stayed with him. But something was off. He'd walked in today with the old familiar feeling of dread hanging over him instead. Was it because now there was an expectation again? No one had expected anything of him for a long time, not in the sense that success was riding on him. Perhaps it wasn't going to give him the closure he thought it would. Perhaps he was erasing the past three years by being here.

'Charlie!' He was relieved to see Ed's friendly face heading towards him from the conference room at the other end of the office.

'Hey, Ed.' They shared a slightly awkward hug that involved a lot of back-slapping.

'Look, I don't want you to think I'm throwing you in at the deep end but I've gathered together the team that's worked on the project so far to help get you up to speed.'

'Okay, great idea.' Charlie followed Ed to the glass box of a conference room where there were six people sat around the table.

One of them was Jessica.

Charlie put a hand on Ed's arm, stopping him before he strode in.

'Is Jessica Martinez part of the team?'

'Sure is. We've collaborated with her company, Digipixel, on the photo-specific algorithm.'

So Jessica's company was an essential part of the work.

'You okay, Charlie? I thought she was a friend of yours. Wasn't she at your party in Tahoe?'

'It's a long story.' He wasn't going to get into the history of his relationship with Jessica.

'That's an "it's complicated" kind of comment, Charlie, so I'm going to deduce from that that you guys used to date or something similar. I don't need to know the details.' He held his hands up to stop Charlie from beginning to explain, not that he was. 'You know I'd do almost anything to keep you here and I could even stretch that to getting a different company to help us out with the algorithm but they're the best. If there's any way you can give it a chance, at least for a bit, I'd love that.'

Charlie sighed, wondering if he was putting himself in an impossible situation before he'd even started. 'Fair enough. I guess we'll see how it goes.'

'Appreciate it.' Ed slapped him on the back and headed into the conference room.

'I'm sure you all know Charlie Mackenzie already,' he said as he sat down at the head of the table and gestured for Charlie to take the same spot at the other end.

Charlie purposely kept his gaze away from Jessica, not wishing to see the self-satisfied smile that had been on her face every time he'd seen her since he'd been back. But he couldn't avoid her forever as she introduced herself as if they'd never met, part of the general introductions with everyone around the table doing the same. She spoke professionally and eloquently about the work her company had done and Charlie felt himself begin to relax. Perhaps she had got the message at the party and had accepted that there would never be anything between them.

They broke for lunch and Ed dashed off to take a phone call before he and Charlie headed out for food. As everyone else left the conference room, Charlie pulled out his phone checking yet again for a message from Maggie. She'd texted to let him know she was back on Bramble Island and to thank him for organising the car that picked her up from the airport. He'd replied with a little more emotion than her perfunctory message to him and had heard nothing back. It hurt, but at the same time he understood that she needed space. He knew he had let her down and that also hurt. More so now that things weren't feeling as amazing as they had a few days ago.

'Charlie?'

He swallowed a sigh and turned towards Jessica who had hung back, presumably to catch him alone.

'Jessica.'

'I know that you would probably prefer I wasn't involved in the project and I completely understand that you might find it difficult to work together.'

That was an understatement.

'Ed's willing to find another company for the photo algorithm if it doesn't work out.' A bit of a stretch of the truth but it was enough to make Jessica's eyes widen and the colour that wasn't down to make-up drain from her cheeks.

'Oh. Well I should probably say that we are the best and I'm not going to jeopardise our involvement in this by playing games. I want to apologise for what happened at the party, with your... girlfriend.'

'Thank you. I appreciate that.' Whether she meant it or not didn't matter to him as long as she did the job and left him alone. A weight lifted off him and for a second he saw the Jessica he'd fallen for before she'd turned into a money-grabbing cheater. 'I had no idea you owned a company or were into this kind of work.'

'I made some money off some shares and bought into Digipixel. They were a start-up a couple of years ago and it's grown from there. You know me, not that technically-minded but I guess I've picked up quite a lot by being involved at the beginning.'

'Well, good for you.' Maybe now she wouldn't need to trap another sucker for their money.

'So we're good, Charlie?'

'I guess so. For now.' He gave a half-smile and she smiled the most genuine smile he thought he'd ever seen from her. It was confusing but oddly soothing to think that maybe she was capable of being a normal person.

'Ready, Charlie?' said Ed, from just outside the door.

'Sure,' called Charlie.

'Welcome back,' said Jessica as he left.

'Everthing okay?' Ed asked as they left the cool of the building for a short walk to the diner in the scorching midday sun, both automatically reaching for their sunglasses before they began strolling down the street.

'I think it'll be fine,' Charlie said, flashing him a confident smile.

'That is music to my ears.'

41

Bramble Island was busier than Maggie could have imagined. It thronged with people and to begin with it was a shock to her and her team after having virtually had the island to themselves for the past few months. The weather had been glorious almost every day since she'd got back from America and every ferry was loaded with day-trippers. The Trust Treks were so popular that they'd had to train more of Clare's casual staff as well as her usual volunteers so that they could cope with the demand.

Being so busy had made it easier not to miss Charlie. Despite her vow to move on and try not to dwell on things, Maggie often imagined that he was out in the woods somewhere rather than thousands of miles away.

Once she had got back from America, she had given herself a week to gather her thoughts before she contacted him, despite numerous texts and emails from him, increasingly despairing at not being able to contact her. She now felt that she had achieved a balance again, somewhere between desperately waiting for him to return, which he had confirmed he would, and forgetting that they had ever met. It was a place she could be happy in and a place where she felt like herself again.

She had agreed that every week she would go to his house so that they could FaceTime with a more reliable internet connection than Bramble Island could offer. Because of the time difference, she had taken to staying overnight which she had mixed feelings about. On the one hand, it was lovely to be in the lap of luxury once a week but the downside was that the place was full of Charlie. His smell, his clothes, his bed. It was for him that she had relented to this kind of contact. Despite her self-preserving promises to herself that she would not wait for him, wouldn't allow herself to be open to the hurt that him not returning would bring, she still loved him. She worried about how he was coping, alert to the fact that he could easily end up going down the same road that had brought him to Bramble Island in the first place.

It was Sunday, the busiest day of the week which would thankfully be followed by the quietest. Not that it would be quiet, just fewer visitors than over the weekend. Maggie was exhausted. Alice had come down with a bug so she'd had to step in and help with the red squirrel Treks over the weekend. The last ferry of the day had just left for Sandbanks as Maggie headed to her cottage to pick up the things she'd need to stay over at Charlie's.

Navigating Charlie's boat around Bramble Bay had become second nature to Maggie and she had even been shopping by herself a few times. She headed towards Charlie's island enjoying the feeling of the early evening summer sun on her face and looking forward to sitting out on the deck with her book until it was 8 pm, midday in San Francisco, the time they always spoke. Even on a Sunday, the call usually found Charlie in the office or working at the desk in his room at The Battery. He'd told Maggie that he preferred to stay in the city rather than be in San Jose all the time because he found it easier to work outside the office. If he worked at the High 5 offices, he got dragged into helping with all manner of other things apart from what he wanted to work on, because he knew the ins and outs of everything and everyone knew that. And besides, if he was living back in the US for a while, he wanted to live somewhere he could really enjoy. She went along with his logic to begin with but found it increasingly worrying that he never seemed to make time to go out anyway; he may as well live at the office.

While she was waiting, Maggie took advantage of Charlie's shower which was far superior to the set-up in her cottage which still necessitated shoving rubber tubes over the taps while managing to reach every temperature extreme possible during even the shortest shower. Using his shower gel made her feel closer to him, yet at the same time made her ache for him. She dressed in one of his t-shirts and towel-dried her hair, leaving it to dry naturally in the warmth of the summer evening air.

It had been two months since she'd left Charlie behind in America. When he'd told her on the night of the party that he was going to stay, he'd alluded to the fact that he didn't necessarily need to be in America all of the time, but he'd made no mention of when he might come back. Despite the fact she'd told herself she wasn't waiting for him, she still found that difficult and as time had gone on, her feelings about what had happened in America had softened. She no longer felt the need to protect herself so fiercely from the idea that he might come back and they'd be able to pick up where they'd left off.

Not all of their weekly FaceTime chats had been great. If Charlie was working, he found it difficult to switch off and concentrate on talking to her. Trying to give him the time and space he needed was getting harder and Maggie was starting to lose her patience with it all. She had been convincing herself that perhaps he was just trying to get the work done so that he could come home for good, but when would that be?

Just before 8 pm, Maggie switched on the computer in Charlie's office and opened the FaceTime app, choosing

Charlie's number which was at the top of the list. He answered straight away and she was relieved to see that he was in his apartment at The Battery, so they had half a chance of a decent conversation.

'Hey Maggie, you're a sight for sore eyes.' He smiled wearily and sat with his chin resting on his fist. He looked pleased to see her and she felt a rush of love mixed with concern for him. He looked so tired which Maggie thought could only be a sign that he was working too hard.

'You look tired, Charlie and it's only lunchtime there. How are things?'

'Well, it has been a crazy week. Deadlines, too many deadlines.'

That worried her. It looked and sounded like he could be working just as hard as when it had been his actual job. As hard as when he'd had his breakdown.

'You look great, honey. I guess the sun's out over there?'

'Yes, it's glorious and really busy. I had to lead a couple of your Tree Insect Treks today.'

'And how are my trees? I miss them,' he said wistfully, 'and I miss you.'

'Everything's good here but I miss you too. I'm worried about you.' She wanted to ask him to come home but she didn't feel like she had any right to. They had been together for scarcely more than a few months but for at least half that time they'd been apart. Was that a relationship where either of them could make demands of the other?

'I'm doing okay. I know I look, y'know, not my best but we're making some real progress with the new app. I know it's tough Maggie but I think another couple of months and I can probably come back and work from there for a little while.'

'Another couple of months?' She couldn't hold it in. 'Christ, Charlie. Do you think you'll make another couple of months? You're letting it happen again.'

'Maggie...'

'I'm sorry but if I thought you were enjoying yourself I wouldn't say anything. It was your decision to stay and I understood your reasons but you look dreadful, you're working too hard. You're going down the same road as you were before and it's so hard to sit here and see you once a week and not be able to be there to help you.'

'I didn't know you could write code, Maggie,' he said, attempting to lighten the conversation.

'Charlie...'

'Okay, I know,' he said with a sigh. 'It's been too long, longer than I wanted it to be too. But I have to do this, I have to see it through. I thought you understood?'

'I did, I do. I just didn't think it would be like this, it's taking such a toll on you.' She sat there, inhaling the scent of his shower gel as she sat watching him and she physically ached for him. If it wasn't for the fact that it was summer, the busiest time of the year on Bramble Island, she would empty her bank account and get on the next flight to see him.

'I'm sorry, honey. I know it's hard and it's worse for you. I get lost in the work and lose track of everything and it seems like just a day or so since we spoke last week. Once this is over, we can be together all the time. You'll be sick of the sight of me.'

'Okay. I —'

The doorbell rang at Charlie's end.

'Hang on a sec. It's probably the maid.' He disappeared from the screen and she could hear him opening the door. 'Hey, come in. I won't be a sec.'

Maggie heard the other person greet Charlie. It was Jessica. She was sure of it.

Before Maggie could really process what had just happened, Charlie was back at his desk, ending their call.

'Maggie, don't worry about me. I love you, I'll call next week.' And he was gone.

What the hell was Jessica doing visiting Charlie? And what worried Maggie more was that he wasn't surprised when he opened the door to her.

42

Charlie had taken to running along the water's edge since he'd been living back in San Francisco. The long hours were taking their toll and he was exhausted but somehow going for a run every morning gave him an energy boost which he badly needed. It also gave him time to think. It was easy to get drawn into working every waking minute and he was, but these moments where he could run, letting his mind wander, had become his favourite part of the day. He thought about Maggie, Bramble Island, the life they'd had which was just beginning when he'd left. He felt guilty about that but somehow this brief introspection that he allowed himself every day also allowed him to tell himself that he needed to do this so that he could go back to her with no regrets. He was wiping the slate clean for them both so that everything that had marred his life before he even met her wouldn't hold him back anymore.

Since Maggie had left he'd worked every single day. In the beginning, he'd had endless meetings with Ed and the team to figure out how they were going to start coding the new app. Quite quickly, Charlie had a plan in his head; he knew how it would integrate with the existing High 5 and how they could use what was already there to save them a lot of work. Ed was beyond thrilled that Charlie had agreed to stay and constantly told him how amazing he thought he was. It was nice to hear but having lived in the UK for a couple of years where it was unusual for people to be so effusive, it sounded disingenuous to Charlie even though he appreciated the sentiment.

Despite all the long hours and being so tired, Charlie was relishing the work and loved being at the sharp end again. But maybe knowing that there was an end to it and that then he'd go back to Bramble Island was part of why he was enjoying it. It wasn't forever.

The only thing in his life which was causing him a problem at the moment was Jessica. Surprisingly, she had kept her word and, so far at least, had been nothing but professional, even when they found themselves alone. But he hadn't told Maggie. Regardless of their feelings for each other, Charlie felt that their relationship was on shaky ground until he went back to the UK for good. He wanted to be honest with her but he worried that she would think there was more to it. He couldn't blame her after what had happened when she'd been in the States but that also made it all the more difficult to explain. No, it was better that she didn't know.

The weekly FaceTime calls with Maggie were hard on him. He knew he would be faring better if he didn't have to see her. He wanted to see her but the feeling of having to justify himself was overwhelming because although she'd not said anything until yesterday, he'd already known she'd expected him to be back in the UK by now. Every week, he'd expected her to ask when he would be back and she hadn't, but the anticipation of it and of knowing that she had expectations of him, even if she didn't voice them, was harder than not seeing her at all. For someone who loved technology, he thought there was a lot to be said for the old-fashioned letter.

The call with Maggie had made Charlie realise that he needed to take time out to visit her. He could really use a break and now he knew that she was struggling with being apart more than she'd let on before, he wanted to reassure her that for him, nothing had changed between them. It might make it harder to come back, but he could maybe stay in the States longer then than if he didn't take a break at all.

When he got back to the apartment, he took a quick shower and then sat at his laptop and booked a plane ticket to London, leaving on Thursday for a week. Then he emailed Maggie to let her know and emailed Ed too.

He felt better already. He couldn't wait to see Maggie and spend a few days on his island with her. He thought about her whenever his mind wasn't consumed with work and he hoped that the time apart wouldn't have changed anything between them.

His cell phone rang, it was Ed.

'Hey, Ed.'

'Charlie, just saw your email about your trip to England. I assume you're coming back?' Ed's tone sounded jovial but Charlie could tell he was calling to make sure he wasn't leaving for good. Despite the flexible arrangement Ed had offered him, it didn't feel like that was an option anymore. It was a little disappointing but not surprising; the offer that Charlie could do it on his terms had sounded too good to be true and that's exactly how it had turned out. But he wanted to see it through despite that.

'Yeah, of course. I'm just taking a week to see Maggie and check on everything back home.'

'How is the Digipixel part of the project working out for you?' asked Ed.

'It's going well. We've integrated most of their code now and we're just working on some additional capabilities that they've suggested.' That Jessica had suggested. It had been a revelation to work so closely with her. Now that she wasn't behaving like an entitled diva, she was pretty smart.

'Good to hear. If I don't see you in the office, have a good trip.'

'Great, thanks, Ed.' Charlie rang off and breathed a sigh of relief. He really needed some time out.

43

Maggie was on her way to the visitor reception having had a call from them to say that she had a visitor from the Trust. She couldn't begin to think who it might be. She always knew if someone was visiting because the travel arrangements were so elaborate, and she always met them from the ferry.

Walking into the cool shade of the building, Maggie's eyes adjusted to the gloom and she saw a man standing to the side of the desk with a large rucksack at his feet. He had his back to her and was looking out towards the quay. Clare saw her come in and gestured silently at the waiting man. As Maggie approached him, even before he'd turned around, she recognised him and her stomach lurched.

It was Ben.

'Maggie. Long time no see.' His smile was warmer than Maggie would have expected.

'What are you doing here?' She hoped she sounded surprised rather than accusatory.

'I'm project managing for Rob Tanner on the holiday lodge project. I thought he'd sent an email about my visit?' He looked genuinely concerned that she had no idea he was coming.

'Oh.' Maggie gathered herself. She had to be professional

about this. Aside from the fact that she'd thought she was the project manager for the holiday lodge project, she had to behave as if this wasn't her Ben, he was a colleague. Not that he was her Ben anymore but it was difficult to think of him any other way. 'Well, no, I don't think I've seen an email from Rob but never mind. Are you here to look at the sites?'

'The site. The decision was made last week. Sorry, I assumed you'd been told.'

It seemed that there was more than one email that Maggie hadn't received.

'Which site is it? The south or the woodland?' She held her breath, already knowing what he was going to say.

'The woodland. It's a superb site, hugely unique in terms of the holiday offer in this area.'

'Since when did you care about marketing over nature?' Maggie blurted out, despite her pledge to herself to be professional.

'Come on Mags, this is my job now. Can't we keep things civil?'

Maggie blushed, annoyed with herself for not managing to do that for even the minute since he'd arrived.

'Sorry, of course. You can leave your bag here and pick it up later when you get the ferry.'

'I'm here for the week. I think some accommodation's been arranged.'

'Well, as you've probably gathered, I didn't get the email about any of this,' Maggie bristled, then thawed quickly as she remembered that it wasn't Ben's fault. 'Look, bring your bag to my office and I'll try and find out what's going on.'

They walked through a passageway of blooming rhododendrons towards the office. When they arrived, Megan was there much to Maggie's relief.

'Megan, this is Ben. He's from the Trust's special projects team. Have you got time to give him a quick tour while I make a couple of phone calls?'

'Sure!' said Megan, enthusiastically. 'Come on Ben, let's see if we can find a red squirrel.' As Megan turned to leave, Ben looked at Maggie. She pointed silently at Megan and mouthed, 'She doesn't know.' Ben nodded.

After a phone call to Rob Tanner's office, Maggie ascertained that Ben was indeed project manager for the holiday lodge project. How he had engineered the change from taking over her job at Croftwood Court to working for head office, she wasn't sure. It was quite a kick in the teeth, made worse because this was the exact reverse of the situation that had led to her and Ben breaking up and she was sure he was going to revel in being her superior. He was here to make preliminary plans as to where the lodges would be situated now that it had been decided that they would be in the woodland. Apparently, Rob's secretary had typed Maggie's email address as .com instead of .co.uk which explained the huge communication breakdown. Ben turning up on her doorstep also meant that she was out of the loop on the project.

The phone call had also confirmed that in the lost emails they had asked Maggie to arrange somewhere for Ben to stay on the island which was completely ridiculous because it was the summer and the only options were for him to stay in one of the holiday cottages which were all booked solidly for the next three months, to bunk in with the volunteers where there was no spare bed or to beg Bramble Castle for a room for him.

The Castle had no rooms to spare and he couldn't even commute to Sandbanks every day because the hotel there was full as well. The last resort was for Ben to sleep on her sofa; there was literally no other choice.

Maggie clicked on her inbox, waiting for the emails from Rob to come through and one popped up from Charlie. He never sent her emails and she was thrilled to see one, it made him suddenly feel closer. Because they used to see each other every day, they'd never got into the habit of messaging and emailing each other and until now, even though he'd been away, that hadn't changed.

To: Mcassidy@Brambleislandtrust.co.uk
From: charlie.mac@techmail.com
Subject: Flying Visit
Hey Maggie,
After our call at the weekend, I booked a flight to come visit. I feel bad that I've been away for so long, expecting you to be there waiting for me with no idea when I'll be coming back. I'll be back on Friday and will come find you. Can't wait.
Charlie x

Maggie's first thought was that she hoped Ben would be gone by the time Charlie arrived. It would be easier if they didn't meet although she had every intention of replying and saying that Ben was here.

But actually, why was she worried about what Charlie would think? He had something going on with Jessica that he hadn't told her about. She hoped he wasn't coming home because he was feeling guilty about anything. She had thought they had got to a place together where they could trust each other but being apart made that hard. Rationally, Maggie knew that Charlie wasn't cheating on her with Jessica but the physical distance between them let that little bit of paranoia enter her head. Especially because she'd had experience of what distance could do to a relationship when she had been with Ben.

At least Charlie was coming back and they could hopefully recalibrate themselves so that they could weather the rest of the time apart more easily.

Ben and Megan arrived back having had no luck with a red squirrel sighting, but Ben was full of praise for the island.

'It's a wonderful place, Mags,' he said, causing Megan to

raise her eyebrows at his familiarity. 'I can quite understand why you left Worcestershire for this.'

'Okay, well there's actually nowhere for you to stay so it'll have to be my cottage. I can stay at a friend's place.' She gave him directions to her cottage so that he could take his bag over there and give her a brief respite from the awkwardness she felt around him.

'Come on then, dish,' said Megan eagerly. Then when Maggie was still sitting there, not knowing where to start, 'Is he your ex?'

'Yes,' Maggie sighed. 'It's a long story, but basically we broke up because I ended up being his sort-of boss and he couldn't handle it and now he's the bloody project manager for…'

'For the holiday lodge thing?' Megan finished for her. 'It's okay, Josh and I put two and two together when that surveyor was here a few months ago.'

'Right. So now it's the other way around and I didn't even know he was coming.'

'You can't let him get to you, Maggie. He might try and throw his weight around but you're the boss here, don't forget that. And you're with Charlie now, that's definitely one in the eye for Ben,' she beamed.

'Thanks, Megan. Actually, Charlie's coming back at the weekend for a visit. Hopefully, Ben will be gone before he gets back or things really will be awkward.'

44

Charlie arrived on the first ferry on Friday morning, a little after 10 am. It was a beautiful day and he couldn't wait to take a walk around the woods and see how everything was doing now that summer was in full swing, but first, he wanted to find Maggie. He headed to her cottage, not because he expected her to be there but so he could freshen up a little, maybe take a shower and change into some more appropriate clothes.

He tried the door which was unlocked as he'd expected it would be and climbed the stairs to Maggie's bedroom.

The bed was unmade and there was an untidy pile of clothes, men's clothes on the chair and a large pair of Converse All Star sneakers underneath. Charlie went into the bathroom and found the shelf above the sink full of a guy's shaving kit, deodorant and toothbrush. And it wasn't the stuff that he'd left at Maggie's.

There must be some explanation, thought Charlie, although he couldn't begin to think what it was. Maggie didn't have a brother and although it would be weird if she was sharing a bedroom with her brother, at least that was a plausible reason. He didn't know what else was.

Feeling like an intruder, he left the cottage without

changing his clothes or washing and went to the office in search of Maggie.

'Charlie! You're back?' Alice leapt up and flung her arms around him.

'Not quite, just visiting. Is Maggie around?' He pulled away from Alice and pushed his hands deep into the pockets of his jeans, feeling a little awkward. Despite Alice's enthusiastic welcome, he didn't feel like he belonged in the same way as before, not helped by the fact that he was wearing his smart clothes and had found another man's stuff in his girlfriend's house.

'She's over in the woods with Ben and Josh. Shall I come over with you?'

'That's okay, I can find them.'

Charlie headed out to the woodland he'd been coppicing before he left. He wanted to take a look at how Josh had carried on with it and there was a chance he'd find Maggie there anyway. He didn't know who Ben was but he was keen to find out.

The trees were a dense dark green canopy now that it was the height of summer. Quite different to when he'd left when everything had been the fresh, bright green of spring. The paths were dry underfoot from lack of rain but the air was cool in the shade of the trees and Charlie realised that was what he'd missed the most about Dorset while being in the heat of the Californian summer.

He could hear voices coming from near the shoreline, although the wood was so dense that he couldn't even see the sea yet.

'Can you mark those trees along there, Josh?' An unfamiliar voice, which Charlie presumed to be Ben.

'Is it necessary to mark out the trees now? We don't have the planning permission yet and I thought we were just discussing likely locations.' He smiled as he heard Maggie belligerently defending the woodland. The holiday lodge project had obviously progressed while he'd been away. He felt bad that he'd not asked Maggie about it, about anything that was going on with her. Silicon Valley made him self-obsessed.

In the absence of a convenient path, Charlie picked his way through the undergrowth towards the beach. He could see Maggie, stood with her hands on her hips, a frown between her eyebrows, glaring at a man who was holding an iPad in one hand and a bunch of plastic ribbons in the other.

'Hey, Maggie!' he called as he emerged into the sunshine, brushing sticky buds from his jeans.

'Charlie!' She shaded the sun from her eyes and grinned at him, her face lighting up. She walked over and threw her arms around him.

'Oh, Maggie honey. It's so good to see you,' he said into her hair as they embraced.

'I'm so glad you're back.'

They pulled apart, Charlie glanced at Ben, then whispered to Maggie, 'What the hell's going on here?'

'Give me a minute. Wait here.' She strode over to Ben and Josh, said something to them both and then came back to Charlie while Josh raised his hand in greeting but stayed where he was.

Maggie took Charlie's hand and led him along the beach to where they would meet a path to take them back to the centre of the island.

'Is that *the* Ben?' It hadn't dawned on Charlie that it could be Maggie's ex until he'd heard her speaking to him in such a tone that it was clearly someone she knew pretty well. Once.

'Yes.'

'Okay. So I don't know where to start. He's staying at your house, in your bed.'

'There was nowhere else for him to stay. He just turned up and I was going to tell you but to be honest Charlie, I was a bit pissed off wondering when you were going to tell me that you'd been seeing Jessica.'

45

'Christ Maggie, I haven't been seeing her, I've been working with her.'

'But you didn't tell me. I heard her arrive at your apartment and I know you wouldn't do that but after what happened with her at Lake Tahoe I didn't expect you to have anything to do with her.' Had he forgotten how Jessica had treated her? Didn't he care?

'Her company is heavily involved in the new High 5 project. I had no choice but to work with her but it's purely professional. We don't discuss anything personal, I made that very clear to her. We're not even friends. Just colleagues.' He looked distraught and Maggie couldn't help but feel sorry for him.

'How can you bear to after what she did to you before?'

Charlie shrugged, 'It's just work, I try not to think about that other stuff. Anyway, she really has been nothing but professional, it's quite impressive.' He took one look at Maggie's face and added, 'I mean, her company's work has been impressive and that's the only reason I went along with it.' He took her hands in his. 'I know it's been a while but I love you, that hasn't changed. Nothing will change that.'

Maggie closed her eyes and leant into him, feeling his arms

wrap around her shoulders and breathing in the scent of him that had almost vanished from his house. 'It's been hard and when I heard her there with you... well, I just wished you were with me instead.'

'I wished that too, honey. That's why I'm here.' Maggie pulled away and looked up at him as he brushed her cheek with his thumb. 'You look beautiful.'

'You look pretty good too, I have a soft spot for smart Charlie. Come on, let's go to mine and have a cup of tea.' She took his hand and began to walk away but Charlie stayed still.

'Ben's been staying there with you? I called in to take a shower and saw his stuff.'

'No!' said Maggie, horrified. 'I mean yes, he is staying there but I'm not. I've been staying at yours. I didn't know what else to do with him.' She rolled her eyes and laughed. 'Oh my god. It's so weird. He's the project manager for the holiday lodges. He just turned up on Monday morning. I'd missed a load of emails so it was completely out of the blue.'

They strolled together through the heathland in the middle of the island where the purple heather bloomed, holding hands and feeling like they were the only people on the island, and it stayed that way for a few minutes until a Pack of Scouts appeared.

'Do you have any time today?' Charlie asked.

'I'm going to see Ben off the premises at 3 pm then I'm all yours.'

'Raincheck on the tea? I'm going to take the boat home and I'll be back for you at three.' He lifted her chin gently with his finger and kissed her.

'I'll be ready.' She watched him walk away then sighed and turned back to see what had happened in the half an hour since she'd left Ben alone with Josh. Hopefully, they wouldn't have managed to condemn too many more trees in that time.

At lunchtime, Maggie suggested that she and Ben have a

working lunch in the office to wrap up the week and so she could make sure he would be packed and ready to catch the 3 pm ferry to Sandbanks.

'What's going to happen now you've marked out where you think the eight lodges are going to be?' Maggie asked Ben as they sat in the office over sandwiches from the café.

'I'll go back with the coordinates we've finalised and that'll be put into the detailed planning application.'

'Presumably, they'll come and survey the trees as part of that?' Maggie felt sure some of the trees were worthy of Tree Preservation Orders but that had never been necessary before.

'I've made detailed notes of what will have to be cleared. That might be enough.' Maggie hoped that there was someone on the council who would want to put a spanner in the works and slap TPOs on the whole island, just to prove him wrong.

Ben had spent the whole week making sure that Maggie knew he was reporting directly to Rob Tanner on the project. It was obviously giving him an immense ego boost and for the most part, she had gone along with it. If they didn't want her to be part of it, that was fine. She loved her job and didn't especially want to be involved in harming the beautiful woodland but it felt rubbish to have been cast aside, especially in favour of someone who would relish lording it over her. But she'd got through it and now, with perfect timing, Charlie was her reward.

'So it'll be a while before anything happens.'

'Don't worry, Mags, I won't be turning up on your doorstep again any time soon. I'll make sure I book my own hotel for next time. Thanks for putting me up.' He smiled and for the first time Maggie allowed herself to think about the good times they'd had and she smiled back.

'It's okay. Weird but okay.'

'So that guy that came to the beach.'

Maggie waited for Ben to form an actual question but when

he didn't she sighed and explained anyway.

'That's Charlie, he's the forester. We're seeing each other,' she said tentatively. 'That's where I've been staying, although he's been away for a while so...'

Ben began fiddling with the wrapper from his sandwich. 'Oh, well that's good, it's good. You probably should have told me though.'

'Why? It's not your business anymore.'

His eyes flashed momentarily with anger, just as they had the day she'd finally left Croftwood Court.

She couldn't help it. 'Are you seeing anyone?'

'No, not at the moment. I've been travelling quite a bit lately so, you know.' He was defensive and she was pleased with that tiny victory.

Maybe Ben had thought there was still a chance. He seemed dejected all of a sudden when all week he'd been bossy and overbearing which was completely out of character. Maggie hadn't thought much of it, had let it wash over her thinking that he just wanted to establish himself somehow as the boss of the project. But maybe he'd been trying to impress her.

He stood up, not managing to make eye contact and said, 'I'd better go and get my stuff together. See you later.'

Maggie let him leave. It was always going to be awkward, the first time they'd seen each other since they'd broken up. She felt relieved that Ben didn't seem to have held a grudge and she almost felt sorry for him now.

She caught up on some emails until it was time to head to the quay to see Ben off. He was stood with his arms crossed watching the ferry make its way across the harbour.

'Have a good trip back,' she said.

'I'm going to need to stay for another couple of days,' he said, and Maggie noticed now that he had nothing with him.

'Really? I thought you'd finished.'

He had finished. Right up until he'd found out about

Charlie.

'No, I need to do a more in-depth inventory of the trees we're thinking of clearing and now that the forester's here it seems sensible to take advantage of that.'

'He's not working at the moment, he's here visiting.' The thing was, Maggie knew that as soon as she told Charlie that Ben wanted to survey the trees with him, he'd want to be involved and although that was good from the point of view of protecting the woodland from Ben's cavalier attitude, it was the worst thing that could happen to her.

'Well, see what he says, could you? The way that Josh has gone on about him, I think he'll be okay about helping out. I can stay another couple of days at yours, right?'

Not feeling that she had any choice in the matter, Maggie nodded and said, 'No problem. I'll see you at the office in the morning,' then walked over to the other side of the quay where Charlie was just approaching in his motorboat.

46

'Don't bother tying the boat off, let's just go now.'

Charlie looked up in surprise with the rope in his hand. Maggie looked flustered and was evidently in a hurry to leave. He threw the rope into the bottom of the boat and turned the engine.

'Quick,' she urged him as she stepped down to the boat, looking desperately up at the quay.

'What's the rush? Is the Beast of Bramble on your tail?' he laughed lazily.

'Bloody hell, Charlie, just hurry up!'

Then he saw what the problem was. 'Okay, we're going.' But the engine was reluctant to spring back into life so soon.

'Hi, Charlie. I'm Ben, I saw you on the beach earlier but didn't manage to get an introduction.' He looked pointedly at Maggie who looked like she wanted to jump ship to get away from him.

'Hey, Ben. Thought you were on the three o'clock ferry?' said Charlie, standing up with his hands on his hips.

'Change of plan. I've got some woodland surveying to do over the next couple of days and I understand you know these woods better than anyone else?'

The last thing Charlie wanted to do for the next two days

was hang out with Ben.

'I'm on vacation. What do you need?'

'I've identified the areas which will need to be cleared but I could do with knowing how that woodland fits in the wider context of the rest of the island. We don't want to be erasing entire species here.' Ben grinned but Charlie didn't let his guard down.

'I'll discuss it with Maggie.' He sat down in the boat with his back turned to Ben and hoped to god that the engine would start first time so that they could make a well-timed exit. It did. It was against Charlie's nature to be deliberately rude to anyone but he had to have Maggie's back on this and he could tell by her face that she was completely mortified by the whole thing. He could see her point. He'd been squirming just as much when Jessica had been within spitting distance of Maggie.

Maggie sat at the bow of the boat with her hair streaming behind her as they made their way across the harbour to his island. He'd missed her so much and he didn't want Ben's visit to come between them. Maggie probably had more to say on the subject of Jessica too; he felt as if he'd got off pretty lightly with that but it was clearly on account of Maggie having bigger problems to deal with right now.

They arrived on the island and moored the boat in the boathouse before making their way up to the house.

'I hope you don't mind but I brought a few things over,' Maggie said just as the back of the house came into sight and Charlie could see a huge parasol shading the deck outside the living room.

'Of course I don't mind, I love that you've been staying here.' He squeezed her hand as she led the way into the living room where she'd filled the couch with pillows and blankets which were folded over the back. Despite his state-of-the-art lighting system, she had felt the need to add a couple of lamps. He didn't mind at all. It looked homely and he loved that she'd made the place into theirs. It wasn't a minimalist, sterile house anymore; it was a home.

'It looks great, Maggie.'

'I'm glad you like it.' She headed to the fridge and pulled out a couple of bottles of beer, popping the tops off and handing him one without even asking if he wanted it.

'Maggie, you don't have to worry about this stuff with Ben. I can meet him and give him whatever he wants. I'm here for a week, a couple days out of that is okay.'

She strode outside onto the deck. Charlie followed sensing that this was just the beginning of the conversation.

'It's not okay, Charlie. All week he's been lording it over me that he's on the bloody project team and I've gone along with it just to get the whole thing over and get him out of my house and off the island and now he's going to get you on his side.' She took a slug of her beer and sat down on one of the loungers.

'I'm not going to be on his side, I'm going to make sure he doesn't fuck up our woodland, that's all,' said Charlie gently. 'Believe me, I know the last thing you want is for me to be anywhere near him but it'll be okay. There's nothing he can say to me that will change anything. I will make it clear that the only conversations I'm willing to have with him are about trees.' He went and sat down next to her. 'Come on, we haven't seen each other in weeks, let's forget all the crap and celebrate being back together.'

'Months, Charlie, not weeks,' she said sadly. 'It's been too long. Can't you stay and finish it from here? Didn't Ed say you could do that?'

He had said that, and Charlie had thought that could be a viable option to begin with but now that he was so deeply involved with the project, he didn't want to work remotely. It seemed that there was too much at stake. He could feel that the end was in sight and the closure he knew it would bring him was almost tangible. He didn't want to resume his life in the Valley, he wanted it to be here with Maggie. He just needed a little more time.

'I know it's been hard but it really isn't for much longer and then I'll be back for good. But right now, I'm not leaving until Ben's left. Me and you, we're in this together.' He clinked his beer bottle against hers and for the first time since he'd picked her up from the island, she smiled at him.

47

Maggie and Charlie arrived back on Bramble Island early the next morning. They wanted to be in the office before Ben so that Charlie could see the plans and the locations that Ben had picked out for the holiday lodges. He had left all of his work out on Maggie's desk, it was a huge mess of paperwork, maps and reference books.

Charlie was frowning as he pored over the maps to work out just which parts of the wood were going to be at risk and was shaking his head as Ben came into the office.

'Morning!' Ben said brightly. Too brightly, thought Maggie.

'Right, let's get started,' said Charlie, as he grabbed the map which had the lodge locations marked on it, and stalked past Ben out of the office.

Ben looked startled and raised his eyebrows at Maggie but thankfully didn't say anything, he just followed Charlie.

Maggie breathed a sigh of relief even though she didn't feel relieved at all. She knew she'd be restless, wondering what was going on until the minute they set foot back in the office. She had thought about going with them but in the end, Charlie had pointed out that there was no need. She would just feel awkward the whole time and if Ben thought that she was chaperoning them, it might make him all the more likely to try and stir up some sort of trouble.

Anyway, it wasn't as if there was nothing to do. She was running some of the Trust Treks; her name had been on the rota before she'd known that Charlie was coming back. She headed to the visitor centre and popped into Clare's office to say hello as she was a bit early.

'I'm glad you've popped in actually,' said Clare. 'We've had a handful of visitors asking about the tape tied on some of the trees. I assume that's to do with the holiday lodge project?'

'Yes, Ben's been marking out which trees he thinks will have to go. Charlie's gone out with him this morning to see what he's suggested. What do you want to do, put some signage up explaining?'

'Well, you know usually we like to be very transparent about what's going on but this is a sensitive issue. Perhaps we could go with some wording that suggests it's to do with a tree survey that's taking place?'

It was half true at least, so they decided on the wording and arranged that Maggie would pick up the signs the following day to place around the woods.

She went out of the back of the building to the meeting point for the Trust Treks and found Megan there waiting to take people on a Squirrel Spotter Trek.

'Hi Megan, how're things?'

'I can't believe how busy it is! I feel like all I do is wander around looking for red squirrels, eat and sleep. But it's brilliant! How about you? Has it been okay with Ben?'

Maggie hadn't told anyone apart from Megan that she and Ben used to be together, just that they used to work together at Croftwood Court. It was simpler that way. She didn't want everyone to know everything about her private life. It was bad enough that she and Charlie were playing out their relationship in front of everyone.

'He's insisted on staying for an extra couple of days and has roped Charlie into doing some surveying, which doesn't sit well with me,' she admitted.

'Awkward,' said Megan making a face. 'Alice has got a bit of a thing for Ben, so she'll be pleased he's sticking around.'

'At least it's working out well for someone.'

'Are they really going to clear the woodland for these holiday lodges?'

Maggie shrugged.

'It seems so at odds with what the Trust stands for doesn't it? I just can't see anyone thinking that it's a good idea.'

'I know. I must admit I was surprised that they'd chosen that area of the island,' said Maggie. 'But hopefully, it depends on what kind of trees are affected so it still might not happen. That's what Charlie's gone to look at with Ben this morning.'

'Well, I'm keeping my fingers crossed for whatever means the woodland stays as it is,' said Megan, as her party of Trekkers appeared.

Once Maggie had finished hunting for wildflowers with her group on the clifftops on the southwest side of the island, she headed back to the office where Charlie was sitting at the computer. He was engrossed in whatever he was doing and didn't seem to register that someone had walked into the room. Maggie bent behind him, putting her arms around his neck and her chin on his shoulder.

'What are you doing?'

'I'm trying to classify some lichen,' he said with a frown. 'Ben thinks it's just regular lichen but I'm pretty sure there's some rare lichen that only grows on ash trees, so that would be something.'

'It would,' agreed Maggie. She leaned round to kiss Charlie, breaking his eye contact with the screen. 'Was it okay then?' She was desperate to know.

'It was okay.' He smiled and pulled her onto his lap. 'He's

a nice guy and if I could forget that you dated him, we'd probably enjoy working together. It was a little awkward but, you know.' He shrugged. 'Anyway, do you have stuff to change into at mine for a night on the town?'

'Which town, because probably all my clothes are fine for anywhere within spitting distance of here.'

'I'm taking you to the Shell Bay Bistro, it's over on the Studland side of the bay, right on the beach. We'll take the boat. It'll be beautiful tonight after such a hot day.'

Maggie was glad to be going out. She was finding being on Bramble Island a bit claustrophobic at the moment and even when they'd been at Charlie's the night before, they'd eaten dinner together and then he'd been working in his study for the rest of the evening. Going somewhere else would be bliss.

48

Shell Bay had a wooden jetty that ran out into the sea. It felt like a Caribbean island restaurant, situated as it was right next to the water, elevated, with wooden steps down to the perfect beach, where the waves lapped gently and glistened in the long rays of the evening sun. Charlie moored the boat at the end of the jetty and they walked hand in hand along the wooden planks into the restaurant where they were seated on the veranda overlooking the water.

They ordered a bottle of crisp, cold Sauvignon Blanc and sipped it in comfortable silence for a moment as they took in the view.

'This is amazing, isn't it?' said Maggie. 'I had no idea it was here and it feels like you're a million miles away from anywhere.'

'I've wanted to visit ever since I moved here but it's a little pathetic if you have to eat alone in a place as romantic as this so I'm glad I waited for you.'

Maggie's eyes lit up as she smiled at him and he fleetingly felt the pain of how hard it would be to leave her behind again.

'I'm glad too.' She reached out and wove her fingers between his, melting away the thought and bringing him back into the moment.

After the meal, they strolled along the beach, carrying their shoes on their fingertips and holding hands. It was still warm although the sun had almost set. They walked all the way to Bramble Bush Beach passing by the couple of old houseboats which were moored about a metre from the shoreline in very shallow water and had sunk into the sand unevenly so that they sloped dramatically from port to starboard.

'And they say there's not enough quality holiday accommodation around here.' said Maggie. 'I bet someone would love to stay in one of those. Do you think they belong to anyone?'

'I guess someone owns them but they look a little neglected.'

'It's a shame. It's a beautiful spot, they would have been amazing once.'

Charlie sat down on the sand and pulled Maggie next to him, enveloping her shoulders in the warmth of his arm.

'So now that Ben's the guy for the holiday lodges, are you off the hook?' He had wondered, ever since Ben had appeared, what that meant for Maggie. The holiday lodge project had supposedly been hers to lead and now it seemed that someone else was doing it.

'No, I spoke to Rob Tanner, who's overseeing it, and he said he got Ben in to save him having to make site visits. Otherwise, I'd be backwards and forwards to head office as well and at this time of year, it's not practical. In the winter when there's less going on, I'll probably take on more of the project work again. Anything to stop Ben visiting too often.' She grinned at Charlie but he felt she was glossing over how she really felt about Ben being there.

Having spent the morning with the guy, Charlie got the distinct impression that he was deliberately messing with Maggie by staying these extra couple of days. Ben had seemed surprised when Charlie started looking at the trees that had been tagged for removal. He didn't know what Ben had expected but Charlie was determined to be professional. As soon as Ben realised that, he'd tried to flex his muscles by using Latin names for the trees and other things which just made Charlie wonder how Maggie could ever have gone for such a dick. He didn't want to let on that that's what he thought because he knew Maggie would worry more about him crossing paths with Ben if there was any hint of animosity. He was planning to keep his feelings to himself and wait for Ben to leave.

'Unless your lichen turns out to be an endangered species, I can't see that anything's going to stop the project. I mean, the planners will know that the Trust has done its homework and will probably be on their side from the start. The only way to stop it is to come up with another solution to the woodland location but we've already exhausted the other possibilities on the island.'

'Maybe it doesn't have to be on the island,' said Charlie, his gaze falling onto the houseboats they'd passed. He nudged Maggie and nodded towards the boats.

'Oh my god, that's a brilliant idea. People would love that! Imagine staying on the water, plus that would solve the problem of needing to cordon off part of the woods for privacy for the holiday people. It's the perfect solution.'

'So who do we need to convince, Ben or someone else?'

'I don't know. Probably Rob Tanner's the best person to approach. Perhaps I should do some research before I mention it. Get some solid ideas together, maybe even try to find out how much it would cost and if it's going to be feasible to do that in the harbour. Have you seen any houseboats apart from these?'

'No, but that doesn't mean it can't be done. I could ask the architect who worked on my house to meet us to talk it through. He's a local guy so should know what's possible.'

Maggie was fired up with enthusiasm and chatted about the

new idea as they walked back to the boat. If the Trust went for it, it would put Maggie in a great position. She could do what she came to Bramble Island to do without feeling compromised between delivering on her mandate and saving the woodland. It seemed like the perfect solution.

49

Alex Parsons, the architect who had transformed Charlie's house, had agreed to meet Maggie and Charlie at his offices in Poole. Maggie had spent the few days since Charlie's brainwave looking at options for the kind of accommodation they could offer, ways to connect the boats to the island and anything else she could think of that would make the idea seem more feasible than using the woodland.

It was just two days until Charlie left to go back and finish off the High 5 project in San Francisco, and although she was loath to waste the precious time they had together poring over ideas for the project, she'd noticed that Charlie had become infinitely more relaxed once she was occupied, leaving him free to carry on with his own work.

Maggie was excited again, just as she'd been before she'd arrived on Bramble Island; the anticipation of being involved in something amazing was back, now that it didn't involve spoiling the beautiful island. It was no wonder they'd brought Ben into the mix; she could see now that she had probably come across as unenthusiastic and possibly unhelpful. Well, that was going to change. After all, it was much better to offer a solution to a problem rather than just moaning about it.

Alex's offices were modern, very white with lots of glass

and Maggie could see how that style translated into the work he'd done on Charlie's house.

'Hello Charlie, great to see you again,' Alex said, shaking hands with Alex and then Maggie as Charlie introduced her.

'This is my partner Maggie, she's the park manager on Bramble Island.'

If Alex was surprised that Maggie was with Charlie now, rather than Jessica who had worked closely with him on the design for the house, he didn't show it.

'Good to meet you, Maggie. I hear you have some plans for Bramble Island you want to discuss.'

They sat in Alex's office on comfortable sofas where they had a wonderful view of Poole Harbour; a much busier, more industrial scene than they were used to in Bramble Bay. Maggie explained the current project proposal and then laid out her ideas for taking the lodges onto the water.

'In principle, it's absolutely possible. It's a relatively calm expanse of water with low tidal impact. It would be straightforward enough to go with a method like this,' he said, pointing to some of Maggie's research material. 'A jetty type system with piles so that there is a controlled rise and fall with the tides and minimal movement from waves. It would work, but it will be expensive.'

'How expensive?' Maggie asked.

'I would imagine for the Trust, prohibitively so. Also, the upkeep of something like this is going to be considerably higher than anything they would do on land. The cost of the accommodation itself would be no different. You could effectively build the same thing on the floats as you could in the woods. I could put some proposals together for you outlining the cost of building the structure for eight units so that you can make a like-for-like comparison with the proposal you have now.'

'That would be brilliant,' said Maggie and then realised that Alex wasn't going to give his time for free. 'I'll contact the special projects office and see if they'll sign off on the cost of your time. Could you email me an estimate?'

Charlie put his hand on her leg and said, 'This is on me for now,' with a pointed look that meant they'd discuss it later if it needed discussing.

'Thanks for your time, Alex, we appreciate it,' he said and they left, heading to a nearby pub on the quay.

'You can't pay for Alex, it's not fair.'

'C'mon, Maggie, it's not going to be much and if you ask the Trust to pay they'll say no because they already have the plan they think is the best one. If you go to them with the backup from Alex, it's a much stronger position. And besides, I love Bramble Island and if putting some of my money into saving the woods makes the difference, that's the best thing I could spend it on.'

Maggie decided to let it go. She had no idea how much money Charlie had, it didn't matter to her but he was right. It was money well spent in her book too.

They had lunch in the pub before heading back to Charlie's island for the evening. Although neither of them had said anything, they were both conscious of the fact that Charlie was leaving in a couple of days and were desperate to wring every last second of being together out of that. Even though Ben had left Maggie's house a few days ago, she'd barely been there since, choosing to spend every spare moment with Charlie. Finally, although he was about to leave again, things between them were starting to get back to how they had been before they'd left for America.

They headed up from the boathouse towards the house. When it came into sight Charlie stopped.

'There's someone here,' he said, holding his arm in front of Maggie protectively, preventing her from going any further.

'How do you know? Can you see someone?' she said, craning her neck to look.

'The door to the deck is wide open and I know I shut it this morning,' he frowned. 'I can see someone inside.'

Charlie began to move slowly along the path with Maggie following. His finger was to his lips as they went, as if Maggie didn't know to keep quiet when they were trying to surprise a burglar. Who would burgle a house on an island anyway? It was such a hassle to get here let alone try and steal anything and transport it away.

Once they got closer, he straightened up and sighed. 'For Christ sake, it's Jessica,' he said.

50

'Are you sure it's Jessica?' Maggie asked. 'Did you know she was coming?'

'Of course I didn't know' said Charlie impatiently, feeling exasperated with Maggie for asking such a ridiculous question. The last thing he wanted was for Jessica to set foot in what had become his sanctuary. The only place, until now, that she hadn't ruined for him. This was his and Maggie's place.

They walked up to the house and found Jessica sitting on the sofa, flicking through a magazine. She looked up and smiled at them when they walked in.

'Hi guys,' she said. 'How are you, Maggie? It's great to see you again.' She was acting like she was supposed to be there. Maggie flicked him a look as if to say exactly that. Christ, what a mess.

'Jessica, what are you doing here? I… how did you even get here?' It was so frustrating looking at her sitting in his house as if she belonged there. Clearly the real Jessica was back.

'The place looks great, Charlie. Just how I'd imagined it.'

'Jessica! For fuck's sake!'

'Charlie, please.' She flinched as if his words had stung her but at least she had stopped smiling. 'I thought if you wanted to be here, with your... girlfriend, then we could shift our base for a while.' The fleeting look of disdain she threw Maggie's way wasn't lost on him and Charlie knew that she wasn't here to make things easier for him. Far from it, he suspected.

'It isn't necessary. I was planning to leave on Saturday anyway.'

'Well, there's no rush now that I'm here,' Jessica said, matter-of-factly.

'Where are you going to stay?' asked Maggie, somewhat naïvely Charlie thought. Clearly, he was going to have to let Jessica stay here because as was the case with Ben, practically speaking there was no other choice.

'I don't remember there being a hotel nearby, I'll stay here. Right, Charlie?' she laughed. He felt beaten and simply nodded in reply.

'Right, I think I'll head back to Bramble Island,' said Maggie, a little too brightly. 'You don't mind if I take the boat do you?'

He could hardly refuse because the look on Maggie's face said she was going to take the boat whatever he said. She clearly just wanted to get away.

'Okay, I guess I can use the yacht.'

'Great to see you again, Jessica.' She barely looked at Charlie as she left through the door onto the deck. He followed her, waiting until they were on the path away from the house, away from Jessica's glare before he quietly pleaded with her to stop and talk to him but she carried on, purposefully walking towards the boathouse.

'Maggie, please, I don't want her here.' In desperation, he grabbed her arm in an attempt to stop her.

'Charlie! Let go of me.' She pulled herself from his grip, her eyes fierce. He was stunned to see no trace of tenderness or love. It had disappeared in the few minutes since they'd been back. Since Jessica.

'I'm sorry, Maggie honey, please. I don't know what to do!'

'Stick up for yourself, stick up for me! Do you really think it's okay to have your ex living in your house? Remember what she did to you!'

'It's just for work,' he said weakly, feeling that he was betraying Maggie as he spoke.

'Okay, well I've got my own work to do.' She strode off down to the boathouse.

Charlie felt defeated. He hated confrontation which was part of the reason why he'd run to Lake Tahoe when he'd found out about Jessica and Jared. Since that day, he hadn't spoken about any of it to Jessica even though they'd been working together. It had seemed better just to get on and leave the past alone.

'Is it too early for a drink?' Jessica asked as he went back into the house.

Charlie stood for a moment, kneading his eyebrows with his fingers before he pushed his hair back and exhaled. It was going to have to be said.

'You shouldn't have just turned up here, you knew I was heading back in a couple of days. What are you doing?'

Jessica put her magazine down and came to stand in front of him. He could smell her perfume she was so close to him, and he had a brief flashback to when this kind of proximity to her used to drive him wild.

'I've loved working with you on this, Charlie. It's made me reflect on what I lost when I let you go. We need to give ourselves another chance, put the past behind us and pick up where we left off.' As she spoke she reached out and took his hand, placing it on her cheek, leaning in and stroking the back of it before he had the chance to take in what she was doing and pull away.

'No, we don't. Your chances ran out with me a long time

ago. I'm collaborating on this with you as a favour to Ed, that's all. If you came for any other reason than the project, you should leave now.' His heart was beating through his chest with the adrenaline and nerve it was taking him to finally be honest with her. 'I love Maggie, we have a life together here. It's over for me and you, apart from the work, it's over. Anyway, I thought you and Drew were together?'

She slipped her hand onto his waist and caressed the skin underneath his shirt. 'No, Charlie. You're wrong. Drew just works for me. It's nothing.' She planted a kiss on his lips and then stepped back to show him her phone. It was a photo of him asleep in his bed in the apartment in San Francisco.

Not able to say anything, Charlie stumbled up the stairs, his lips tingling, all he could smell was her and he thought he was going to throw up. What the fuck was she doing to him?

51

Maggie moored the boat at the quay on Bramble Island, her guilt at taking Charlie's boat overshadowed by her anger at his inability to stand up to Jessica. What was it about that woman that she couldn't leave him to get on with his life? And why couldn't he seem to bring himself to tell her that?

She headed straight for the office. While she was feeling like this, frustrated, raving mad, it was best to throw herself into something. Work was the answer. As she walked through the woods, the smells and sounds of the island soothed her and she felt calmer by the time she opened the door. None of the volunteers were there, it was the middle of the afternoon so they'd be out leading Treks.

Maggie sat down at her desk, it was familiarly cluttered with her notes and piles of paperwork and post to check through. It had been a while since she'd had a normal day in the office what with the Treks, Ben's visit and then Charlie coming back and she had a bit of a backlog. Scanning through the frightening number of emails, she came across one from Ben to Rob Tanner with her cc'd in.

To: rob.tanner@project.trust.org.uk
From: ben.kirk@project.trust.org.uk

Hi Rob,

To update you on the progress on site at Bramble Island: all trees have been identified and confirmed expendable by Charlie Mackenzie, the forester. I propose planning consent be applied for based on the attached grid references. Some concern was raised by Clare who runs the visitor centre – the tree marking has prompted questions from visitors about what is happening. It may be wise to actively manage an information release as soon as possible, in advance of the planning application.

Best, Ben

Maggie hoped that Alex would get back to her quickly so that she could pitch her water lodge proposal before the planning application was submitted. She had a feeling that if it was afterwards, it would be too late to change anyone's mind. But in the meantime, there was something else she could do.

The island was quiet. Rain was forecast and Maggie could smell it in the air before the drops began to fall. It was warm, summer rain so she didn't mind getting wet and didn't change her pace at all. It felt good to defy what she would normally do. Instead, she revelled in the absurdity of letting herself get soaked through. She headed for the lodge site and wandered through the wood untying the plastic ribbons from the trees. After all, they were marked on a map now, why invite speculation when it might all come to nothing?

Back at the office, all of the volunteers were taking shelter. Maggie hung her soaked fleece on the back of the door and pulled on a hoodie which she'd left there at some point.

'Hey, Maggie. Long time no see,' said Josh.

'What are those?' asked Alice of the ribbons which Maggie had dumped on the floor.

'They were marking the trees for the lodge project but now that the locations have been mapped and Charlie's had a look at the trees, there's no need for them.' She shuddered as she thought of how Ben had described the trees as expendable and how he'd made it sound in his email as if Charlie thought that too. As if.

'I think Ben wanted them left, actually,' said Alice as Megan rolled her eyes.

'Visitors are wondering what they're for and we don't want to alarm anyone before we know what's going to happen.'

Alice looked sulkily at Maggie but didn't say anything else.

Maggie made a snap decision, 'I've got Charlie's boat. Who wants to go to Sandbanks for fish and chips?' She needed to get away from the island and being alone would be a terrible idea. 'Megan, you can drive.'

'Brilliant!' said Megan. 'Give us twenty minutes to get ready and we'll meet you on the quay. You look like you could do with drying off anyway.'

It had been so long since she'd been in her cottage that it felt almost like someone else's place. Ben had left it very tidy and she discovered he'd bought a really good bottle of wine from the island gift shop and left it on the kitchen table with a note.

Maggie, thanks for lending me your place. It was good to see you again and I'm glad we can be friends. I'll be back for the next phase but I'll try and find somewhere else to stay to save you the commute! Best, Ben

Well, that was nice, she thought as she ran upstairs to get changed.

The fish and chip trip was a huge success. The rain had cleared up so they sat on the edge of the quay at Sandbanks and ate with their feet dangling over the edge as they watched the activity around the harbour.

'How's Charlie doing?' Josh asked Maggie as she swirled a chip around in her pot of curry sauce. 'I've not seen much of him since he got back.'

'He's fine. He's been working a lot. He's got a colleague over here with him as well, so he's pretty busy.'

'It's not the same working the woods without him. Do you think he'll be back before the end of the season?'

At the moment she found it hard to imagine him ever coming back. 'I don't know, Josh. I wish I did.'

52

Charlie stood in the shower letting the hot water run over him, removing all traces of Jessica's kiss. How had she got that photo of him in bed? She'd been to The Battery a few times to work with him but he'd never slept when she'd been there. Nausea washed over him as he thought what Maggie would say if she saw it. He hoped she'd know that he wouldn't sleep with Jessica but the photo was going to be hard to defend when he had no idea how it had happened.

He dressed and went downstairs. Jessica wasn't on the sofa anymore. She was sitting at his computer in his study. Unfortunately, as he lived alone he hadn't bothered with too much security on it and he saw that she was using his account.

'Christ, there are no boundaries with you are there? Get off my computer.'

She turned to him with a self-satisfied smile. 'Just checking my emails.'

'I'm taking you to the mainland. It's up to you what you do then, get a hotel, fly home, I don't care but you can't stay here.' He didn't trust her at all and did not doubt that she would find a way to show the photo to Maggie, whatever he agreed to.

'I don't think so, Charlie. Unless you're coming with me?'

'You know I'm not. I never should have gotten involved with you again.' He pushed her aside and shut down the computer trying not to think about what she might have been doing. He'd deal with that later. Her case was still beside the door and her handbag was on the sofa. Charlie grabbed both and headed out of the house.

'Charlie! I'm not leaving!' she shouted as he dragged the case behind him down to the boathouse.

He didn't look behind, but as he had all her stuff, he knew she'd be following him. He threw the case and bag into the boat and climbed in after them. Jessica appeared, flustered and angry which cheered Charlie no end. At last, he felt like he was winning the battle with her and he did an imaginary fist pump as she got in the boat.

'What do you expect me to do? I don't have a flight booked.'

Charlie shrugged. She was off his island. That was all that mattered to him.

'You can't just abandon me!'

'You got here, you can get back.'

'God, Charlie, you are going to be so sorry. This is the end of you and Maggie.'

'No, it's not. She's nothing like you, Jessica. She's not scheming and manipulative, she doesn't lie to get what she wants. She'll know that photo's not what it looks like. She'll believe me,' he said, with more conviction than he felt. The evidence was pretty damning and he was not going to give Jessica the satisfaction of asking her how she came to take the picture.

As they approached the quay at Sandbanks, he saw Maggie sitting with all the volunteers. She'd already seen him, he could tell by the look on her face. He raised his hand and waved. Maggie stood up and presumably suggested it was time for them to leave because they all followed suit. Then

Josh noticed him, waved and pointed him out to the others who also waved. They looked like they might wait for him to moor, as there was a debate going on but he saw Maggie shake her head and they all got onto their boat. His boat. Josh stood and shrugged in apology to him.

Charlie's elation at getting Jessica off his island had now dissipated in the face of Maggie's coldness. She wouldn't even wait to talk to him. But maybe she didn't want to see Jessica, that was more likely and he consoled himself with that thought as he watched them pass across his bow as they left.

He moored the yacht behind the Bramble Bay Ferry which had finished for the day, tying off with just two lines as he planned to leave almost immediately. He gestured to Jessica that she should go first, then he passed the case and her bag off to her before standing on the quay himself.

'I'll finish the project but I don't want to see you. We can do it remotely and if anything else is required, I can brief someone else to help out.'

'If that's what you want,' she said, picking up her bag and pulling the handle up on her case. 'So long, Charlie.'

He got back on the yacht but watched her walk away, heading towards the Sandbanks hotel. It wasn't quite far enough for his liking, but it would do for now although he still wondered how she had got to his place. What he wanted more than anything was to see Maggie and make things right with her. He had no idea whether Jessica was going to send the photo or not but he had decided to warn Maggie and try to explain since they'd promised to be honest with each other. It wasn't worth betting on Jessica's better nature because in his experience, she didn't have one.

He cast off and headed towards Bramble Island. It might be too soon to talk to Maggie but he couldn't imagine going home, let alone being able to sleep, before he had spoken to her. Jessica could easily have been sending the photo when he caught her in his study which would explain Maggie's reaction in Sandbanks. He just had to know.

When he reached Bramble Island, he moored the yacht on the Bramble Bay Ferry berth. It was the only part of the quay big enough to take it and as long as he didn't stay past 9 am the next day, it should be fine. There was no sign of Maggie or the volunteers so he headed straight for Maggie's cottage. As he walked across the shingle, he felt a wave of exhaustion hit him. It had been a tough day, emotionally; it was a long time since he'd had to deal with any of this stuff. He stopped and realising he didn't have the energy left for arguments and explanations, turned back to the quayside.

He reached the yacht, taking a few minutes to bring his motorboat around and tether it to the stern to tow it home. The next time he saw Maggie, he wanted to be ready and if she had no boat, the timing of that would be down to him. He needed to feel some control over his life again.

53

When Maggie got back from Sandbanks she headed straight for the kitchen and opened the bottle of wine that Ben had left. Whatever his faults, at least Ben wasn't some psycho ex who couldn't leave her alone. She sat on the sofa, pulled the throw over her legs and put the television on hoping to find something distracting to watch.

She couldn't believe that Charlie was going to spend the night in his house with Jessica. It made her blood boil. He was so bloody useless around that woman. If Jessica threw herself at him, Maggie honestly wondered what might happen. They'd had two days left together and now that was ruined. He might as well be back in America because she was not going to set foot back on his island while that woman was there. What made it even worse was that he was taking her out for the evening. He'd never taken Maggie to Sandbanks. They were probably going to Rick Stein's restaurant. Maggie bet Jessica couldn't eat anywhere that wasn't expensive.

After a couple of glasses of wine, she began to feel better. 'Sleepless in Seattle', one of her top ten films, was on and she'd only missed the first half an hour. But the story seemed to mirror the way her own life was going; Meg Ryan and Tom Hanks never quite met in the same place, they kept missing each other for the whole movie right until the very end. That was just like her and Charlie but now she was wondering if they'd ever have the ending they'd both wanted in the beginning.

By the end of the film and the bottle of red, Maggie had streaks down her face from crying and had exhausted herself. She burrowed into bed and slipped into a deep sleep.

When Maggie woke the next morning, her head felt foggy, much like the view from the window. It was drizzling to match her mood. She'd probably drunk one too many glasses of wine the night before, but at least in this weather the only visitors would be hardened bird watchers who probably wouldn't be interested in Trust Treks.

She got up and headed to the kitchen. Sweet tea would make her feel better. Sleeping on things had made her realise that she needed to leave the next move to Charlie. As long as Jessica was there she didn't want to visit him at home. She had no idea whether he was still planning to leave in a couple of days or whether he and Jessica were just temporarily shacking up together while he finished the project. Maggie had no idea how much longer his project was going to take but she honestly would have preferred him to have stayed in America rather than for Jessica to be staying here. Until now, she had quite successfully managed to operate on an 'out of sight, out of mind' basis so that she didn't miss Charlie too much to bear. Now, he was all she could think about. Him and Jessica.

Once she'd showered, she felt better. It was the first time she'd battled with the tap-shower for a few weeks and she fleetingly yearned for Charlie's power shower but this was homely, she told herself. She had fallen too easily into treating Charlie's house as her own and it wasn't. If it was her house too, she would have been able to insist that Jessica should leave. Charlie would have cared what she thought.

Maggie pulled on her waterproofs for the walk to the office. She strolled, in the rain, via the quay to check on Charlie's boat but it wasn't there. Maybe Megan had borrowed it?

When she arrived at the office everyone was there.

'Does anyone know what happened to Charlie's boat? It's not where we left it last night.'

'Maybe it's been stolen,' said Alice, looking stricken.

'It's unlikely. Someone would have had to come here specially, or they were already on the island,' said Eric. 'Maybe Charlie picked it up?'

'Yes, maybe. I'll email him,' said Maggie, thinking that she ought to do that anyway. She had no idea whether he was still leaving tomorrow and it would be good to know what was going on, for her own peace of mind. 'Actually, would you mind emailing him, Megan?'

'No, that's fine,' said Megan, firing up the computer and tapping out an email while Maggie went over the priorities for the day with the others. With few visitors expected, they could get on with some routine maintenance like cutting back overgrown paths.

Maggie felt her mobile vibrating in her pocket and pulled it out. It was Charlie. He rarely called her because he had no signal at his house.

'Hey, Charlie,' she said, ducking outside for a bit of privacy.

'Maggie, I'm so sorry, I just got the email from Megan. I picked up the boat last night after I'd dropped Jessica off.'

He'd dropped Jessica off! She hadn't stayed the night after all and given how intent she'd been on staying, Maggie wondered whether Charlie had finally put his foot down.

'Oh, okay. That's fine. We just wanted to make sure it hadn't been stolen. Where are you?''

'I'm on my way to the airport. I had a call from Ed, there's been a major hack of High 5. I've got to go back and help them out. It'll probably be in hand by the time I can get there but, you know. I was going back tomorrow anyway and Ed's freaking out.' He paused. Maggie had the sense that there was something he was waiting for her to say. Was she supposed to beg him to stay? Offer to go with him? Ask about Jessica? She didn't know. There was so much to say but it wasn't the time.

'I hope it turns out okay. Let me know how you're getting on.'

'Bye, Maggie. I love you.'

She hung up. It had been a chaotic couple of days, added to a few weeks of not having seen each other properly; Maggie wasn't so sure how things were going to end up. If she'd said she loved him, they would have been empty words because she didn't feel the same now as she had before their trip to America. She had been so sure then. Nothing could touch them, they'd been solid. But the first time they'd ventured out of their Dorset bubble, it had almost broken them.

54

Charlie had taken a direct flight from London to San Jose so that he could go straight to the High 5 offices. It was a hive of activity when he arrived, with even a couple of TV news crews filming on the sidewalk.

Ed looked terrible, ashen-faced and exhausted. There were a few other Cumulus.com executives in the conference room looking very serious, having seemingly endless meetings with specialist teams, trying to find out what had happened.

'It looks like a DDoS attack on a massive scale,' explained Ed.

'Really? That's actually quite impressive.' Charlie began, then once he saw Ed's face, changed tack. 'It's devastating, but to pull off a denial of service attack on a company like this with so many hosting locations, I mean, it's seriously complex.'

'It is and that's the problem. We can't stop it at the moment, we don't have a plan and we've been down for almost 18 hours now.' Ed shook his head. 'It's unprecedented.'

'I need to take a look at it. I'm no expert on this kind of thing but man, the more of us looking at it the better, right?' It was a terrible situation but Charlie used to thrive on having to fix problems, maybe not as big as this one, and it gave him a huge adrenaline rush which he was struggling to control in front of Ed. The stakes were so high and even though the outcome didn't directly affect him anymore, High 5 would always feel like it was his.

Jared had stepped away from High 5 completely since the take-over but Charlie knew that he would want to help. Plus, when they were in college he did his fair share of hacking, just amateur stuff but he could be a valuable resource. He got the okay from Ed and made the call.

'Hey, Jared. I've got an offer you can't refuse.'

'Are you here, Charlie? Have you seen what's going on with High 5?'

'I'm at the office now. You need to get over here. We need all the help we can get.'

'Have you heard from Jessica? She's pissed, man.'

Charlie sighed. Why did Jessica have to be everywhere? He'd assumed she'd still be in the Sandbanks Hotel.

'No. Jared, I haven't heard from her and I don't want to talk to her. She crossed a line by following me to the UK. I'm done with her.' He felt a lightness sweep over him as if saying it out loud had made him realise it was true; he was done with her, for good this time.

'Okay, I'm on my way.'

At Ed's request, Charlie met with the incident response team. They were confident they'd find a way to stop the attack but in the meantime, it was costing the company a fortune and the race was on to resolve it over the weekend before the markets opened on Monday. It was terrifying to think about the impact it would have on their share price if they couldn't show that it had been nipped in the bud.

While Charlie was making a coffee, Ed came into the kitchen.

'They have a lead, an IP address which they've traced to the dark web,' said Ed, looking more relieved than the lead warranted, Charlie thought.

'That's great. They must have forgotten to cover their tracks with that one. It could be a breakthrough.'

'Let's hope so. I'm going to take a break. I've got a room at the hotel across the street. If you want to do the same, put it on the company account.'

'Thanks, Ed. I think I'll stick around until the jet lag kicks in. Can I have a quick word about the project while you're here?' Charlie suddenly wanted to get everything Jessica related off his mind. 'I can't work with Jessica on the rest of the project. I know that makes things a little tricky and I am sorry but there's no way around it.'

'The history caught up with you, huh?' Ed smiled knowingly.

'Something like that. I want to do a great job for you, Ed, but I can't do it with her.'

'It's no problem, Charlie. Kyle can deal with Jessica from now on. Go through him if you need something from her. I'll talk to Jessica, let her know the new structure.'

'Thanks, that'd be great.'

Ed gave Charlie a friendly punch on the arm. 'Call me if there's any development.'

Jared arrived and set himself up next to Charlie on one of the hot desks in the main office.

'Charlie, you need to call Jessica. She's going fricking crazy. Have you blocked her or something?'

'Yes. I have nothing to say to her and I don't want to hear anything she wants to say to me.'

'Something's going on with her. I know her, and this is serious. Charlie, I think she might be behind this attack.'

Charlie leant back in his chair and laughed. 'C'mon, Jared! Jessica's not a hacker, she's not capable of pulling off something like this.'

'She's seriously rich, she doesn't have to have done it herself,' Jared insisted. 'That guy, Drew, who works for her?

I bet he's no stranger to the dark web.'

She had been pretty pissed at him and had threatened to finish him. But this was more than that, it wasn't just an attack on him. This attack was hurting countless other people, from the shareholders to the investors, even the users. Whatever he thought about Jessica, it seemed to Charlie that this was beyond what she was capable of. Perhaps Jared was onto something by suspecting Drew.

55

Maggie looked at the picture on the screen in front of her and tried not to think the worst. But she couldn't see how Jessica came to have a photo of Charlie sleeping, without her having been there when he fell asleep, and that opened up all kinds of other questions because why would he fall asleep while someone who is just a work colleague was in his room? And it wasn't that he'd dozed off while she was there working; he was in bed, his shoulders were bare and the other side of the bed looked slept in. Plus, she could see it was a recent picture because the scar on Charlie's arm was clearly visible.

It wasn't the right time to confront Charlie about it. The High 5 hack had made the UK national news so Maggie knew it was a huge crisis and although he didn't own the company anymore, he would be trying his best to help them and could be putting himself under a lot of pressure. That Charlie wasn't the person in that picture. He wouldn't sleep with Jessica, Maggie knew that. And yet, based on the evidence, what other conclusion could she come to?

Maggie closed the email and decided that the only thing she could do was to put it out of her mind until she knew Charlie had time to talk. Yet again, it was so hard to deal with things when he wasn't here and unfortunately, she was beginning to get used to it.

Alex had sent through a basic plan, along with costings, for building the infrastructure of the water lodges. It was possible, expensive but possible. Maggie emailed Rob Tanner to set up a meeting. He came back to her almost immediately and said that he was happy to make a site visit the following week to review the work that Ben had done and although she hadn't told him what her reason for wanting to meet was, he said he was happy to make time to see her.

Rob looked at his iPad and then looked at the trees.

'I thought Ben had marked the trees up. Are we in the right place?'

'Sorry, I took the markers off because they'd been causing some concern with visitors. I didn't think it would matter now that the locations are grid referenced?' Maggie was sorry now that she'd taken off the markers. She didn't want Rob to be annoyed with her before she pitched her idea. 'Basically, the front couple of metres all along the beach were marked,' she said, gesturing towards the edge of the woodland, 'and the sections marked in yellow on your map are here.' She walked along the tree line and stopped periodically to illustrate to Rob the positions of the lodge plots.

'Okay, I can see now. It probably is affecting more of the woodland than I'd envisaged from the drawings,' he said, and Maggie saw her opportunity to pitch.

'I've been doing some research on an alternative.'

Rob pursed his lips, 'We've already ruled out the other areas on the island.'

'This isn't strictly on the island,' said Maggie, producing the artist's impression that Alex had prepared.

'Wow, that's seriously inventive,' said Rob, looking impressed, 'but probably seriously expensive.' He handed the picture back to Maggie who handed him the costings from Alex in return.

'Yes, the infrastructure would cost more but we can charge more for such unusual accommodation, plus it has a much lower impact on the island itself.

Rob scrutinised the costings while Maggie studied his face, trying to guess what he thought.

'It's very interesting,' he said after a minute of silence. 'I think it's worth considering.'

'That's brilliant, thank you so much!' In her most optimistic daydreams about what Rob would think of the idea, he hadn't been as keen as this.

'Don't get too excited. We'll need to have a proper look at the proposal. I can understand that people want to preserve the woodland and I think that's the best argument in favour of this plan, it just depends whether your costings stack up with what we think the increased revenue could be.'

Even with Rob's caveat, Maggie was delighted that he had readily accepted the idea as a valid alternative and she felt sure that it was such an attractive idea, it would win over anyone else that might be involved with the final decision.

She saw Rob onto the ferry and headed over to the Scout campsite where the volunteers were clearing and tidying up after the last camp of the summer holidays. There was hardly any opportunity during the summer to cut back the rhododendrons and other leafy shrubs which encroached over some of the paths and if they didn't cut it back now, it would get out of hand quite quickly.

'Hi, Maggie!' called Megan from her vantage point near the top of a ladder where she was pulling ivy off the roof of the toilet block.

'Doing a good job there, Megan!'

'How was the meeting with Rob Tanner?' Megan asked, climbing down the ladder as Maggie came over.

'Very positive.' Maggie hadn't told anyone about the water lodge idea but now that Rob was willing to consider it, it seemed like it would be okay to tell the volunteers that there was a different option. 'I pitched him the idea of having the holiday lodges on the water instead of in the woods.'

'Oh my god, that would be amazing!' said Megan. 'That makes the best use of the setting and saves the woodland, it's perfect.'

'It is,' agreed Maggie, 'but it's also expensive. Whether they go for that option depends on whether they think they can make more money from the fact they are on the water, to justify the extra cost. But he did seem really keen.' Maggie couldn't help a huge grin spread over her face.

'Well, fingers crossed. I've never heard of anything like that before. What made you think of that?'

'Charlie came up with it when we went to Shell Bay for dinner. There are a couple of old houseboats moored over on Bramblebush Beach.'

'And how are things with Charlie? You didn't manage to spend much time with him when he was back.'

Maggie shrugged. 'It's just hard work with him not being here. There's been a hack at High 5 so he's helping with that but I could do with talking to him. His ex, Jessica sent me a photo of him in bed.'

'What? With her? That seems so unlikely,' said Megan, shaking her head.

'It's a photo of him, sleeping.'

'There could be an innocent explanation.'

'I don't know, Megan. It's weird, and she obviously sent it to me to cause trouble which she's managed to do before without photographic evidence.'

'Well, at least give Charlie a chance to explain. I find it hard to believe that he would cheat on you, Maggie. You two are great together. Once he's back, it'll be okay, you'll see.'

But Maggie had a horrible feeling that it was never going to be the same as it was in the beginning. Too much had happened.

56

Jet lag had finally forced Charlie to book a room at the hotel across the street from the High 5 offices. Having felt like he was going to sleep forever when he got there, he woke up just a couple of hours later feeling refreshed enough to go back to the office.

Jared's theory that Jessica could be behind the cyber-attack had gained traction with Charlie while he'd slept and he knew it was something they had to rule out and that meant seeing Jessica one last time.

Her visit to Bramble Bay had made him realise that any attempt he made to cut her out of his life was never going to work. Confronting her and addressing the past, was the only way to tackle it. But he couldn't do it alone.

Jared was still in the office, exactly where he'd been when Charlie had left. They were no further forward in the search for the source of the denial of service attack.

'I'm buying into your Jessica and Drew theory,' Charlie began. 'I think we go over there and see if we can find anything out. You okay with that?'

'Shit, Charlie, she's never gonna confess to us.' Jared looked pale and Charlie realised that he was frightened of Jessica. That could have been how things turned out as they did; maybe Jessica had played on Jared's fear of her to get what she wanted. Perhaps Jared had experienced this other side to her before.

'Maybe not but we might be able to find something out. If one of us can distract her maybe we can get a look at the history on her computer or check her messages or something.'

Jared grinned, 'Like Magnum PI.'

'If you want,' said Charlie. 'C'mon. Let's go.

Jared's Tesla was parked out back. Charlie found it slightly perturbing that Jessica's address was already programmed into the Sat Nav.

'We were still together when I got the car. She programmed it in.' Jared said, reading Charlie's mind.

'What's the plan then?' asked Charlie.

'Man, this was your idea. You don't have a plan? It's obvious. She wants to get back with you so you can distract her while I look for something.'

The thought of having to tell Jessica that it was over, that he didn't want her, ever, terrified Charlie. He'd made a half-hearted attempt when he threw her off the island but this was it and he didn't know how she'd take it.

Jared pulled over just before they turned onto Jessica's street.

'Okay, you drive in, I'll get in the back so she doesn't see me on the cameras and I'll head around back while she's letting you in.'

'Okay,' agreed Charlie, reluctantly. 'I'll give you as long as I can.'

Charlie pulled up to the gates of Jessica's house and pressed on the intercom. She answered after a few seconds.

'Charlie, this is a nice surprise.' She sounded genuinely pleased to hear from him. Not at all like someone who was almost forcibly removed from his house the last time they met. She buzzed the gates open.

Jared snuck out of the back seat as Charlie headed for the

front door and made it around the side of the house before Jessica opened the door.

She looked immaculate as ever, wearing a bathing suit and a flowing robe. She leaned forward and kissed Charlie on both cheeks. He went along with it; he had to for now.

'It's great to see you, Charlie. Can I fix you a drink?' She floated over to the kitchen island and draped herself along the side of it.

From the corner of his eye, he could see Jared waiting next to the open patio door and Charlie focussed on why they were there.

'Come and sit down,' he said, positioning himself on the couch so that she would be sat with her back to the door. As soon as she sat down, he took her hands to make sure he kept her attention. He saw Jared come in and head straight for her office.

'Jessica. I want to clear the air between us,' he began. 'I was angry when you came to England and it wasn't fair of me.'

'All I wanted was for you to realise what we had and come back to me. I thought if you saw me away from here, you might see things differently.' She seemed almost sincere.

'Well, it's not as simple as that.' He placed her hands onto her lap and took a deep breath, hoping that Jared was getting on with his side of the job. 'It hurt me that when I had the breakdown, the time I needed you the most, I couldn't count on you. I didn't know where to turn without you and Jared being there for me.' He'd never talked about his breakdown with anyone except Maggie but being able to tell Jessica how he'd felt was cathartic. 'You didn't try to make things right, you didn't seem to care.'

'I had no idea that's what had happened to you until a while afterwards. I thought you had just left me because of Jared and I felt bad about that.'

As if that wouldn't have been reason enough, thought

Charlie but he bit his tongue and let her continue.

'There was nothing between me and Jared, it was just sex. He paid attention to me and all you were interested in was work. It was you I wanted Charlie.' It was incredible how differently she saw the past given that they had lived it together.

'I'm never going to get over that, Jessica. It was a betrayal but more than that, you were oblivious to what was going on with me. It must have been obvious that I was struggling, not coping with work. If you'd loved me you'd have seen it instead of jumping into bed with my friend because I wasn't paying enough attention to you.' She stood up and put her hands on her hips. Charlie's heart jumped into his throat; he'd said too much, pushed her too far when the main aim at the moment was to keep her talking.

'God, Charlie! You've forgiven Jared, what's the difference with me? We've been working great together and now you're dragging up the bad feeling again for no reason. We could have carried on and it would've been fine!' She was getting angry now and what Charlie didn't want was for her to start pacing around and find Jared snooping.

'I'm sorry,' he said, hoping that he sounded it. 'I should have been clearer about things when I came back.'

'You've been perfectly clear, Charlie. It might be over for us but it's over for you and your new girlfriend too.'

Charlie could feel the colour drain from his face. 'You sent the photo.'

'I did.' She paused, smiling with one eyebrow raised. 'I guess there's no coming back from that for me. It really is over but know this, Charlie, if I can't have you, I'm going to fucking mess with you so that no one else will want you either.'

He had to get out. He was shaking with rage and fear; the terrible feelings that had overwhelmed him on the day he'd finally broken down, were all back. Suddenly, he couldn't think straight but he knew he had to leave.

'Look at you,' she called after him. 'Running off to try and win her back. You're fucking pathetic!'

He reached the door and headed to the car. Shaking, he could barely start the engine but once he did, he headed at high speed towards the gates which were only just open enough for him to get through. In no fit state to drive, he pulled over and rested his head on the steering wheel.

It took a few minutes for him to compose himself and then he remembered. Jared.

57

Maggie still hadn't heard from Charlie. She was fed up with waiting for him. Whether it was waiting for him to finish the work, waiting for him to come back from America or waiting for him to finally tell Jessica where to go. All of it. So she'd decided it was time to take back control of her own life, just like she'd come to Bramble Island to do in the first place.

Rob Tanner had come back to her and said he had spoken to the trustees and they loved the idea of the water lodges. There was overwhelming support for the idea that they would preserve the woodland but the snag was the money. The Trust had put aside an amount of money for the project and the new plan would take it way over budget.

'What I wondered, given your passion for the project,' he said on the phone to Maggie, 'was whether you'd be interested in crowdfunding for the extra funds? It was hugely popular when the National Trust did a similar thing to buy the White Cliffs of Dover and it gave them invaluable publicity.'

This was what she'd come here to do; get this project off the ground, and now it seemed like she had some control of it again, she was more than happy to start crowdfunding.

It was so easy to set up. She'd set the target amount to raise and decided on a suggested donation amount. David, the area manager, had allowed her to offer an annual pass to Bramble Island for anyone who donated over £1000 and Will had persuaded his boss at the Bramble Bay Ferry Company to offer unlimited ferry trips for the same donors.

Maggie donated the first £50 herself to get the ball rolling and to check that it worked. She was proud of herself for pushing the project forward. It might have been Charlie's idea but he wasn't here now. This was all her now.

She'd drafted a press release and sent it to Rob Tanner and Verity for approval. Once they'd given it the okay, as well as sending it to every news outlet she could think of, she'd asked Clare to send it out to her database of people who'd signed up to the Bramble Island newsletter and the word began to spread from there.

Less than a week later, they had raised half of the target amount. Rob Tanner was thrilled and was sending one of Verity's colleagues to help manage the burgeoning press attention. The local news wanted to cover the success of the crowdfunding and the BBC's Countrycase wanted to do a piece on how thinking differently about development can benefit the environment. That meant another visit from Ben who was going to talk to them about the impact on the woodland from his newly adopted persona as saviour of the trees.

Maggie was happy to field most of this attention herself but she needed a bit of expert guidance on how to spin things the right way so she was looking forward to having a helping hand from a PR expert.

She waited on the quay for Ben and Verity's colleague. Knowing that they would be staying for a few days, she had arranged rooms for them at the Sandbanks Hotel. Now that the summer was almost over they finally had rooms free, otherwise she'd have had to bunk in with Megan and Alice and give her cottage up again.

Once the ferry was close enough, she could make out Ben sat inside, next to the window with his companion beside him; she could see them get up ready to disembark as the ferry tied off at the quay. When they emerged from the cabin, Maggie recognised the man Ben was with straight away. It was Nick, the man she'd had a fling with before she broke up with Ben. It seemed unthinkable that he could be here on Bramble Island, when she felt sure she'd never see him again but the holiday lodge project was just at the point the Trust Treks had been when Nick had been brought in before and the Trust tended to work with people they knew. She felt stupid for not realising it could have been a possibility.

For a second, she thought she might be sick and briefly leaned over the railing on the quay until the feeling passed.

'Hey, Maggie.' Ben was behind her. 'Are you okay?' She felt his hand on her shoulder, put a bright smile on and turned around.

'Hi! I was just looking at the fish, a shoal of mackerel I think…'

'Right. Well, this is Nick. Nick, this is Maggie Cassidy, the park manager of Bramble Island.'

What should she do? Pretend it was the first time she'd met Nick? Ben had no idea that this was the man. How could he know? She tried to remember back to those difficult, emotionally charged conversations; had she mentioned Nick by name?

'Nice to meet you, Maggie.' Okay, so he was going down the road of pretending not to know each other. Had Ben told him that he was her ex? She supposed it may have come up fairly innocuously if they'd been talking about her.

'Welcome to Bramble Island, Nick. Have you been here before?' Maybe this was the way to go. Ignore the past and just start from now.

'No, it's my first visit. I did some work for the Trust a couple of years ago when they launched the Trust Treks but I don't visit many properties otherwise.' Amusement played in his eyes as he looked straight at her.

'Maggie came up with the Trust Treks idea,' said Ben, with what sounded like pride.

'Wow, really? It was a great initiative. Are you running them here?'

'Yes, the Squirrel Spotter Treks are the most popular, obviously, but we do quite a few different ones.' She was leading them towards the office, dreading the moment that she might be alone with Nick or that he might refer to something that would make Ben realise who he was.

'I hear you've managed to book us into a hotel this time,' said Ben. 'Last time Maggie didn't know I was coming and I ended up having to stay in her cottage,' he explained to Nick.

'I wasn't there,' Maggie said, realising too late that she was over-explaining and noticing Ben raise his eyebrows in surprise. Why did she do that? Nick didn't care whether she was there with Ben or not. 'Anyway, here we are. Make yourselves at home. I don't know what you want to do first, Nick?' she asked.

'I think it'd be wise to see the locations so I know what we're talking about. Is now a good time?'

Before Maggie could suggest anything else, Ben piped up.

'I've arranged to meet someone for lunch if you can manage without me for an hour or so.' He looked shifty and Maggie could only imagine it was Alice he was meeting. Finally, someone had fallen for her charms.

'No problem. Nick, let's go.' Maggie led the way towards the woodland, striding purposefully as if that would somehow mean they weren't able to hold a conversation, but as soon as they were off the main path and into the woods, Nick stopped.

'It's good to see you again, Maggie, and great to be working together again, like old times.' He smiled solicitously and it turned Maggie's stomach to think that she had fallen for his charms the last time.

'Well, I can't say the feeling's mutual, Nick.'

He looked surprised. Perhaps he'd thought the way he'd treated her last time was acceptable but she needed him to know that there was no chance of a repeat. 'Just to be clear, it's not going to be like old times. I'd appreciate it if we could keep it professional and say no more about what happened before.' She turned away from him and carried on walking, feeling elated at finally having stood up for herself. This was how things should be. Take control of your own life and don't let things get messed up by other people.

'So, Ben's your ex, I hear?'

Maggie said nothing, but her elation quietly slipped away as she realised that if Nick wasn't going to get what he wanted, he was probably going to make her pay in some way.

'That's the guy you dumped for me?'

God, he was such a dick. How had she not realised that before?

'I didn't dump anyone for you. As I recall, we didn't have a relationship, more a series of unfortunate one-night stands.' It stung her to refer to their liaison in terms of how he might remember it when it had been more than that to her, at the time.

'He doesn't know that was with me though, does he?' She could hear the smirk in his tone.

Now Maggie stopped and turned around to face him. 'No, he doesn't and if you feel he needs to know, fine. Go ahead. We've both moved on and neither of us is going to get upset about something that happened two years ago and meant nothing. Apart from to you, it seems.'

Nick looked taken aback and Maggie was relieved to see that her dismissal of him seemed to have taken the wind out of his sails.

He put his hands up in defeat. 'Okay, fine. I'll say nothing more about it,' he said and began to trudge after her as she carried on walking.

'So, this is where the lodges were going to be sited,' explained Maggie as they passed through the woodland where it met the beach. 'Right from that huge oak over there to that silver birch,' she pointed. 'And most of the trees in between would have needed felling from here to around ten metres inland.' She turned around to face the water. 'And this is where the new jetty will be which will lead to the water lodges.'

Nick had thankfully managed to adopt a more professional approach and asked a few pertinent questions which Maggie was happy to answer now that she was sure he knew where they stood. In fact, now that he wasn't being a dick, she caught glimpses of why she'd fallen for him when they'd worked on the Trust Treks. He was incredibly clever about how you could play on certain elements of a project to make it appealing to either the media, customers or whoever you wanted to target, and it was that business-like side to him that she'd found most attractive. But not anymore.

58

Charlie sat in Jared's car wondering what to do. He couldn't believe he'd left Jessica's place without a second thought about how Jared was going to get out. But also, he couldn't believe the effect Jessica had had on him. Now that he'd had a few minutes to catch his breath, he could feel his mind clearing, which was good because he needed to think about how to get Jared out without having to go back there himself.

He pulled out his phone, about to call Jared but realised that if he was still undiscovered in Jessica's house, he wouldn't be for long if his phone wasn't on silent. He couldn't take the risk. Then in the rear-view mirror, he saw something moving and realised it was Jared sprinting towards him. The adrenaline that must have been coursing through Jared was almost palpable and jolted Charlie into action. He started the car, leant over and pushed open the passenger door and thanked god they were in a Tesla with superior acceleration for a quick getaway.

'Go, go!' said Jared breathlessly as he slammed the door.

'Shit, what happened?' asked Charlie. 'Did she catch you?'

Jared shook his head but was still getting his breath back so didn't say anything more.

'Is it her? The hack?'

'She's involved in it at least.' He took a minute, then elaborated. 'She'd left her emails open and there were some between her and Drew. I took a couple of shots of what I could find. I think it'll be enough. I know I said it might be her but now we know, Christ, I can't actually believe it.'

'So, I guess we tell Ed and the team and let them deal with it.'

'They're gonna have to tell the cops. They've been doing it through the dark web from what I could see. They won't be able to trace the hack without Drew's help.'

'Well, we've got to hope she's willing to end it.'

They got back to the office and as soon as they'd told Ed and Jared showed him what he'd found, they called the police. There was nothing more that Charlie could do to help. He just hoped that Jessica would do the right thing.

He took an Uber to San Francisco having arranged a room at The Battery.

'Good Afternoon, Mr Mackenzie. Great to see you again.' said the receptionist.

'Thanks, it's good to be back.' He signed the check-in sheet and waited for the key.

'We have a key outstanding from your last visit?'

'Oh,' said Charlie, surprised. 'I'm pretty sure I gave it in before I left.'

'Let me check the records.' She tapped the keyboard for a couple of minutes. 'It seems there was a duplicate key issued during your last stay?'

Charlie frowned. He had never asked for a new key but then maybe it hadn't been him that asked. 'Do you know which receptionist issued the duplicate?'

'It was Daniel.'

Daniel had worked at The Battery for years and Charlie knew him well. And he knew Jessica well and unfortunately hadn't been working at all while he was staying there with Maggie. Perhaps Daniel had thought he and Jessica were still together when she had been visiting for work lately.

'It was issued to a friend and I don't like our chances of getting it back. Charge it to me if it's a problem.'

'It's no problem, Mr Mackenzie. We just have to make sure the keys are accounted for. We can disable the missing one on our system.'

Daniel. He could imagine Jessica sweet-talking him into giving her a key and that was how she'd got the photo of him sleeping.

He let himself into his room, stripped off and collapsed into bed. Asleep almost before his head hit the pillow.

Charlie woke up and switched the news channel on. The High 5 hack was still leading the news and they were showing footage of Drew being arrested at his apartment while the voiceover informed him that he was a 'disgruntled employee' of one of their collaborators. Clearly, Ed was aiming to downplay the link they had with him.

He lay back and closed his eyes again, wondering how it had come to this with Jessica. She must be completely unhinged to have gone to these kinds of lengths to hurt him.

His phone vibrated with a FaceTime call from Maggie.

'Hey, Maggie, how are you?'

She looked great. She was sitting in the office on Bramble Island. Before, she'd always called him from his house but since he had taken the motorboat to Sandbanks when he left, she had no way to get there now. He knew she didn't like calling him from Bramble Island because the connection was slow and they could get interrupted, so he thought it was a little odd.

'I'm fine thanks. Did I wake you up?'

'No, I was already awake. Just been watching the news.'

'Are you alone?' Who would she think was with him?

'Yeah, of course.' Then it hit him. 'Oh. She sent you that photo?' His heart dropped into his stomach.

'What's going on Charlie? I want you to be honest with me. If you're involved with her again, well... I don't know what to think.'

'I'm so sorry, Maggie.' All he seemed to do was say sorry to her lately. What had happened? 'There is nothing between me and Jessica, believe me. She showed me the photo and it looked bad, I didn't know how to explain it. As far as I knew she'd never had any opportunity to take a photo of me like that, at least not since I got back to the States. But I know now and I swear it's nothing to worry about and I guess I was hoping she wasn't going to show it to you.'

'I can't believe you still let her into your life after what happened. All she's tried to do is make things bad for you, for us, and you never stand up to her.'

Maggie was absolutely right but he was shocked to hear her spell it out to him. It wasn't like her.

'You're right and the last time I saw her I told her that was it. For good this time.'

Maggie's expression told him that she didn't believe him. And who could blame her? He had made some terrible decisions lately, not only for himself but for their relationship.

'I can't do this anymore, Charlie. It's too hard to be waiting for you, wanting to be with you and not knowing if you feel the same way. All this business with Jessica as well... I can't take her being part of your life, I'm sorry.'

'Maggie, you have nothing to apologise for at all. I'm sorry it's taken me this long to realise what she was doing. I should have protected you from her... protected both of us,' he said quietly.

'I think we've missed our chance, Charlie.'

Her face told him that she was upset, but her tone told him she was decided.

'Maggie...'

'Charlie. There are so many things that have gone wrong for us since we went to America. And since you've been away, you've taken no interest in what's happening here. This was your life, Charlie and now you're not interested in it at all.'

'That's not true, Maggie,' he said, while knowing that what she said was true. But only because he'd had to mentally distance himself from Bramble Island to keep his mind on the job. And to stop his heart aching for Maggie quite so much. 'It makes it so much harder to think too much about home, that's all. I have to keep it separate, it's not because I don't care. I know it's been hard but I want to be with you more than anything.'

But as he said it, he heard how it would sound to Maggie because if that was true, he would be there right now.

59

Maggie looked at the computer screen trying to see in Charlie's eyes whether he meant what he was saying. She wanted more than anything for him to put the phone down and come home. He looked terrible. She had seen on the news that the hack problem with High 5 had been solved but she didn't think for a minute that would mean Charlie was coming back.

'I'm almost done, Maggie. I'll be back real soon and—'

'No Charlie. It's over. We've been apart longer than we were ever together and it's too hard. If it's meant to be, well, maybe one day things will be different.'

'Maggie, no. look, I'm going to fly back tonight—'

'Don't fly back for me, Charlie, not unless you're done. I want you to be ready to come back because if you come back for me before you're ready, you'll never feel like you got it out of your system. That's what you need to do.'

It was the hardest thing she'd ever had to say and was completely at odds with how she actually felt. But she knew that she deserved more than this. She had finally managed to get her career back on an even keel and felt back in control of her life for the first time in a couple of years. Seeing Nick and telling him exactly how she'd felt had been empowering and she couldn't risk all of the gains she had made for someone who was too self-involved to notice her triumphs. It felt like déjà vu; Ben had never been her cheerleader either. She was not going to let history repeat itself. There was too much at stake.

Charlie put his head in his hands and when he looked at her again, he had tears in his eyes.

'You mean everything to me, Maggie. Coming back here was harder than I thought. All this stuff with Jessica has made me feel like I did three years ago and the only thing keeping me from being right back there is the thought of you being there when I get back. I couldn't have done any of this without you.'

'I love that you've found yourself again after so long but that was you, not me. You were ready to get back out there and that's great. I'm glad I was there for you and maybe helped you to make the final leap but I can't be here just waiting for you.' She saw with total clarity what had been happening. 'I've let relationships dictate my life for too long. I came to Bramble Island for a fresh start, to make my mark and do something I could be proud of. I love you, Charlie but I came here for me and I have to put myself first.'

She wished with all her heart that Charlie would say something that would make everything okay. She wanted him to be her protector, champion, partner in everything.

'That's a good decision, Maggie. It's right for you to put yourself first. That's what I did... good decision.' He wiped his eyes and smiled at her. Too brightly, defeat just below the surface. 'Okay then, I guess this is it. I guess I'll catch up with you sometime when I get back.'

'Okay. Take care, Charlie.'

She had barely clicked the button to end the call before a heaving sob escaped from her, and thank goodness she was alone because there was nothing she could do but let it out.

Once she had gathered herself, she left a note on the desk

for Nick and Ben saying that she would catch up with them the following morning. The Countrycase team were arriving on Bramble Island at lunchtime the next day and it was Ben and Nick's last day on the island.

She went back to her cottage, keeping her head low to hide her swollen eyes and in an attempt to avoid having to speak to anyone. She changed into leggings and her favourite sweatshirt, made a cup of tea and sat on the sofa mindlessly watching back to back episodes of 'The Big Bang Theory', hoping it would be enough of a distraction to stop her mind from going over and over the conversation with Charlie.

Maybe she should have said yes when he offered to fly back. That was what she wanted, but that wouldn't have put an end to it. It would be like the last time he'd come back when he was grabbing every spare minute to carry on working. He had to get it out of his system, otherwise there would be no future for them.

A few weeks ago, before the water lodges idea, she had seriously thought about jacking it all in and flying to San Francisco. Why not just set up a life there with Charlie when it had felt like there was nothing for her in Dorset. But now things had changed. More than anything, she knew that seeing through this project on Bramble Island would be one of the most fulfilling things she would ever do. How was being with Charlie when all he wanted to do was work twenty-four-seven going to ever fulfil her? It just made her realise that the few weeks they had at the start of their relationship, before the real world had seeped into their blissful Bramble Bay bubble, had been perfect but not real-life. Not sustainable.

The best thing she could do was give herself the greatest chance she could to make a success of the holiday lodge project, and if she kept busy, she wouldn't even notice that she was no longer waiting for Charlie to come back.

The crowdfunding page took ages to load on Maggie's ancient laptop. She could never be sure how much of that was due to the terrible Wi-Fi on Bramble Island and how much was because her laptop was so old.

When the page opened, it took her a minute to realise what she was looking at; the total raised had exceeded her target. She refreshed the page, maybe there was an error. The page loaded again, this time with a slightly higher total. It was incredible. They had hoped this might happen after the Countrycase piece aired but not before. Obviously, word had spread.

She smiled to herself then stood up to go into the kitchen for more tea. She glanced out of the window as she often did. What had started as her hoping for a glimpse of Charlie on the quay had become a habit. Instead of Charlie, she saw Nick walking towards the quay where the ferry was waiting to do its last trip to the mainland for the day.

Watching Nick board the ferry, she wondered what it would be like if Charlie ever came back and became the forester on Bramble Island again. It was hard to imagine him picking up his old life where he left off and the thought of watching him arrive and leave on his boat, without him being hers anymore was heart-breaking and she wondered for the hundredth time since the FaceTime call, whether she'd made the right decision.

60

Maggie couldn't wait for him. She'd said she would wait; he still had the note she'd left him in Tahoe, but she'd changed her mind. Because of him. Charlie felt wretched. It was entirely his fault for coming back to America, leaving her for work which he didn't have to do. He didn't need the money, that was for sure. He'd just been doing it to try and finish off High 5 properly. And that wasn't a good enough reason.

The work was progressing well but he didn't get the same buzz from it that he used to. He had started to see that it was because nothing was riding on it for him anymore. Back in the day, he and Jared had worked so hard to build the company. Then, they were doing it because everything was riding on it, their hearts and souls were invested in the success of it and now there was no reason he could cling onto, no high waiting for him at the end.

He sat in front of his laptop, in his room at The Battery, wondering what to do next. Maggie didn't want him anymore. He didn't know what would happen if he went back to Bramble Bay now. She would think he'd left unfinished business in the US and might not think he was ready to be back there with her. He knew she hadn't meant to force his hand into going back and that was really why she'd broken it off completely; she wanted him back but not at the expense of his quest for closure.

He called Ed.

'Hey, Charlie, great work from you and Jared on the hacking. I hear they charged Jessica with aiding and abetting computer intrusion but she's out on bail because she gave up that guy Drew. Boy, she really had it in for you, talk about a woman scorned.' Ed chuckled down the phone.

'Uh-huh. I'm glad to help. Look, Ed, I—'

'You want out.'

'I do. I'm sorry. I know I promised you I'd see out the new project to the end and I really wanted to, but things are different now. I came back as if I was the same person that left three years ago and that felt great for a while but that's not who I am now.' Charlie was shocked at how easy it was to articulate how he was feeling given that since the call with Maggie, he'd barely been able to keep a thought in his head for going over and over what she'd said.

'You've done us a great favour even to get it this far. We can take it from here, Charlie. If your heart's not in it, it's time to go and find somewhere else to put your heart.'

Feeling like a weight had truly been lifted off his shoulders, Charlie got dressed and headed out for a walk. He didn't know where he was going and it didn't matter. He walked towards Union Square, then along Market Street and onto Hayes Street. Then, suddenly, he knew where he was heading. A place where he knew he'd feel close to Maggie, even though they'd never been there together.

The Botanical Gardens in Golden Gate Park was somewhere Charlie had known about when he'd lived in San Francisco but he'd never been there apart from to a couple of corporate functions which were back in the day when he'd had little appreciation for nature, not like now.

The trees on Bramble Island had helped to heal his heart the last time and that was where Maggie had found him.

Maybe the trees here would help just as much. He headed for the Redwood Grove. The majesty of those trees and the magnificent woodland that they formed had just the same vibe as the woods on Bramble Island. He left the path and chose a tree where he sat down and leant back against the trunk. As he pushed his shirt sleeves up to his elbows, he caught sight of the scar on his forearm and had a momentary flashback to being sat like this after he'd fallen out of the tree, when Maggie had found him. That day seemed a world away from where he was now but somehow, sitting in this woodland at the bottom of a beautiful, majestic tree he felt connected to that day when he and Maggie had finally found each other.

How had it ended like this? He knew the blame lay solely at his door. How had he let this happen when he thought he'd found everything he'd wanted in the world in Bramble Bay.

His phone rang. It was Josh.

'Hey, Josh, good to hear from you, man.'

'Hi, Charlie. How's it going?'

'Um, okay I guess. I've finished up the High 5 work…'

'So you're coming back?' Josh sounded relieved.

Charlie sighed. 'I don't know. I don't think Maggie wants me to.'

'Did she say that? Because she's been looking pretty miserable since you left.'

Charlie didn't want to wish misery on Maggie but he was glad to hear that she hadn't shrugged off the break-up as if it didn't matter. Maybe she was finding it just as bad as he was.

'She called it a day.' He could hear Josh whispering to someone, presumably Megan.

'Oh, well that might explain it then.'

'What?'

Charlie could hear Josh taking a deep breath. 'Eric overheard Maggie crying in the office yesterday. I probably shouldn't have said anything but Meg thought it was the right thing to do.'

It broke Charlie's heart to think of Maggie feeling that way because of him. 'Do you think she's okay now?'

'I don't know. Meg seems to think you should come back.'

'Shit, Josh. I don't know if I can sweep in and you know…'

'Give me the phone, let me talk to him,' he could hear Megan say in the background.

'Hi Charlie, it's Megan. Look, you need to get your arse back here. What are you doing?' Wow, she was really angry with him.

'Hey, Megan. I don't think that's what she wants. She told me not to come back.'

'Really? Look, I know it's like, none of my business.' Charlie rolled his eyes. 'But she said you should finish up the High 5 stuff and not come back until then. Is that right?'

'Uh-huh.' How did they know what she'd said. Did Maggie tell Megan?

'And Josh says you just said you've finished. So, I don't get what the problem is?'

'Okay, I hear you. I'll call her and straighten it out.'

'Come on Charlie, we're way beyond that now. Do you want her back or not?'

61

Maggie stood on the beach watching Eva Ranj interview Ben, who had been heavily briefed by Nick, about the woodland and how important it was to the fabric of the island. She had butterflies in her stomach because, in a minute, it was going to be her turn.

'Right, let's change for the shots by the water's edge!' someone from the TV crew shouted once Ben and Eva had finished. Eva headed over to Maggie, smiling; they'd met very briefly earlier.

'Okay, Maggie. Are you ready for this?' she asked.

Maggie was slightly star-struck. She loved Countrycase and even if she'd secretly been hoping it would be Joe Davis coming to see them, Eva was a good second best.

'Yes, I think so. We're going to talk about how we came up with the houseboats idea and about the crowdfunding.'

'Perfect! And don't be nervous, you're a natural once you start talking about the project. Just pretend the cameras aren't there.' Eva walked down to the water's edge to help them decide where to position the next segment.

Easier said than done, Maggie thought. But at least she was armed with facts about their crowdfunding. Nick had pulled all sorts of stats together about other crowdfunding the Trust had tried which showed how successful this round of funding had been. She was ready with an update of the total raised and how they were continuing to run the crowdfund until the deadline, with a plan to use the extra money to improve the fabric of the island and to have a pot for future maintenance of the houseboats.

'Maggie, you're the park manager here on Bramble Island and it's your idea which has saved the woodland.'

'Yes, my partner's idea, really. We went across the harbour to Shell Bay and there are a couple of abandoned houseboats near there. From having the idea, we looked into the feasibility of having the holiday lodges on the water rather than in the woods.'

'But that's a much more expensive option.'

'Yes, it was way over the amount which had initially been set aside so we decided to crowdfund, to save the woods.'

'And it's been a huge success, hasn't it?'

'Yes, we hit our target just a few days after launching and now that we've exceeded it we're continuing to raise money for the future maintenance of the project as well as to improve the fabric of what we already have on the island.'

'Congratulations, that's a huge achievement and I understand it's the most successful fundraising ever undertaken by the Trust?'

'Yes, I think the speed at which we reached the target surprised us all. And it was from lots of people making smaller donations which I think shows how much the island and the woodland means to so many people.'

'And I understand that it's extra special for you, Maggie. You met your partner Charlie when you were both working on the island.'

Maggie lost all focus. She could see Charlie abseiling down the tree he'd been working in when they first met. All the moments they'd shared on the island seemed to hit her all at once in a torrent of memories.

'Okay, cut there!' shouted someone, breaking into her thoughts.

'I'm sorry, Maggie,' said Eva. 'Ben mentioned it and I thought it would be a nice touch. I apologise if it was inappropriate.'

'No, not at all,' said Maggie, trying to compose herself and not start crying on camera. 'It's complicated, that's all. Sorry. Do we need to do that again?'

'No, don't worry. We'll cut that out and finish on the previous comment and I'll do a piece to camera to round off. You were great,' she said encouragingly.

Maggie really didn't feel great, so now that her minute in the spotlight was over, she headed to the office, knowing that no one would be there because they were all watching the filming on the beach. Nick and Ben were due to leave that afternoon, after the filming, and although she knew she ought to see them off, she couldn't face it. She just wanted to be alone.

She left a note on the table beside the office door explaining that she was sorry she couldn't see them off but she wasn't very well and had gone home to bed. She knew Megan and Alice would take care of things for her.

Back at the cottage she changed into her pyjamas and poured herself a large glass of wine before finally letting the tears fall that had been threatening since Eva Ranj asked her about Charlie.

Perhaps she had made the most enormous mistake breaking things off between them. It had been so easy to forget how wonderful it had been in the beginning but if it was meant to be, she should have been able to stoically wait for him, been able to keep herself going with the memories. The problem was that the great times were tainted by the slightly-less-than-amazing ones. Since America, their relationship had been at the mercy of other people. It hadn't been about them anymore, and that had changed things.

It had been the right decision, it was just hard to take. Things would get easier and in the meantime, she had the water lodge project to keep her busy over the winter months.

62

As soon as Charlie had spoken to Josh and Megan, he knew with sudden clarity what he had to do. It was no good allowing himself to go down the road of letting something he knew he wanted, *someone* he knew he wanted, slip away from him. The only thing making him feel bad right now was knowing that Maggie thought he didn't love her enough to make their relationship a priority.

He could see now how it was one thing to have her blessing to come to the US and finish something he never had a chance to finish properly before, but quite another thing for that to be seemingly never-ending, involving his ex-girlfriend and not actually making him as happy as he'd thought it would.

All that mattered was winning Maggie back and he figured he could do something about that.

He looked again at the scar on his arm and grinned. That was the catalyst that had brought them together in the first place and was the best reminder he had of how he'd felt about her then. He'd never been happier than right after his accident, at least, once he'd been working again and spending every waking minute with Maggie. Before their trip to the US. And he'd be the first to admit that he'd begun to forget how great life had felt all those months ago. It had disappeared in a fog that had enveloped him ever since he'd been back in the Valley.

He walked back to The Battery with a spring in his step, a plan beginning to formulate as he walked. He booked himself on the first flight to London, checked out of his room and took an Uber to the airport.

Josh had mentioned that a TV show was going to be filming on Bramble Island the following day, to do with the houseboat project, and that gave Charlie the beginnings of his plan. The flight gave him chance to research the show, find out the email address of the producer and plead for them to let him have 30 seconds of their time. They'd agreed and when he landed, the waiting car took him straight to Sandbanks where he pulled the tarp off his little motorboat and went to Bramble Island. He'd had it on good authority from Megan, via a text when he was almost there, that Maggie was well out of the way and he'd filmed his part of the story which he hoped would be the beginning of his plan to win her back.

So as not to alert Maggie to the fact that he was back, he'd sworn everyone that had seen him to absolute secrecy, cryptically promising them that he would reward them if they managed to keep the secret until the show aired the following week. Then he took his boat and went home.

The house had been shut up for weeks and felt a little stuffy until Charlie threw open the doors and let the sea breeze fill the place with its fresh air. Despite the journey, he wasn't tired; he was on a high and wanted to make a start on the next part of his plan.

Maggie wasn't interested in his money, he knew that, but he also knew that to win her back would take some magnificent attempt on his part to sweep her off her feet given what she'd been through the last few months. Besides, he wasn't planning to shower her with gifts, more of an experience.

63

The volunteers were leaving, but not without a party. Megan and Josh had organised it and had invited everyone who worked on Bramble Island, including all the staff at the ferry company – tactically necessary because otherwise none of the day volunteers and workers would be able to get home afterwards. The Countrycase episode was due to air that evening and they had been offered the use of a large television from the Castle for the occasion. Luckily it was a beautiful day so they were able to set it up on the quay, just outside the café so there was plenty of room for everyone to watch and then they would spill onto the beach near Maggie's cottage afterwards for a beach barbecue and drinks.

Maggie sat cross-legged on the floor in front of the TV with the volunteers and a few others. Everyone else was sat in picnic chairs which they'd brought with them and Clare had provided a few bottles of prosecco that were being passed around and poured into various plastic glasses and beakers.

'Oh my God, I'm so excited!' said Alice. She had come out about her relationship with Ben, as she had been unable to stop herself from announcing that her boyfriend was going to be on Countrycase.

'They did some shots of us cutting back the bracken round

by the clifftop path so me and Josh might be in it too,' said Eric.

'Shhhhhh!!' everyone said as the programme started. Given how many people were there, you could have heard a pin drop while the theme tune was playing, then when they did the overview of what would be on the episode and showed a shot of the island, everyone cheered before shushing again when they started talking.

'It's Ben!' squealed Alice, when his segment about the woods came on. He looked very charismatic on film, Maggie had to admit, and he did a great job of explaining the best features of the woodland.

Then there was a segment on a dairy farmer who had branched into making gourmet ice cream along the coast in Lulworth, then it was back to Bramble Island.

'It's Maggie!' a few people shouted when her bit came on. Maggie cringed as it got near to the end, wondering how it was going to be with the cut and Eva rounding up, but what actually happened was even more surprising than she'd expected.

It was Charlie.

'So, Charlie, you're the forester here on the island and I understand that the island has an extra special place in your heart,' said Eva.

How was Charlie on this programme? He hadn't been here. Had they filmed it afterwards? Eva was wearing the same clothes but that didn't really mean anything. Maggie glanced round at the others but everyone was avoiding eye contact with her.

'Yes, I met my partner, Maggie here.'

'Yes, we spoke to Maggie earlier about the houseboat project that was the brainchild of both of you.'

'She's done a fantastic job since she arrived in the spring. I'm only sorry that I haven't been here to see it all.'

This was some kind of weird dream, thought Maggie. It

was the only explanation.

'And I think there's something you want to say to her?'

Charlie looked straight into the camera and said, 'Maggie, I've been a jerk. I love you so much, I'm never leaving again. All I want is you and this beautiful island.' He smiled, his eyes brighter than Maggie had seen them since they'd left Bramble Bay for San Francisco. 'I love you, honey.'

There were gasps and a few cheers from the crowd.

'Thank you, Charlie,' said Eva, then she turned to the camera. 'Maybe our first Countrycase wedding is on the cards! Now let's see what we can expect with the week's weather from Sarah.'

Maggie stood up and looked around, half expecting to see Charlie in the crowd somewhere. Everyone was cheering and clapping as the credits began to roll and people started to leave the quay for the beach now that Bramble Island had had its five minutes of fame.

'Well, that was a surprise,' said Alice looking around at the other volunteers incredulously. Only Megan and Josh seemed not to be surprised or at least were not doing a very good job of pretending to be.

'Over there,' said Josh, pointing to where William from the Bramble Bay Ferry was waving a hand and grinning at her.

'Go on,' said Megan, giving Maggie a light shove between her shoulders.

'Over here, Maggie love!' yelled William.

Once he could see that Maggie was following him, he made his way to the ferry.

'Special Service for Miss Maggie Cassidy. Welcome aboard!' He elaborately waved to the ferry as Maggie approached.

'Seriously William, what's going on? I thought you were running the ferry to take everyone back to the mainland later on?' She stood with her arms crossed, hoping that her fake indifference would force William to spill the beans.

'All in good time. Now, are you coming or not?'

She stepped aboard, her curiosity getting the better of her while trying to suppress the hope that this was something to do with Charlie.

Maggie sat on the top deck and once the ferry was underway, William came up to join her.

'Come on then, now I'm on here you might as well tell me,' she said.

William grinned, looking pleased with himself. 'No way! Just wait and see.'

Maggie hoped they were heading to Charlie's island. He heart was beating faster and she had butterflies in her stomach just as she had the first time she'd taken the ferry to Bramble Island. Surely he was going to be there. Where else could they possibly be going?

'If we're going to Charlie's there's nowhere for the ferry to dock.'

William grinned and shook his head. 'You're not going to get me like that,' he said.

Maggie rolled her eyes. He would be there and she wasn't sure she was ready to see him but at the same time, the flurries of anticipation in her stomach were telling a different story

As the ferry inevitably skirted to the right to approach Charlie's island, Maggie saw that next to the boathouse was a brand new jetty. It was adorned with lanterns hanging from posts all around the edge. How long had it been since she'd been here, wondered Maggie, for this to be so different?

The ferry docked at the jetty, dwarfing it and the boathouse and necessitating William to manhandle a gangplank into place as it was so much lower than the quays at Sandbanks and Bramble Island which were the only places the ferry normally docked.

William led the way down the gangplank onto the jetty. The path next to the boathouse was lit with storm lanterns every metre or so on both sides, leading up towards the house.

'This is where I leave you,' he said, with a flourish of his hand and a bow.

'Okay,' said Maggie uncertainly. 'Thanks, William.'

'No problem. We're all rooting for you,' he said with a grin, before lifting the gangplank and heading away. Maggie watched until the ferry was out of sight, then she took a deep breath and began to make her way up the path.

The decking at the back of the house had thousands upon thousands of twinkling fairy lights stranded above it and she could see Charlie standing underneath them, waiting for her. He was wearing a white shirt with the sleeves rolled up and some navy blue deck shorts. The more dishevelled Charlie that she had fallen in love with was back and her heart leapt as she realised it but she kept her pace deliberately slow, forcing herself not to throw herself into his arms until she heard what he had to say, however much she might want to.

'You're here,' he said, a tear escaping down his cheek before he could brush it away.

'Yes,' she said softly, her heart breaking for him but trying to hold onto the fact that she wasn't going to compromise. His grand gesture apology on television wasn't going to sweep her off her feet. She had to think with her head, not her heart.

'Did you see it?' he asked.

'I did. Why are you back?' It sounded harsh, but she had to know.

'I realised that I'd tried to go back to being a person I wasn't anymore. I thought when I'd met you, you'd helped me get back to being my old self, but actually, I wasn't that person at all anymore. The High 5 stuff, when you were there with me, it felt like I had the best life again but when you left, it was empty. It just took me a little while to realise why I wasn't happy anymore.'

'So you've finished working?'

'Sorry, yes. I'm not explaining very well. I've quit and I'm back for good.'

He reached out his hand and Maggie felt her heart skip a beat as she thought he was going to touch her. He held his arm out, showing her his scar. Maggie fought the urge to take his hand.

'Remember this day?' he asked.

She nodded. 'It was awful.' Maggie still wondered how she'd ever made it from the woodland to the quay with a barely conscious Charlie.

'But that night, when I woke up in the hospital, I knew I loved you, Maggie.'

She smiled at him, because she had felt the same but had put it down to the heightened emotions of the day. Surely, no one can fall in love that quickly.

'I knew then too.'

Charlie raised his hand and stroked her cheek with his thumb, moving in to gently kiss her when she couldn't help but nestle her head into his caress.

'I love you, Maggie.' She could feel his breath on her mouth as he spoke, both of them unwilling to pull apart. 'I'll never leave you again.'

She looked into his eyes which were deep brown pools of sincerity and she knew that he meant it.

'I love you too, Charlie. But I need to know that this life we have here is enough. What if you miss that... computer stuff again. What then?' What about me, she wanted to say but wasn't quite brave enough.

He smiled, 'Computer stuff isn't going to tempt me away from you or the woods again. I love writing software and I got that part mixed up with the rest of it which I know for sure I won't ever miss. And if I want to write software, I can do that from anywhere. From here, with you.' He paused, his eyes searching hers for reassurance. 'Okay?'

'Yes, definitely okay.'

He briefly kissed her again then pulled away and knelt in front of her, holding out a ring box.

'Maggie, will you marry me?'

It was the easiest question she'd ever had to answer. 'Charlie, yes, I would love to marry you!'

He pushed the ring onto her finger then stood up and pulled her into a hug, lifting her off her feet and twirling her around. 'Oh my god, Maggie. I love you so much.'

It was so perfect. The late summer evening was warm and the lights twinkled more brightly in the deepening dusk.

They walked towards the woodland that led to the beach. The path through the wood was lit with lanterns and Maggie felt her stomach flip with the anticipation of something else that Charlie had up his sleeve. It was exciting and although it was sudden, it felt so right. Even holding hands with Charlie again was making her tingle as if it were the first time again.

The path opened out onto the beach which had been adorned with yet more lanterns, some strung on ropes between the trees and there was a fire pit which was already roaring and a tub full of ice and bottles of champagne.

'Did you do all this? she asked, reaching up to kiss him softly, lingering on his lips for not quite long enough. It might never be long enough. 'This is incredible, it's gorgeous,' she said, taking the hand that he held out to her.

'You're gorgeous, I wanted it to be perfect.' He pulled her towards him so that she had to tip her head to still be able to look at him. 'For you.'

'Thank you. You're amazing.'

'I had a little help. But there's something else I want to do before the party starts.'

'What do you mean the party?'

He shrugged. 'I had to pay everyone back somehow, they kept it a secret from you that I'd been back for a week before that Countrycase show aired and then they still managed to keep it a secret that it had ever happened. So, I'm throwing a party for everyone.'

They made their way back to the house and Charlie swept her up into his arms before they walked through the door. 'I know we're not married yet but I'd love it if you'd move over here permanently?'

She nuzzled into his neck. 'I'd love that.'

He carried her over the threshold with the biggest grin on his face and straight up the stairs where they discovered each other all over again, making up for the weeks of being apart.

And in the time it took for the Bramble Bay Ferry to make the return trip to Bramble Island, everyone was there, from Clare and her team to Jan and the café staff and all the volunteers. They all cheered and clapped as Maggie and Charlie came out of the woods onto the beach.

'It's amazing,' said Maggie, incredulously. 'I can't believe we're going to get married!' She looked down at the sparkling ring on her hand.

'And this can be our engagement party.' He took a bottle of champagne and poured a glass for each of them then sat on a blanket next to the fire, patting the space next to him.

'Here's to us.'

'To us.'

'So, what do you think about San Francisco for the wedding?'

'Charlie! Don't push your luck,' said Maggie, pushing him backwards so that they were lying next to each other on the sand. 'Right here is where we belong.'

64

One Year Later

They lay amongst the blanket nest they had made on the deck, looking up at the stars.

'I can't believe we're finally here,' said Maggie, taking Charlie's left hand and twisting his new ring around his finger.

They had been married that day in the little church on Bramble Island, followed by a reception on their island, Charlie's island, for all of their friends and family. Their parents had been left the run of the house while Maggie and Charlie escaped to the solitude of Bramble Island.

'If you hadn't worked like a crazy person for the last six months, we wouldn't be here. I mean, we'd be married, obviously,' he said, 'because nothing was going to stop that happening, but we might be spending our wedding night in the Sandbanks Hotel instead of in a beautiful Bramble Island Water Lodge.'

'Honestly. I thought I'd be so sick of the sight of them that I'd have been willing to go anywhere else for our wedding night, but now, it's the most perfect place.'

'Well, I was going to suggest San Francisco,' he said, waiting for the inevitable look from Maggie.

They had been back to America together for the launch of the new High 5 app which was all the closure that Charlie needed and they'd finally managed to put the ghosts of their first trip there to rest by having a wonderful week, alone, at the Lake Tahoe house.

The best thing to come of all the ups and downs was that Charlie and Jared were best friends again. Jared had been over to stay with them on their island with his new partner, Celeste, and he had been the best man for Charlie at the wedding.

Jessica, thankfully, was out of their lives. She had lost everything following the hacking scandal after Jared's evidence showed that she had been the instigator of the idea even though Drew had done the work for her. She had completely disappeared from Silicon Valley life, and from Charlie's.

Megan and Josh had wanted to stay on Bramble Island and had managed to fund themselves over the winter, having moved into Maggie's cottage together. Since then, Maggie had successfully petitioned the Trust to have them both be paid members of staff now that the water lodges meant that there was more work on the island keeping the guests happy. They were in charge of the day-to-day running of the lodges and offered bespoke tours of the island to the visitors as part of the package.

'So, are you ready for the honeymoon?' asked Charlie, pulling one of the blankets tighter around Maggie's shoulders.

'I think so. I'm still a bit nervous about the thought of going all that way on the yacht. It'll be the furthest we've been by miles.'

They planned to sail to the Greek Ionian islands, just as they'd talked about on their very first sailing trip together.

'A month on the Ionian Sea,' he said. 'Just us. Me and Mrs

Mackenzie.'

Maggie grinned. 'I've never heard of a more perfect idea.'

The End

Author's Notes

Bramble Island is my fictional name for Brownsea Island, a real place in Poole Harbour, Dorset. Brownsea Island is a bit different to Bramble Island in that it is part National Trust parkland and part nature reserve run by the Dorset Wildlife Trust. My fictional version is loosely based on the National Trust part of the island purely because that is the part I have visited. It has a fascinating history and is thought to be where Enid Blyton based some of the Famous Five stories.

The name Bramble Bay comes from Bramble Bush Bay, a little beach just across the water from Brownsea Island and home to a couple of houseboats which are permanently moored there. As a child we spent several family holidays on the beach at Bramble Bush Bay. We used to park on the side of the road and wend our way through the bushes to the shore and in all the days we spent there, we never saw a single other person. It was like having our own private beach. The other appealing thing was that there was no seaweed and no waves – ideal for pottering around in our dinghy. In those days I had no idea that it was called Bramble Bush Bay and no idea that Brownsea Island was somewhere I would visit years later and love.

Thank you so much for reading The Island in Bramble Bay. I hope you enjoyed it, and if you did I'd be so grateful for a review on Amazon. Reviews make such a huge difference to authors.

Huge thanks to my daughter, Claudia who was my first reader and had some incredibly useful and constructive feedback. Thank you to Catrin for her diligent proof-reading, again on the promise of cocktails which I will deliver on this year when we go to Yarndale. Thanks to Kate for being an early reader and to Alison for some fantastic feedback and for giving me confidence that my yachting references were passable. Thanks to Berni Stevens for another gorgeous cover and for managing to come up with a variety of choices when I gave her nothing to go on and had no idea what I wanted. James and Jake, thanks for reading your second romance book ever and for the IT advice. And special thanks to my dad for finding Bramble Bush Bay in the first place.

Check out my blog www.victoriaauthor.co.uk for more on all my books and what's coming next…